♦ Missing You ♦

Michael R. Jennings

ISBN — Paperback:
978-0-9855412-3-1 (13) – 0985541237 (10)
ISBN — E-Book:
978-0-9855412-4-8 (13) – 0985541245 (10)

Library of Congress Control Number: 2014920946

For bulk order and other information, please contact the author at: mjenni45@aol.com.

Author Website: MichaelRJennings.com

Printed in the United States of America
Copyright © 2015 by Michael R Jennings

For Agnes Marie Jennings
1918 ~ 2005

This novel is dedicated to my mother,
who encouraged both the creative and
educational aspects of my life for as long as
I can remember. Her undying support and
belief in my abilities is reflected in all that I
accomplish.

Acknowledgments

As with my previous publications, this novel would not have reached fruition without the assistance of a number of dedicated individuals; and oftentimes that "dedication" is simply manifested in the encouragement I have received from family, friends and loved ones. Fellow author Arion Golmakani (*Solacers, Alireza*) ranks high on my list of acknowledgments for showing me the "ins and outs" of the mechanics of publishing a novel. Though three years and three publications have passed since his "teachings," his patience in showing me the ropes with my debut novel will always be remembered with deep gratitude.

As with my previous works, I received steadfast support from my two sons, Brendan and Ryan—and oftentimes that support was a gentle "kick" to keep writing. While the physical location has changed, I am blessed with being afforded the opportunity to write in a home on a six acre tract, complete with running brooks, deer, foxes and yes, even vultures—a writer's paradise. Another thank you goes out to professional copy editor Diane Alexander. No author with a sense of pride could survive without the assistance of a copy editor. With my first novel, *Flight Surgeon*, I became a firm believer in her knowledge of everything "grammar." Again, thank you Diane for willingly taking on my latest effort and treating it as if it were your baby.

Another round of thanks goes out to Jeff Fielder, who designed not only this cover, but *Flight Surgeon's* as well. You are definitely a cut above in the design arena. As with my first novel, I would be remiss in not expressing my appreciation for all of the fellow writers (my online friends) who provided the right amount of humor along the way when I needed some diversion from the writing process (you "Bantering Authors" know who you are). A special thank you goes out to a fellow "Bantering Authors alumni," Stewart Farquhar. You graciously accepted the first ten pages of my draft and performed a critical analysis upon those pages—as only you know how. Your critical feedback prompted this writer to go back into the first draft and make major revisions. Though, in all fairness to you, I hold you entirely blameless for the end result.

Last, but never least, to the multitude of others in my life for your vocal wishes that I provide you with a follow-on novel. Thank you one and all for your support and encouragement. To my beta-reader Stacey McKelvie, what can I say but thank you many times over?

Also, it's been said that behind every male writer in a

committed relationship is a woman who understands the individual mindset that writers encompass along the path of writing. I have been personally blessed with a "main squeeze" that has been totally supportive—not only for this particular novel, but my first novel, as well. Your patience and understanding of my need for "space and time" is truly appreciated. It goes without saying that I have been blessed by you, Barbara Rosen, to have not only your understanding of the idiosyncrasies of this writer (and there are many), but your undying love and belief in me as both a human being and a writer. You are truly loved in return.

1

FOLLOWING THE CONCLUSION of mass, Brent makes his way to the back of church where the pastor was greeting parishioners as they exited.

"Father Pat, you outdid yourself with your homily this morning. I'm not sure where you derived your inspiration from, but I actually stayed awake for once," his smile enveloping them both.

"Brent, good to see you. Thank you for the compliment. I'm so glad you stayed awake for a change; however, I have a major confession to make. This has been such a busy week, what with marriages, funerals and what have you, that I never found the time to craft a new homily. I did the next-best thing—I resurrected one from 20 or so years ago. Don't tell anyone," he adds with a wink, followed by his typical, wide Irish smile.

"Father, your confessions are always safe with me," Brent whispers. "Speaking of reasons to confess, will you be joining us outside for your usual calorie-free donut and coffee?"

"As always, and don't you be taking the biggest apple fritter, either. My belt still has one more notch in it before I have to buy a bigger one," Fr. Patrick remarks, all with a big Irish laugh as he turns back to greeting another in a long line of exiting parishioners.

Brent walks out the main doors of the church to where the refreshments were set up every Sunday. A number of people were already consuming sugar-laden coffees and feasting on an array of donuts that would make a weight-loss clinic cringe. The cemented canopy roof kept everyone and the donuts safely protected from the warm morning sun of Scottsdale, Arizona. The birds were busy singing their morning songs and Fr. Pat's dog was busy barking over the chatter of human voices — much as he did every Sunday when mass let out.

And then, as if the world had stopped in time, the birds ceased their chirping and the dog's barking went silent — an eerie silence that Brent recalls experiencing twice before. Memories of those two moments cause Brent to suddenly stop from the chills that ran up his spine. Without giving any thoughts to the possible repercussions if his premonitions were wrong, he yells "run" before racing from beneath the canopy.

Before a young woman knew what hit her, Brent's momentum forces her backward as he tackles her onto the grass running alongside a cemented, three-foot-tall retaining wall. Her yet to be tasted coffee and donut appear to hang momentarily in mid-air before falling to the ground.

With Brent's body fully covering hers, she immediately lets out a series of blood-curdling screams. Her fingernails dig deeply into the back of his immaculately pressed white dress shirt.

She instantly ceases her struggles as the ground begins to shake violently beneath her body. The world appears to explode around her. She finds it difficult to breathe as the weight of the stranger's body pushes against her lungs. At the same time, every muscle in Brent's body tenses to the maximum. The vibrations beneath them both were simultaneously accompanied by a thunderous roar. Brent makes every attempt to cover her entire body with his. His chin, lips, nose and forehead presses tightly against hers. Bricks, mortar, dust and glass rain down on everyone and everything; Brent feels bits of debris hitting his backside.

With what seems like an eternity, in five or six seconds, the earth beneath them eventually ceases to shake. The deafening noise that greeted them a few moments ago was replaced by the same eerie silence before the quake hit—minus the human chatter. Brent was at an immediate loss to explain what had just taken place. Earthquakes, of any meaningful magnitude, were virtually non-existent in Arizona—until now.

Glancing down at the unknown person below him, her eyes remain tightly closed. Her body continues to lie motionless as if frozen in ice. If she were breathing, he couldn't tell. Dust had quickly covered her olive-skin face and begins to turn her disheveled, dark hair to lighter shades of black and gray. As Brent turns his head and glances down the buckled walkway leading to the parking lot, he notices a number of parishioners struggling to get back on their feet. Cocking his head farther to the left, he catches his first glimpse of the church that was no more. Sticking out from the collapsed canopy were two outstretched arms — arms Brent knew were no longer attached to the owner's body. He instantaneously feels nauseated. For the first time in his adult life, he finds himself close to tears — a trait not becoming his professional being.

As he pulls himself away and kneels beside her, she begins to stir. Her eyes remain closed. Brent takes her right hand in his while observing the heavy coat of dust that darkened the two sides of her yellow blouse and light-blue slacks. Only the areas of clothing where he covered her with his body were free of dust — but not for long, as heavy layers of dust continue to settle down around them. Twenty seconds later, she finally opens her eyes, though the expression emanating from them was blank. He had to believe she was in a state of shock — unable to register the significance of what had just taken place.

"Oh my God," she remarks so softly that Brent isn't sure what she had said. And then, almost knocking Brent over backward from his kneeling position, she rose instantly to her feet and starts screaming, "My baby! My baby!" Tears rapidly flood her face. She cries out again, "My baby! My baby!" Her hands quickly covering her face as she sobs.

Brent jumps to his feet, grabs her by the shoulders and asks, "What baby? In the church?"

No," she cries out, "In my apartment...with my neighbor."

"How far away is your apartment?" Brent inquires.

"Seven, no eight blocks," she answers, still in a somewhat confused state of mind. "Where you see those five tall palm trees... over that way," she adds, while pointing directly to the west of the church. "It's on the corner of 88th and Villanueva. I need to find my baby. Please help me find my baby," she pleads.

Brent glances at the scene around him, sirens already wailing in the distance. Only one partial wall remains in an upright position—the wall holding the large crucifix behind the main altar. Without really knowing it to be a fact, he feels that far more than the church met its demise this beautiful Sunday morning. The thick dust that surrounded the area all but blocks out the morning sun. Taking in the scene before him, he wonders about the condition of his own house.

"Are you going to help me?" She asks again, pulling him away from his own thoughts.

"I'll help you," he answers, a bit reluctantly, "but first we need to see if we can help anyone here."

"No," she responds emphatically, "I need to get to my baby. Now!"

"I know you do, but there may be people here that simply need a piece of lumber removed to save them. I can't just walk away. Look around you...the devastation appears to be everywhere. We may not be able to even make it to your apartment safely."

"We don't know that to be a fact until we try, do we? Then I'll go by myself. My baby needs me. I've got to find out if she's okay," she adds. She turns without so much as a goodbye and begins walking quickly around the buckled walkway and debris leading to the street.

Brent's feelings of remorse are immediate as he watches her walk away. He could understand her personal anguish, but he also knew that he couldn't just walk away from the current situation to help just one person. Once she was out of view, he turns his attentions to the massive pile of rubble that, but for a few minutes before, was a house of worship. As he glances around, he somewhat realizes that no one would be found alive under what was the canopy. As he carefully makes his way up the mound of bricks, cement and broken lumber, he was astounded at how three of the church walls managed to fall perfectly inward—explosive technicians could not have done a better job.

Making his way to the crest of the rubble, he isn't shocked in the least at seeing no signs of life—outside of two couples standing on the far sidewalk surveying both him and the rubble. Looking about the ruins, he sees no arms, no legs, or any other bodily parts protruding anywhere; the roof apparently snuffing out the lives of all those within the church itself. Brent hears no moans, no cries for help—the hush of death beneath his feet grips his stomach. He remains standing in place. Feelings of total helplessness overcome him. Never in his thirty-two years of life had he felt as alone and disconnected from life as he did this very moment. He stands there pondering the hows and whys of a religious gathering, in a matter of seconds, could turn into a massive graveyard of many souls. And how was it that he was among the few who would live to see another sunrise?

Knowing no answers would be forthcoming, he turns and begins to navigate his way back down the debris—wondering all the while if his own home had survived. Finding his way to what was left of the sidewalk and street, he turns in the direction of his house. No sooner than traveling but a few feet into his walk, he comes to a halt, as he remembers the young lady and her baby. The very thought of her brings forth a series of questions that trouble him. Can she make it safely to her apartment on her own? If her building is totally demolished, like that of the church, what good would his presence be to her? Would she single-handedly tear at every ounce of debris to find her baby? Could I even find her or her apartment? Not knowing any of this begins to tear at his conscience. Could he live with himself by just walking away from it all? What about my own house? Is it still standing?

2

MAKING AN ABOUT face, he heads back in the direction of the church. Passing the church, he holds back at even taking a glance in its direction—a sense of hopelessness still gnawing at his stomach. The church parking lots, both to his right and left, were totally demolished by the quake; the various cars inhabiting the lots reminds him of an auto junkyard he had driven by outside of town. The sidewalks were almost buckled beyond passable. He notices billows of smoke dotting the horizon. Sirens could be heard from every direction, though he believes there were no direct routes to wherever they were headed; not if seeing firsthand the devastation around him was any indication of what the emergency personnel had to deal with.

After taking it all in, he continues around buckled sidewalks and begins making his way down the main street that ran alongside the church. It was then that he notices his first signs of life—outside of those few who were walking to their cars following mass and the couple across the street. He spots those lucky enough to have made it out of their homes and apartments. All were either milling around or hanging onto each other — wondering privately not only what happened, but the bigger question, what happens now?

As he continues to make his way down the street, he becomes acutely aware that not a single structure was left untouched by the quake's force. Those structures left standing, in many cases, leaned precariously to one side or the other. Windows were shattered everywhere he looked. Structures made of brick are mostly brick-less. The entire block appears to be uninhabitable — for not only immediate use, he gathered, but for the foreseeable future as well. Glancing farther down the block, he notices a house fully engulfed in flames. Given the impassability of the streets for emergency vehicles, he knew the structure would be totally consumed by the fire — and more than likely, those homes around it. If the residents were fortunate enough to get out alive, they would be watching helplessly as their past, present, and maybe their future, went up in flames. At the very least, they are to be counted among the lucky ones to have survived the quake.

He stops along the way and offers his condolences to any and all gathered outside of their homes. He makes a point of asking them if they had seen a dark-haired young lady pass by. The response was always no. By the time he makes his way to the end of the first block, ten minutes already passes. Climbing over a few uprooted trees, buckled sidewalks and streets all combined to take their toll on the clock. He had a hunch there would be no direct route to her apartment—and to her baby.

Heading up a short side street, Brent was quick to observe a small group of people with heads bowed as if in prayer. By the time he was twenty feet away, he clearly sees what appears to be a large sinkhole. Coming up closer to the edge, he glances in and was stunned at what he was seeing. Some thirty feet down was the young lady from church. There she was, standing in a pool of water that reached up to her chest. As the eyes of the people shifted his way, so did hers.

"Help. Please," she cries out.

"Stay calm," Brent shouts into the hole. "We'll find a way to get you out. Try not to move. I'll be right back, okay?" Looking over at the five people standing near the edge, Brent asks, "Would you mind staying here for a minute? I may need your help."

A few seconds pass before the oldest man in the group answers up. "We'll be here. It's not like we have a place to go to anyways."

"Thanks," Brent responds. He could hear the pain in the gentleman's voice. Quickly turning, five sets of eyes watch as he races to the closest house. Not finding what he was looking for, he hurries away to the second house—disappearing down the side of what was left of the house. A half minute later, he reappears carrying a garden hose with a sprinkling device still attached to one end.

Speaking to the group, he says, "I think it's obvious what I have in mind. I'm not convinced that she has the strength left in her to pull her way up the hose, hand over hand. So, if the four of us men grab hold and start walking with the hose, we might be able to get her up. If you two ladies wouldn't mind keeping an eye on her and letting us know if she stumbles or falls back down, that would be appreciated."

"We can do that," answers the same man.

Brent begins to slowly guide the hose down the side of the hole. "Okay," Brent yells back down into the hole. "I have to ask you first, are you okay? Any broken bones or anything like that?"

"No," she weakly answers back.

"Good. You have two choices. One is to grab onto the sprinkler and we'll pull you up, or you can wrap the sprinkler and hose around your waist and cinch it tight. Either way, we'll do the pulling. Got it?"

An exhausted sounding "Okay" makes its way up to Brent. He remains standing near the edge and watches as she ties the hose around her waist.

"When we start pulling," he yells down at her, "lean back a little and try to plant your feet against the wall of the hole...as if you were walking up the side. Okay?"

"I'm ready when you are."

"Ladies, yell if she slips. Gentlemen, easy does it." The four of them quickly grab hold of the hose and slowly start walking away from the hole. Fifteen feet into the pulling, one of the two women yells, "Stop." Ten seconds pass by before she gives the thumbs up to start again. By the time they reach the opposite side of the street, the woman once again yells, "Stop. Don't move." The four of them watch as the two women get down on their knees and help to pull the young lady up and over the edge to safety.

Brent and the three men immediately drop the hose and make their way over to where the young lady was sprawled out on her back. The two women set about undoing the hose around her waist. She was breathing heavily, as if she had just finished a full marathon race. With eyes completely closed, she continues to lie there. With the hose pulled out from beneath her, one of the women pulls a handkerchief from her pocket and begins to gingerly clean the muck from around her eyes and face.

As Brent looks down on her, he sees a body covered from head to toe in mud — and who knows what else. From the looks of her face and clothing, he surmises that a major sewer line had broken apart, thereby creating the sinkhole. Her right pants leg was slit all the way up the side, exposing muddied panties. From all the mud covering her, or whatever it was that was covering her, he couldn't make out if she was bleeding as well.

When her breathing returns to almost normal, she slowly opens her eyelids, but says nothing as she takes in all those staring down at her.

"Don't try to talk just yet," the younger of the two women advises her. "Just lie there and rest until you feel like getting up."

"Thank you, everyone, for getting me out," she ekes out with an emotional stutter in her voice.

"Thank the gentleman here for finding a way to get you out," comments the youngest of the three men.

"I couldn't have done it alone," Brent responds. As he glances around the neighborhood, he then adds, "I'm sorry for your loss. I only wish there was something I could do to repay you for your kindness. But at the moment, there's nothing I can do to restore your homes…your lives."

"One way or another, we'll get by," responds the young man. "I've been through war situations worse than this," he adds.

As he glances back down at the mud-covered woman, Brent notices her attempting to get back up to her feet. Reaching down with extended hands, she takes hold and allows him to pull her up to a standing position. The moment she lets go of his hands, she immediately begins to fall. Brent straight away grabs her wet soiled body and pulls her into him. Not only wet, he realizes, but smelly as well.

"Your mind is ready to get going, but your legs obviously didn't get the message," Brent semi-whispers into her ear. "Maybe it's just your sense of balance, or your legs are still weak from climbing up the sinkhole wall. Just chill for a minute, and when you're up to it, I'll help you find your daughter."

With his admission of offering to help her, she emotionally loses it and instantly throws her arms around Brent. With her head pressed tightly into his neck, she lets loose with a burst of uncontrollable sobbing. All of a sudden, Brent finds himself in unfamiliar territory. He is best known for making women happy — not making them cry.

After two minutes of clinging to Brent, she pulls herself away. "Thank you."

"You're welcome. Now take my hand and walk with me for about ten yards. I want to make sure you *really* are ready for what lies ahead. Reaching out, she takes hold of his hand and does as requested. "You did well. I think you're ready for the next challenge."

"I'm ready," she responds, with a look of gratitude in her eyes.

Glancing over her head at the five people zeroed in on them, Brent makes one last comment. "Thanks again everyone. We now need to go in search of her baby. And good luck to each of you," he adds.

"God speed you on your journey," replies the middle-aged man with an Irish brogue. Brent immediately wonders if the gentleman knows Father Patrick.

With the goodbyes behind them, Brent reaches out and offers up his hand; a hand she quickly takes for dear life as they start rapidly walking away. "My name is Brent. Brent Masterson, by the way. And yours?"

"Shimie. Shimie Jamison. That's my maiden name...not my formerly married name."

"And your child's name is?"

"Brianna Lynn."

"Shimie is an unusual name. Though I'm sure you've been told that before. I'll ask you later where it came from. Right now, we need to stay focused on the journey ahead."

"Thank you. I kind of like it too," she responds, with the slightest twinkle in her eyes.

As they turn right and cross the main street, they soon enter a street where another group of people stood in front of their homes—all with dazed looks on their faces. No sooner had they started walking down the street when Brent came to a complete stop. Clutching her hand even tighter, he swirls her around and rapidly leads her back in the direction they came from.

Startled by his actions, she asks, and not in a pleasant tone, "Why are we turning around? My apartment is this way."

"I think I smell gas—not a good sign. We need to find a detour around it."

"No!" Shimie screams. "I need to get to my baby. This is the quickest route."

"Listen to me," Brent yells back. He grabs her shoulders and looks directly into her large, brown eyes. Barely six inches separated their faces. "If you get blown to smithereens by a gas explosion, who in God's name is going to take care of your baby then? Have you even thought about that possibility? Quit being so damn stubborn and listen to me."

"I'll go by myself then," she yells back at him.

"Oh no you won't. Look what happened to you the last time you took off by yourself." He immediately bends down, scoops her up and throws her over his left shoulder and begins running. Shocked by his actions, she starts pounding her fists against his lower back. It was then that she notices large amounts of dried blood on the back of his shirt. She at once stopped her pounding.

By the time Brent reaches the end of the block, a loud explosion rocks both the air and ground beneath his feet. Again, Brent finds himself on the ground on top of her. He glances back over his shoulder and observes a number of homes exploding in flames simultaneously. As he watches, he can only imagine the fate of those standing out in front of those same houses. He now feels a sense of guilt for having not yelled down the block. He knew if the two of them hadn't left when they did, they too would have been counted among the fatalities.

"Look here, you little ingrate, if you have any desire to live long enough to see your baby again, you had better start listening to me. I've risked my own life to save your life—three times now—no more. Do I make myself perfectly clear?" he yells, only inches from her face.

Shimie didn't respond immediately—with the exception of tears streaming from her eyes. "I'm sorry...again," she finally responds after regaining her composure. Continuing to look up at Brent, she states, "An FYI...while you had me unceremoniously draped over your shoulder,

I noticed the back of your shirt was heavily covered in dried blood. And even your dress pants have large spotted areas of blood on both legs. Do you feel anything?" She asks. Her compassionate tone surprises Brent.

"Oh, every now and then I feel some pain back there, but nothing crippling…nothing to slow me down. The fact that you say it appears to be dried is a good sign, huh?"

"Yes, that is a good sign. I'm a surgical nurse. Once we get my baby back, I'll take a look at it. If that's okay with you?" she adds, then smiles as she looked deep into his eyes.

"That would be fine. Thanks. Ready?"

"Ready as you are. By the way, thank you for saving my life again."

"You can thank me later…after we find your baby. And no more of this not listening to me stuff. End of subject." Brent helps her back up to her feet. Leading her back down the main street, they stop only briefly to say a few words to those able to make it outside of their homes. With her hand tightly gripped in his, he abruptly turns left and heads once again in a southerly direction—hoping to find a street that had the appearance of being passable. Two blocks later, he finds a street that he feels they could safely make their way down. The street itself was in shambles, but by watching their steps, he thinks they could safely make it to the other end. With some careful stepping, and with Brent leading the way, they manage to make their way to the other end of the block.

What was clearly weighing on Brent's mind, and was keeping him on edge, were the periodic tremors, or aftershocks. He was experiencing a number of them since leaving the ruins of the church. For that reason, he makes a point to stay away from any structures that were two or more stories in height. Of course, his nose was always sniffing the air for signs of natural-gas leaks. Brent knew all too well that the Phoenix metropolitan area was heavily dependent on natural gas for its heating, air conditioning and cooking needs; the same natural gas that supplied his own house. If he had a house left, that is.

Not wanting to get too far off a straight path to her apartment, Brent makes a right turn at the intersection and heads back north. He soon finds they can only make their way one block before reaching another insurmountable obstacle—another in a line of buckled streets and collapsed houses. Broken water mains and sewer lines had added to the destruction everywhere they were turning—though even these water breaks had now joined the silence of the morning.

Glancing to his left, he observes Shimie's five tall palm trees. Surveying the street, Brent concludes they could safely make their way down this particular street. As before, there were any number of people standing around— wherever they could find a patch of flat ground to stand on. If there were no residents gathered in front of some homes, he was of the belief they either never made it out in time, or were away from home when the quake hit.

Those that made it out were huddling close together — not for warmth — but for consolation. It would be sometime before the shock wore off. For many, the experience of this morning would alter their lives forever. For the time being, however, all they could do was cry and hold onto one another. And wait for the unknown.

With no apparent smell of gas in the air, Brent guides Shimie down the street. As before, they acknowledge those they pass — but there was little to be said. Each resident was caught up in their individual and collective grief. Brent and Shimie were thoughtful enough to at least acknowledge their presence with a nod of the head as they passed by. Under normal circumstances, Brent might have stopped and offered assistance, but right now he was on his own mission — to reunite a baby with its mother; a mother who was putting her whole faith in Brent that he would do just that. This too was weighing heavily on his mind. He was used to assuming responsibility, but not of this nature.

Tightly holding her hand, least she fall or stumble, Brent makes his way past the usual obstacles, including a large number of uprooted trees, before eventually reaching the end of the block. He gives off a slight smile while glancing up the next street. It appears to be passable, he observes; outside of a few fallen trees that he felt they could either go over, around, or beneath. Without further hesitation, they began making their way up the next street. At that moment, his cell phone rang. He knew from the ring tone, it was his father.

"Good morning, father, how's things in D.C.?" He said while continuing to move at a brisk pace down the street.

"Of course I'm okay. Would I be answering the phone if I weren't?"

"No, I suffered no injuries. I had just walked out of church when the quake hit. A half minute earlier and you and mother would be making my funeral arrangements."

"I'm out of breath because it's getting hot out and I'm moving as fast as I can."

"Nope, haven't made it home yet. I'm currently on a mission to reunite a mother with her baby."

"Yes, you heard me right…a mother and a baby. We're getting close to her apartment, so it won't be long. What are the news channels reporting?" A long silence ensues as his father explains what he saw on the news.

"Well, I can easily attest to what they're reporting…it's like a war zone everywhere we go."

"Don't worry father, I'll be careful. I need to hang up now…it's hard to walk at this pace and talk. Give my love to mom."

"You too, dad. And don't you two start worrying about me every two minutes…I'm a Masterson, remember." With that, he hit the off button.

He glances sideways at Shimie, and remarks, "As you probably guessed, that was my father still being a parent. What about your parents?"

"Mine are both deceased," she answers with a hint of pain in her voice.

"Siblings, by any chance?"

"An only child."

"Sorry. I appear to be striking out here with the personal questions."

Another ten minutes would pass before they were able to reach the end of the long street. Brent's heart almost stops when he takes a hard look at the street before them; a street that was once lined on both sides with multi-story condos or apartments. For whatever reason, those buildings that came down did so into the center of the street. It was almost eerie to see no one outside of the buildings. After a quick survey, Brent knew right away this block would not be an option to them. With that in mind, he turns right once again and heads north. Upon reaching the next intersection, he realizes that turning left was not an option either. Making their way up to the next intersection and glancing to the left, he felt a sigh of relief. While there appears to be substantial damage to both sidewalks and the street itself, he thinks it looks negotiable.

Crossing the intersection that was awash in muddy water, they continue their journey in silence; a silence they both accept given the current circumstances. Three-quarters of the way down the long street, however, they were stopped by a rather large Arizona Ash tree that was uprooted by the quake; a tree that was almost impossible to go around given the collapsed, sunken roadway. The upper part of the tree managed to fall directly onto the owner's house — almost flattening it in the process. Brent made a number of running attempts at jumping on top of the tree's trunk before giving up on that idea.

"Well, we may just have to see if we can work our way through the branches. Either that or find another street to go down. What are your thoughts, Shimie?"

"I'm all for going through the branches," she answers, not wanting to waste time finding another street.

"The branches win out then. I'll lead the way."

Following the tree line up to the house, Brent begins making his way through the branches. Two minutes and a lot of scratches later, they both make their way safely out of the maze.

"Were you in the Marines by any chance? You got through the branches as fast as I did," Brent jokes.

"No, but I've climbed my share of trees as a kid. My dad wanted a son, but he got me instead."

The first thing Brent notices is a slight smile on her lips and a gleam in her eyes when she said that. "Well, your youthful training as a pseudo-son obviously paid off. Now, back to the task at hand…how many blocks do we have left to go?"

"It should be three," she answers. "One this way and two that way…see the five palm trees?" she adds, while pointing in their direction.

"Yep, I see them. Let's get moving then."

"Oh my God, I am so nervous right now I'm shaking. After looking at all of this destruction, I can only think the worst for my apartment and daughter."

"Don't fear the worst until it's staring you right in the face."

"I know what you're saying," she responds, "but this isn't your daughter we're talking about."

"Point well taken, but right now we have two long and one short block to travel, so let's get moving, okay?"

"Okay, sorry. I was just trying to express my feelings, and you started getting all philosophical on me. I don't need that right now. Understand?"

"I understand fully," he responds, with a slight note of contriteness in his voice.

While Shimie feels justified in calling him on his so-called philosophical approach to the situation, she also knows that she needs his skills right now in the worst way. As far as she was concerned, the mini-debate was now history.

Hand in hand, they once again find themselves working around the many obstacles created by the earthquake. Brent picks up the sound of helicopters in the distance. As with other streets they've traveled along, they came upon people who were either crying, hugging or just plain sitting down with their hands over their faces. While Brent feels a sense of sadness for all of them, he is particularly saddened by those who were alone in their grief. Were they always alone, he wonders, or were their loved ones in the house and didn't make it out with them? A question that would go forever unanswered, though deep down, he knew both cases existed.

The two of them were able to get down the current block more quickly than the previous ones. There was destruction all around, but they were fortunate in being able to walk around most of it without too much difficulty. Looking across the intersection, Brent observes nothing that would prevent them from reaching the other end of the street. Making their way across the street, it was the same scene as the previous street — people all around trying their best to deal with their grief.

The act of making it to the end of the block turned out to be more arduous than Brent had first envisioned. Two-thirds of the way down the street, they were met by a large sinkhole full of brownish-colored water — similar to the one he had helped Shimie out of. To the right of the sinkhole were two houses fully engulfed in flames. To the left was a two-story home that was leaning precariously toward the sinkhole. Brent knew that a decision had to be made — and made quickly. Either turn back or find another street to go down, or take the inherent risk of racing past the leaning house. One more aftershock and that house would be history — and aftershocks were never predictable.

Turning to Shimie, he asks, "Well, you see the situation before us, what do you think?"

"It's obvious we can't run into a fire. I can see that this house can't hold itself up for much longer. So, as I see it, we only have two choices. Turn around and go back, or go through the side yard of the house, or the house next to it, and come out on the other side."

"Damn good option. I never thought of that. Let's see if we can get to the backyard of the house next to it and go around through the backyards. If it falls, that's okay, as it will fall toward the street."

Taking her hand once again, they make their way back up the street and step over a fallen side gate to a home that had already totally collapsed. As they made their way across the backyard, they were stopped by an upright, wooden fence.

"Okay, we have no choice but to scale the fence," Brent remarks discouragingly. Here, put your left foot in my hands and I'll boost you up. Grab the top of the fence and swing yourself down to the other yard. Can you handle that?"

"Piece of cake," she responds, without reservation.

Once her foot was securely in his hands and her one hand on his shoulder, he lifts her up. Shimie immediately grabs onto the top of the fence and swings herself to the grass below. "Oh my God," she cries out.

"Are you okay? What's the matter?" Brent promptly asks, concerned that she had hurt herself going over the fence.

"Oh my God, there's a body lying here."

Brent quickly scales the fence and lands right next to where Shimie is standing. And sure enough, not ten feet away was what he knew to be a man lying face down — with a portion of the patio roof lying across his back. Brent kneels down and checks the victim's carotid artery for a pulse.

Looking up at Shimie, he says quietly, "There's nothing we can do for him. He's already gone. The house is obviously leaning toward the street, but the patio's roof fell into the backyard, which is a little odd."

"How sad," Shimie says more to herself than to Brent.

Rising back up, Brent reaches for her hand and swiftly leads her across the yard to the next fence. "We could go out this side gate, but it's too close to the house for my taste," he remarks. "Let's climb one more fence and play it safe."

"Fine by me," replies Shimie in a subdued voice.

"Okay, you know the routine," states Brent as he bends down and locks his hands together. In less than ten seconds, the two of them are over the fence, landing five feet from a half filled pool.

"Perfect timing," Brent comments while looking at the pool. "Given that you're still caked in mud and who knows what else, why don't you get into the pool. I fully realize you want to get to your daughter, but cleaning yourself up is important too…if for no other reason than to rid yourself of possible germs."

Without saying a word, she walks to the other side of the pool and proceeds down the ladder and into the water. Given her sense of urgency concerning her daughter, Brent is somewhat surprised at the amount of time she spent in the pool attempting to clean the muck off her face, hair and clothing. Climbing back out, she immediately rejoins Brent.

"You look much better." He couldn't help but notice the nipples bulging out from her wet blouse. Even with her wetted look, she was absolutely gorgeous.

"I feel a hundred percent better, thank you. I stunk badly, and I knew it," she adds with a partial smile.

"Gee, I never noticed," he replies with a grin of his own. Taking her hand, he hurriedly leads her to the far end of the yard. Brent unlatches the side gate and they both find themselves safely back on the sidewalk. In short order, they make it to the end of the street with only one short block to go before reaching her apartment complex. They both stand in place while watching a National Guard personnel carrier, a Humvee, a military first aid vehicle and, holding up the rear, an oversized bulldozer pass by in front of them. Brent was in awe of how quickly they were able to mobilize and begin rescue operations.

3

_____

"Oʜ ᴍʏ Gᴏᴅ!" exclaims Shimie, as the tears start to flow in a flood.

Brent looks up the street in the direction she's staring. He could make out the end unit of the two-story apartment complex—a unit that lay in ruins. He immediately pulls her close to him and slips his arm around her shoulder.

"What unit number is that?" Brent asks calmly.

"That's 100," she barely gets out between sobs.

"And what's your unit number?"

"106."

"Okay, let's not make any assumptions just yet until we get there. You are six units down from that one." Reaching down, he takes her hand and begins walking in the direction of the apartments. Going both around and over a few obstacles, they make it to the apartment building in less than two minutes.

Shimie frantically glances down the row of apartments.

Her unit had not been totally leveled, though it had buckled and sat at a 45-degree angle. She immediately lets out a long sigh as a ray of hope passes through her mind — even though her body begins to tremble from apprehension from the unknown fate of her daughter.

Given the number of apartments, Brent is a little surprised at seeing only five or six people standing in the middle of the courtyard. At the end of the complex, he observes two men frantically working to clear the rubble in front of one unit. He could only surmise that they were in the process of helping someone who was trapped inside. He heard no pleas for help coming from any of the units. Nor did he hear the cries of a baby — but he had the sense about him not to mention it.

"Which unit is yours?" Brent asks calmly.

"That one," she replies, pointing in the direction of her unit. "The one with the white chair in front of it," she adds. Rather than wait for Brent to take the lead, as he had up to this point, she quickly makes her way down the courtyard as Brent follows on her heels.

Standing in front of her apartment, they quickly survey the damage. The door was partially crushed to the point of not opening. The picture window was gone except for huge chunks of jagged glass sticking up from the base of the window. As with the unit itself, the window casing was crushed to a 45-degree angle. After ten seconds of assessing the situation, Brent was the first to speak.

"I'll go in through the window. It won't take much of

an aftershock to bring the unit down, so no reason for the two of us risking our lives. It appears to be a small unit, so it won't take long to search. Which room is the baby's bed in?"

"Her crib is in my bedroom, which is just off of the living room…down the hallway," she states in a shaky voice. "And no, I'm the one that should be going in. It's my daughter in there, not yours."

"I'm well aware it's your daughter in there. But I fully expect to find things strewn all over the place. If any of it has to be moved aside, I'm obviously better equipped to do it. Trust me, I'm not going to spend much time in there…it's a small unit. I'll find your daughter and your neighbor."

"Oh my God!" Shimie yells out, bringing her hands up to her mouth. "I forgot all about my neighbor."

"That's my other point. There's no way you would be able to bring your neighbor out. I'll first go in search of your daughter and bring her out. I'll be right back."

Shimie was dying on the inside from the helpless feeling of being left outside. Wanting badly to go inside, she reluctantly gives in to Brent's going alone. She watches as he breaks away the jagged glass lining the bottom of the window frame. The seconds pass like minutes. Never in her life had she experienced so much anticipation as right now — and on top of that — anticipation with unknown results.

Once he clears the glass away, Brent stoops down and

lifts one leg over the base of the window frame. In a matter of seconds, he's out of sight. With the leaning nature of the apartment, Brent is required to go down on all fours. With enough light coming in the living room, he quickly surveys the entire room at a glance. Various wall pictures were scattered everywhere, along with lamps, end tables and nick-knacks. Assured that no baby or neighbor was in this room, he begins crawling down the hallway to the single bedroom. He was met by a lot of water on the carpeted hallway floor.

As with the living room, the one large window in the bedroom was broken out. Taking in the room, he is heartened by what he sees; the room as a whole is relatively unscathed, with only the changing table lying on its side. Glancing across the top of the bed, he finds nothing but pillows. With glass lying on the floor where he needs to go next, he pulls the bedspread off the bed and throws it over the glass. As he crawls over to the right of the skewed window, he rises up partway and looks into the baby's crib—only to find it empty. Checking under the bed, he finds only miscellaneous items placed there for storage. That leaves only the bathroom and kitchen, he surmises.

As he makes his way out of the bedroom, he makes a sharp right turn and crawls three feet farther down the hallway to what he assumes is the bathroom. He immediately notes that door is closed and wedged in place. This bothers him immensely as any attempt at freeing the door could cause the unit to collapse entirely. He has no idea what part of the support structure keeps her apartment from totally caving in. After giving it some thought, he decides to check out the kitchen first before returning to tackle the bathroom — if need be.

Meanwhile, Shimie stands in place and nervously wonders what's taking him so long; not being fully aware that Brent has only been inside five minutes. The apartment was small — she knew that well. It shouldn't take him this long to search every room. She desperately wants to go inside and check for herself, but she was also afraid — afraid not of going inside, but what she might find. As long as he was inside, she deduces, there was still hope.

Crawling back down the hallway, Brent makes two right turns before he enters the kitchen. As his eyes adjust to the dim light of the slanted window, he freezes in place. The sight before him is not what he hoped to find. The body lying before him, he could only assume, was the neighbor lady. She lay motionless on her back as if in a deep sleep. Her head was cocked to one side on the tiled floor in front of the upright refrigerator. Once again, his stomach begins to churn.

He inches closer to where she lies. The gleam of light shining in through the broken kitchen window was just enough for Brent to spot a pooled mass of dried blood on the left side of her head. Placing his fingers on her neck, he hastily pulls his hand back as if bitten by a snake. Outside of bodies lying in a casket, he had never experienced dead people before today — and hopefully never would again.

Her neck was cold upon his fingers. He knew rigor mortis had already started its unforgiving process of decay. As the feeling of nausea instantaneously hits him, he finds it necessary to divert his attentions away from the body.

He notices a wrought-iron skillet lying on the floor close to her lifeless body. Glancing upward, Brent observes two pots hanging from the ceiling over the stove—though many more had shaken loose by the quake and fell to the floor. He surmises the heavy skillet found its mark when the earthquake hit. Looking to his right on the floor, he takes in what he knows to be a broken baby bottle in front of the stove—its milky contents splattered across the floor.

"Are you okay in there?" A loud voice startles him. "Did you find my daughter? Is she okay?"

"I haven't found anyone yet," Brent yells back. Now was not the time to increase her worries by mentioning the fate of her neighbor, he concludes. "It's slow going...a lot of debris in here," he shouts back. "I've got one more room to check."

"Hurry...bring me my baby," she yells back.

Finding her neighbor in the kitchen, he considers, all but eliminates the chance of finding the baby in the bathroom. There's no plausible reason one would leave a baby in there while warming her bottle. Before leaving the neighbor woman, Brent removes his cell phone from his belt and snaps five quick photos—not only of the neighbor, but the surrounding area as well.

Reaching for a dishtowel lying on the floor, he brushes

aside the broken glass. Moving aside the various pots and pans strewn on the floor, he crawls around the stove island to the small dining area. He had high hopes of seeing the baby in either a highchair or one of those...he momentarily forgot what they were called. He just knew it was similar to a car seat, but that it generally sat on the floor with a baby buckled in.

Instant dismay sets in. Scouring the entire area, he finds nothing more than busted chairs, an overturned highchair and an almost flattened kitchen table. Looking high and low, left and right, he sees no child; all of which leaves him extremely puzzled. The neighbor taking care of the baby was here; albeit dead, but she's here. Then a massive earthquake strikes and, a couple hours later, poof—the baby is gone—vanishes without a trace or a clue. He forgot to ask Shimie the age of the child, but with the presence of a baby bottle, highchair and crib, he finds it highly unlikely that the baby found a way out on her own. Or was she, he wonders, actually in the bathroom? He knew there was only one way to find out, though he didn't like the possible dangers involved while attempting to gain access to the bathroom itself.

And then it hit him. The bathroom is on an outside wall—as most bathrooms are. That means it must have a window—and most likely a broken window. With any luck, he figures he should be able to go around to the backside of the building and basically just look in the window. It's worth a try, he thinks. Besides, he also knew he had better reappear outside — and soon. He pictures her standing in front of her unit tearing her hair out. Once he tells her what happened inside, including the missing baby part, she will absolutely lose it. And after what she has been through to get to this point in time, he knew deep down that he would lose it as well — if he had a child, that is. Getting married and having children were not exactly on his bucket list of things to complete anytime soon — if ever.

And sure enough, as he carefully steps out of the living room window, there she was, standing with a look of horror on her face — a look he already knew would greet him without her child in his arms.

"Oh my God! Don't tell me my daughter is dead. Please don't tell me that. Oh my God!" She screams out louder than the first time. The residents down the courtyard turn in their direction and then just as quickly return back to their own grief.

"Get a hold of yourself," Brent says as he approaches her. "Your daughter is not in there. I checked every room but the bathroom, which I couldn't get into. We'll go around to the back and see if we can look through the window. There is an outside window to the bathroom, isn't there?"

"Yes...one of those smoky ones," she replies haltingly, tears streaming down her cheeks. "Does that mean that my neighbor and daughter made it out of the apartment okay? Maybe they went for a walk before or after her morning feeding," she adds, wishfully.

Brent immediately finds himself at an unpleasant cross-road. Do I tell her that her neighbor was lying on the kitchen floor dead? Or do I allow her to think, even if it's just for a bit longer, that maybe the two of them did go for a walk? At some point, however, he would have to be honest with her. As an attorney, he's used to hurting people, but only in a legal setting. The current situation he inadvertently finds himself involved with is personal—as personal as it can get between a mother and her missing child.

"Ahem, I think I was talking to you. Is there something you're not telling me?" She asks.

Jarred by her voice back to the present situation, Brent makes a quick decision—one he hopes he would not later, or currently for that matter, regret. Picking up the lone chair that sat outside her front door, he carries it out to the safety of the courtyard. "Come here, please. And no, this is not about your daughter." When she walks over to where he stands, he motions for her to have a seat. Once seated, with both a puzzled and worried look on her face, he begins.

"First off, just to set your mind at ease, I know for a fact that your daughter is not inside. We'll check the bathroom in just a minute, though I find it inconceivable that your neighbor would place her in the bathroom, with the door closed no less, while she warms your daughter's bottle. Secondly, I did locate your neighbor…on the kitchen floor. And no, she will not be counted as one of the lucky survivors."

"Oh no!" Shimie cries out, immediately bringing her hands to her face. The sobs quickly follow. At this point, Brent was feeling extremely powerless. He has made many a woman cry on the witness stand, but that was his job — to break them down emotionally. Once he broke them down, it wasn't his job to put them back together. The situation confronting him now was totally out of his league of expertise.

"Are you...sure?" Inquires Shimie between sobs.

"Yes...I'm quite sure," he answers in a low, calming voice. "There was no pulse. Her body was stone cold." After a moment's hesitation, he continues. "If it's any consolation, I strongly believe she died instantly."

There is a long moment of silence between them as Shimie tries to get herself under control. Before she has a chance to fully compose herself, Brent offers up a plausible answer to her missing daughter. At least he was hoping it would partially set her mind as ease.

"I can't say with any certainty, but I would lay ten to one odds that someone heard the cries of your daughter and went in and took her out."

"Do you really think so?" She responds, with a renewed ray of hope in her voice.

"I'm simply offering that up as one possible answer. By the way, how old is your daughter?"

"Nine months. What does her age have to do with anything?" She inquires with curiosity.

"In my mind, it has a lot to do with solving this mystery

that confronts us. If nothing else, it eliminates certain possibilities. If she were a five-year-old, she could easily have gotten out on her own. At nine months, she was obviously carried out. At nine months, it is highly unlikely that your sitter — your neighbor — would have left her in the bathroom alone. Before we get into this discussion any deeper, let's go around back and see if we can peek into the bathroom. If nothing else, it will rule out the only room I wasn't able to check."

No sooner had he finished the sentence than Shimie was up and out of the chair. Taking Brent's extended hand, they walk side by side down the courtyard in the direction they had first entered. Turning left, they skirt around two sections of buckled sidewalks before reaching the alleyway.

"Oh no!" Exclaims Shimie as she surveys the street.

"What now?" Asks Brent, wondering what had caught her attention.

Pointing across the street, she answers, "That's my car. The blue one on its side."

"Just be thankful you weren't sitting in it…obviously totaled. Come on, we've got to keep moving."

Returning his attention to the alley, Brent takes note of the fact that each of the units apparently has small backyards with wooden fences on the alley side — and with individual gates for taking their garbage out. He also notices the 300-gallon rubber garbage cans that didn't fare too well when the quake hit. Wild and stray animals will be feasting for a while, Brent thinks as they skirt around the strewn garbage. He was thankful upon seeing that most of the wooden fencing had come down during the quake—which let him count the number of units as they proceeded down the alley.

"Okay, from the looks of the way that unit is leaning, I'm going to guess that it's your unit. What do you think? Am I right or wrong?"

"Oh, that's mine alright," Shimie quickly answers. "That Mexican Sun God was put up by my ex. He bragged that it would take a killer of an earthquake to break it away from the wall. For once, I'm glad he was right."

"Then I take it that smaller window to the left of the Sun God is the bathroom window?"

"That's it," Shimie answers, with the rising sounds of anxiety in her voice.

"There's a lot of debris in the yard to climb over...you stay put and I'll go have a look in the window. As I mentioned before, I don't really expect to find your daughter in the bathroom."

Shimie said nothing in response. He was right earlier when he said he was better equipped, being a man and all, to tackle this sort of thing. If she had to, however, she knew she would have taken on the same tasks in order to find her daughter. Nothing would have stopped her—not even at the risk of injury or death. Her daughter was her whole life.

Brent swiftly makes his way over the fallen fence before

encountering huge piles of broken roofing tiles, tar paper, lumber and an old, rusted-out swing set. Finally making his way to the broken out bathroom window, he sticks his head inside. Though his head blocked some of the light coming in, he was still able to survey the small room—or what was left of it. The bathtub was intact, but the sink and medicine cabinet had pulled away from the wall. And, just as he had surmised from being in the hallway earlier, there was water everywhere. Water—but no baby.

Pulling his head back out of the window, he immediately turns to where Shimie is standing and shakes his head. She stands there with a thousand expressions on her face. Beaten. Discouraged. Unbelieving. Brent quickly picks up on her look of hopelessness. What was he to say now that would give her even a glimmer of hope? He isn't sure, but he knew he had to find something that would give her at least an ounce of encouragement—even if it were false encouragement. His kindness was drawing him into a scenario he never thought possible in his lifetime. But then again, who would ever think that Arizona would experience an earthquake? Not just any earthquake, but a devastating one at that.

Making his way back to where she anxiously stood, he hesitates for a moment before finally saying, "Okay, as you have probably figured out by now, your daughter is not in the bathroom. That leads us to the last and final conclusion. Some well-meaning Samaritan has rescued your daughter. Just who, I haven't anymore a clue than you do.

But I do know one thing for sure…we need to go back into the courtyard and start asking questions of those standing around. I would like to think that someone has to know something. At least, I would like to hope so. The bottom line is…your daughter is safe…we just don't know where or with whom."

"I'm feeling sick. I don't know if I can take anymore of this. My daughter needs me. I need my daughter," Shimie cries out, and promptly begins sobbing all over again.

Brent reaches out and pulls her into him. Shimie in turn throws her arms around him and unleashes a torrent of tears and bawls uncontrollably. Brent does his best to comfort her justifiable fears, but this is new ground for him. As an adult, even his younger sister never needed consoling of this magnitude—and her worries concerned only money or boyfriends.

With their arms still wrapped around each other, Brent is the first to speak. He does so in a quiet tone. "I'm try-ing my best to help you, but admittedly I'm not a miracle worker or a psychic. I don't claim to have all the answers. The earthquake, and what has happened to you personal-ly, is obviously a new experience for both of us. We have no choice but to push on…to exhaust every possibility. But now we need to return to the courtyard while the apartment complex people are still there … providing they haven't already moved on."

Arching her head up to look him directly in the face, she says, "I know what you're saying. I'm just sick from not knowing where my daughter is. I need to find her. My daughter means everything to me."

"I know what your daughter means to you. That's what I'm willing to help you do…to find her. No matter how long it takes, I promise to help in any way I can."

"Trust me, I appreciate you being here…and helping me. You have to be concerned about your own home, and here you are helping a total stranger. I can't even begin to thank you enough," she concludes, still looking straight into his blue eyes.

"Yes, I'm concerned about my own home, but my home only represents a material object. Fr. Pat was right in his homily this morning…material items don't fulfill or nourish the soul. So, thanks to his homily, you caught me in the right frame of mind. Though, to be honest with you, I most likely would have helped without the benefit of his homily."

"That was one of his better homilies. Thank you for wanting to help me. And you know what? We've been together for probably the last two hours, probably more, and I don't even know if you are married or have a family waiting for you at home."

"I'm not only *not* married, never have been married, and no one is waiting for my return…with the exception of the koi fish, perhaps. Not to change the subject, but right now we have some people to talk to."

As he reaches out to take her hand for the hundredth time today, they begin making their way back down the alley and into the courtyard. Luckily, the same five people are still standing there—along with the two men throwing debris left and right in front of one of the units. As they approach the five—three women and two elderly men—Shimie realizes that she doesn't know any of them by name. Oh, she had seen them around the complex before, but had never spoken to them other than to say hi. Being a large complex, people were always moving in and out. Shimie was the first to speak up.

"Hi, I'm Shimie...from 106...or what used to be 106. My nine-month old daughter was with my sitter Gladys while I was at church. We searched my unit, but my daughter wasn't in there. Did any of you by any chance see anyone who might have brought her out?"

There was a stony silence as they glanced at each other. One of the women finally spoke up.

"The three of us women were on our morning walk when the quake hit. It took us a good half-hour to get back here. And no...I personally didn't see anyone with a baby. Having a daughter with a newborn, I think I would have paid attention to something like that." Turning back to the other four, she asks, "Did any of you?" The shake of their heads said it all. The enormity of all that had taken place this morning was clearly visible in their weary eyes. For the first time this morning, Shimie finds herself feeling sorry for someone other than herself.

"Thank you," Brent responds as he reaches down for Shimie's hand. Moving around the five of them, he leads her toward the two men still frantically throwing debris away from one of the units. Approaching as near to the men as physically possible, Brent instructs Shimie to wait for him. Climbing over the rubble, he stops five feet from the men. They both look his way, but continue what they were doing—too transfixed on their own mission to concern themselves with a nosy stranger.

"Pardon me," Brent calls out. At this, they glance his way once again, but this time remain focused on what he may have to say. "Did either of you see a baby being removed from 106 this morning? Either before, during, or after the quake?"

"Not I," responds the younger of the two. He then glances at the other man who simply shakes his head. With that, they resume what they were doing before the interruption.

"Thanks," Brent says as he turns and walks away to rejoin Shimie.

"Well?" Shimie inquires, with an anxious look in her eyes.

"Dead-end with those two. They saw nothing."

"I can't believe that my baby just vanished in thin air," she says in response. All the energy and hope she had up to this point appears to have drained out of her like water over a fall. As quiet tears once again fill her eyes, she looks up at Brent and dejectedly asks, "What now?"

"I'm not quite sure myself," Brent replies somberly as he gazes into her swollen, troubled eyes. He, like her, is filled with more questions than answers. And right now he's feeling some responsibility for Shimie. He knew himself well enough to know that he couldn't just walk away from either her or the situation that was thrown at him. At this very moment, she still needs help—if for no other reason than simply to be a shoulder to lean on—someone to talk to. Always in the back of his mind, however, were concerns for his own home. Was it still standing? Was it habitable? Could he even get to it from here? So many questions—but the answers remain as elusive as her missing child.

"What are you thinking?" Shimie asks, breaking the silence along with his chain of thoughts. She waits for his response as they walk back in the direction of her apartment.

"I'm trying to plan out our next move. Only I'm not sure what our next move would or should be. Your apartment is obviously destroyed, so we can't wait it out here. Eventually, we'll need to eat and get some much-needed water to drink. And yes, I realize that eating is probably the furthest thought from your mind right now, but if we don't eat, we'll have no energy to do anything."

"You're right...I'm not hungry right now."

"I don't know about you, but I'd like to make it to my place...or at least attempt to make it there. Having lived in LA for a few years, I had my home built here with the potential for earthquakes in mind—at least a minor level earthquake. So, with any luck, it might still be habitable. Are you game?"

"I'll go with you, but first I'd like to put a note on my door...in case someone comes back with my baby."

"We can do that...but only if we had a pencil and paper."

"Right inside my front door is a tall table that I throw my keys and purse on when I come home. There's also a notebook with a pen inside. I can't ask you to go inside again, so I'll go."

"No you won't," Brent states commandingly. "I can be in and out of there in a flash...if I can locate the notebook right away, that is."

Before she has the opportunity to respond, he heads in the direction of the window. Climbing back in the way he had before, he quickly finds the notebook lying on the floor by the overturned table; he shoves the notebook down the front of his pants. He then scoops up keys, lipstick, a makeup kit and what appears to be a birth control pill packet and places them back into her purse.

Before he makes it back to the window, however, a thought strikes him. A second later, he finds himself crawling on all fours as he heads into the kitchen. He carefully slides the neighbor's body to the right—only to be greeted by a pool of dried blood where her head was positioned. Recovering from the momentary shock, he opens the door to the refrigerator. Even though the light didn't come on, he quickly spots what he had hoped to find—a loaf of bread and, more importantly, three large bottles of water. Placing a bottle in each of his pants' pockets, he hastily retreats back to the living room and climbs back out the window.

Walking over to where she was standing, he presents her with both the purse and a water bottle. "Thirsty?"

"As a matter of fact, I am thirsty. Thank you."

"And I grabbed a loaf of bread while I was at it. At least we won't starve to death...today anyway."

Shimie glances up at Brent—and for the first time since this ordeal began—gives off a relatively large smile.

"You look beautiful when you smile. Oh, and here's the notebook too. Sit down and write whatever it is you want to write. Do you have a cell phone on you by any chance?"

"It should be in my purse you retrieved...but why do you ask?"

"If someone is looking for you, or has your daughter, then they need some way of contacting you. You may want to add my number to the note, as well...just in case yours goes dead. Here's my business card with the number on it."

"Oh no!" My charger is inside...by the door."

"No it isn't. I saw it plugged into the wall by the notebook, so I slipped it in my pocket."

"Do you think of everything?" She responds, while sitting in the chair, beginning to write.

"Generally speaking, only when it comes to my profession," he replies. "I'm a stickler for detail while working on client cases. The rest of my life...not so much. I have a house cleaner twice a week—who does my laundry also. And I'm the world's worst cook. That about sums me up."

"And just what is your profession...if you don't mind my asking?"

Before he had the opportunity to answer, his opening words were drowned out by a huge explosion some two or three blocks away.

"That was too close for comfort. Anyways, I'm an attorney...primarily for large corporations. It's on my business card."

"Sounds exciting."

"Only when I win," Brent replies. "And I usually do," he adds, more as a statement of fact than bragging. "So, you're a surgical nurse. For a hospital I assume?"

"Yes...Scottsdale General," Shimie answers, while at the same time rising up from the chair. "I was in med school, then unexpectedly got pregnant, so had to drop out. Will you slip this in the doorframe for me, please?"

"Gladly...I'll slip my card in with it...you never know." Brent heads over to the door and wedges it in between the door and the frame before returning to Shimie. "Okay, if we're going to my place, we had better get moving. The sun is getting just a little too warm for comfort. Oh, if you happen to spot a bag of some kind while we're walking, grab it. We can put the bread, water bottles and notebook in it. Easier to carry that way."

"I can do that. How far away is your house?"

"Somewhere around a mile and a quarter from here...

sort of on the opposite side of the church. I'm thinking we should head north to the main boulevard. The streets are cemented, which means that rebar was probably laid down. With any luck, they won't be as buckled as the side streets we traveled on to get here."

4

"Brent." She said his name as if a question mark should follow—but she said no more.

"Okay, what's on your mind?" Brent asks gently.

"I feel guilty leaving here…as if I'm abandoning my daughter."

"That would be true if your daughter were here, but she isn't. Whoever it was that rescued her will take good care of her…or they wouldn't have rescued her in the first place. They heard your baby crying, went in and brought her out. At great risk to their own lives, I might add. I don't mean to imply that it's a case of survival of the fittest—meaning us—but you can't take care of someone who isn't here. The best thing you can do for your daughter right now is to take care of yourself."

"I know you're right, Mr. Philosophical Man, but it's still hard to just walk away."

"Call me insensitive—call me what you want—but one of us has to look at the reality of the situation that's been forced on us. Right now, you are thinking with your heart...your emotions." He's done his best to be understanding of her situation, but right now they were faced with their own survival. If he had to leave her here, he would.

"Okay, enough with the speeches," she responds, a note of dejection in her voice. "I've had a change of mind. I think its best that you go on without me. I need to be here in case someone comes back with my baby. You men all think in terms of survival of the fittest—women don't. We take care of and protect those who aren't able to take care of themselves—especially our children. I don't expect you to understand my decision, but it's a decision any mother would make who found herself in the same situation."

"Shimie, there's chaos, death and destruction all around us. You've seen it firsthand. I hear what you're saying, but I sincerely doubt that anyone is going to be foolhardy enough to risk injury or death simply to return a baby right now. We left a note on ..."

"Hey, you'll have to vacate the area...now," came a bullhorn-speaking voice from the same personnel carrier that passed them earlier. "There are high levels of natural gas in this neighborhood...you need to clear out."

"I'm waiting for my baby to be returned to me," yells Shimie to the lone figure sitting atop the personnel carrier.

"Sorry lady, but that's an order. You must vacate the area immediately," he yells back, without the use of the bullhorn this time.

"But you don't understand," she yells back, "I need my baby. My baby needs me."

"Lady, you two, and the people way behind you, either move or I'll have you all arrested without hesitation. Do I make myself clear?"

Brent immediately holds out his hand to her, but she doesn't bother to take it. Though he was only a few feet away, she somehow felt all alone as if her heart had been ripped out. This time she would show him that she was capable of overcoming whatever obstacles lay before them. Besides, without her daughter, she has nothing to lose. With feelings of abandonment coursing through her veins, she begins to walk.

Turning left out of the courtyard, they head north toward the four-lane thoroughfare some four blocks ahead. Their experiences during the trek north were the same as before—buckled sidewalks and streets, uprooted trees, smoldering ashes where homes once stood, and people milling around as if in a daze.

Sirens could be heard dead ahead, which was a welcome sound to Brent as it meant that at least a part of the main road could be traveled on. Twenty minutes later, they reach the principal east-west road he was hoping to get to. Quickly surveying the situation, he could easily see that this would be a much easier road to travel on. While parts of the sidewalk and roadway were torn up, emergency and National Guard vehicles were shifting back and forth from one lane to the other; oftentimes having to travel where oncoming traffic would normally be.

Aside from vehicles traveling to and fro, the two of them took in the sight of hundreds of people walking the same roadway — moving aside only when an emergency vehicle came upon them. The scene was reminiscent of ants setting out to forage for food in a single line and returning along the same path. Sadly enough, he hears few voices as the people pass by where he and Shimie stand. Everyone appears to be caught up in their own thoughts, their own grief and their own degrees of shock. Inwardly, Brent knew that when the dust settles and the rebuilding begins, the psychiatric community, including traumatologists in the metro area, would have more patients than they could handle. Post-traumatic stress disorder — but in civilian life.

As Shimie glances up at Brent, he simply motions in the direction they were to go. He instinctively knew that Shimie was not happy with him right now, but there was little he could do about it. He had been taught, both by his parents and in law school, to set aside emotions when making life-altering decisions or — in the case of his profession — winning. And right now it was all about survival; especially with the sun beating down on them and depleting the moisture in their bodies. Two of the three bottles of water had already been consumed and tossed aside. Brent wastes no time in consuming two slices of the apple-cinnamon bread while they stood there. Though he offers the bread to Shimie, she refuses to eat. He isn't sure if she refused out of defiance, or simply had no appetite. At the moment, it made no difference to him.

Given the detours they were forced to make, coupled with having to fight their way through the oncoming crowds, it took an hour and ten minutes to make it where Brent knew they had to turn off the main road. Looking southward to the road that would eventually get him close to his own house, Brent's heart skips a beat. A quick glance down the street reveals the same conditions he and Shimie had faced when going from the church to her apartment. The roads — and in some parts, the sidewalks — were built of asphalt, and they were buckled as badly as ones they had already faced. Trees were unceremoniously lying everywhere; homes had burnt to the ground and the same faceless people stood around in total disbelief and grief.

"Well, are you up to this?" Brent asks. He said this knowing full well that she, at this point anyway, had no choice but to push on.

"I don't like the looks of it, but I don't think we have any other alternatives. Unless some of the other side streets are better than what we're looking at right now."

"My guess is they aren't. And we could waste a lot of precious time trying to find the perfect street to go down — if one exists. Like our earlier travels, we'll just take it one block at a time. And just so you have some idea, we have six blocks to go straight ahead and then two east. We'll eventually hit cemented roads, so hopefully those will be in better shape than what we're looking at now. Oh, and by way, the sweat is pouring off of you; please drink some more water before you become dehydrated."

"Thank you...I will. Any chance you want to share some of that bread with me that you've been hoarding?"

"I think I can manage to share a few crumbs," he replies, while he hands over the sack. He was heartened to see a little more sparkle in her eyes than when they first set out on this particular stretch of their trek. Without looking at his cell phone, he knew that it was well past noon by the position of the sun. He was grateful that the quake hit earlier rather than later. As he found out when he moved here, the afternoon sun in Arizona can be unbearable at times; especially in the afternoons.

Handing the loaf of bread back to Brent, and after taking a swig of water, she extends her hand to Brent. Without hesitation, he takes her hand in his and they set off down the street together. The going, as Brent first anticipated, was not easy on the two of them. Sometimes it felt as though they were climbing a mountain. At other times it was as though they were going down steep hills—and at any moment they could fall into a deep hole. It was a nerve-wracking experience for them both. Six blocks and forty minutes later, they make it to the point of now having to turn east.

"Okay," Brent says, while still clutching Shimie's hand. "My house is two blocks straight ahead. That tall gate you see ahead opens up to my driveway. Fortunately, given that the remaining two streets are cemented with rebar, the going looks to be quite easy. What we'll see beyond the gate is anyone's guess."

"Wow! A private gate no less," Shimie remarks, while trying to envision what lay beyond the gate itself.

"Every house on that side of the road is gated...simply for security reasons." Following that little discourse on his gate, Brent begins moving once again with Shimie at his side.

"Doesn't the gate open by electricity?" Shimie inquires.

"It sure does," Brent quickly replies.

"Well, with the electricity apparently out everywhere, how do you propose that the gate is going to open for you? Or does everything do as you tell it to?"

Brent notices a strong hint of resentment, or was it envy, in her question, but chose to ignore it. "I have a backup generator that is electrically tied into the gate. This will be a test of whether or not the generator kicked in." After approaching the gate, Brent keys in his four-digit pass code and the gate immediately begins to open. "Well, at least one thing is working around here."

The driveway itself, paved with decorative bricks, wove up the hill in the form of a large S. While not necessarily steep, it took some effort on their part to get to the front of the house. By this time, they were both worn out. Shimie is left awestruck upon seeing the house. Brent, for his part, conducts a quick visual survey of the house for damage. Outside of a large number of roof tiles that shook loose, he is pleased that the outside of the house appears to be intact. And to think that his design architect laughed at him when instructed to make it partially earthquake proof. As it turns out, Brent is now pleased that extra money was invested in the house.

"My God...that's not a house...that's a mansion," Shimie states in almost disbelief.

"Whatever you choose to call it, Shimie...it's simply a home to me."

"Wow...business must really be great," she remarks, still in awe of it all.

"I didn't pay for most of it...my parents did. It was a gift when I graduated from Harvard law school. They already had the property picked out. It was left up to me to design the house and have it built to my specifications. I knew pretty much what I wanted before I left law school. While it was being built, I was working out of our LA offices; two-plus years later I moved in and set up a satellite office in downtown Scottsdale."

"Interesting. Your parents must have more money than they know what to do with."

"Let's just say they have done well for themselves."

"And just out of curiosity, what line of work is your father in?"

"Not just my father. Both he and my mother are attorneys as well. They met in law school. In fact, I am but one arm of their law group. Their main offices are located in D.C., but they have various offices around the country. I was eventually put in charge of the western six-state region."

"So, your parents felt that you needed a house that you didn't pay for to entertain the rich CEOs that find themselves in trouble, huh?"

"Something like that." Brent quickly picks up on the obvious sarcasm in her voice. "We deal with only the richest companies out there. Which is why you won't ever see our company's name listed in the yellow pages. They know who we are and how to contact us. That is exactly what establishing a good reputation does for a firm — and with winning — no need to advertise. We take pride in what we do and hire only the best and most aggressive attorneys out there. And trust me, they are well paid. But enough of this — let's go inside where it's hopefully cooler."

Shimie, still in a state of wonder, quickly follows Brent into the foyer of the house. She finds the foyer even more beautiful than the exterior of the house. Intricately designed marble graced the foyer floors. Two Romanesque columns stood ten feet inside the front door — though she had to believe they were there more for show than for support. As she follows Brent off to the right side of the foyer, she is once again enthralled at the choice of furnishings in what appears to be the living room. Almost everything in the room was pure white — the huge leather couches, the end tables, the coffee tables and lamps — everything was white.

"From the outside, and now being inside, the house appears to be circular," she remarks after finding her voice again.

"Looks are deceiving," he responds. "The house is actually half a circle...if that. To the left you'll find three guest bedrooms and a mini-bar/kitchen area. Each of the guest's bedrooms also has their own full bathroom. Oh, and the main laundry facilities are also located to the left. To the right here, down that hallway, are the master suite and a guest master suite, though slightly smaller. The main kitchen, gym, my office, etcetera are all on the right. You can obviously see the main living room, which we're standing next to. What you don't see from the foyer here is the courtyard, pool and outdoor kitchen. The wall straight ahead of you, which is forty feet wide and sixteen feet tall isn't exactly a wall. With a push of a button it disappears, thereby providing direct access to what people generally refer to as a backyard; though the main access is right from the foyer. I wanted something different in a house and what you see is what the architect and I came up with."

"Wow! I'm impressed already...and I haven't even seen most of the house."

"Let's head to the right where we will most likely end up spending a fair amount of our time."

Continuing to follow Brent through the house, she finds herself in the kitchen. Not just any kitchen, she quickly realizes. This one could easily handle fifty guests just milling around while talking shop with champagne glasses in their rich little hands. There were enough stovetop burners, microwaves and ovens to feed an army at one sitting.

She had to smile when she recalled him earlier saying he didn't even know how to cook. She knew from his earlier remark that he wasn't married, but a part of her had to guess that some lady friend did the cooking for him.

"And this is the one room we both need to be in if we don't want to die of starvation...where all the beverages and foods are located. There probably isn't much in the fridge, but I'm sure there is at least something you might want to munch on. If nothing appeals to you, then try the freezer or the pantry over there. One look in the fridge and you can tell that I eat out a lot...or have my dinners delivered. On some occasions, a friend will cook. Something tells me, however, that delivery is definitely out of the question right now. And another thing, consider this your home until you and your daughter are reunited."

Without responding to his statement, she opens up the refrigerator, and sure enough, there isn't much in there. A chunk of cheddar cheese — with mold on it — a dozen or so bottles of artesian water, a waxed container of orange juice that she was afraid to open, a small loaf of what appeared to be moldy bread, three apples and two oranges in the vegetable drawer that were sickly looking. He was right, she thinks, there isn't much in there — and what was in there is generally inedible. Playing it safe, she settles on a bottle of water, but carefully checks it over for an expired pull date.

Glancing at the water in her hand, he asks, "Not hungry, huh?"

"Yeah, I am a little hungry, but I swore off eating mold when I was a child."

"Ouch...that bad, huh?"

"Take my advice," she freely offers up, "don't ever allow a client to look in your refrigerator...or you will soon lose a client. Or possibly kill him if he eats anything," she adds for good measure.

"Double ouch. I guess I'll just have to fire the house cleaners for not properly scraping the mold off the food," he throws out to keep the mood light. And it works as he watches her smile. "Okay, I don't know about you, but I need to change clothes in the worst way. My back is not feeling all that well at the moment."

"I promised to look at your back...and I still will if you want me too. You also appear to have a pretty good slice on your chin...however that came about."

"If I'm not mistaken, I think I cut it on that piece of medal jewelry hanging from your neck when I threw you to the ground; whatever it is that the medal represents."

"This medal represents a gift handed down from my grandmother to my mother and then to me. It's a symbol of St. Gemma Galgani, from Italy. She is, among other things, the patron saint of hope and love. She is the saint I chose for my confirmation name. I wear it every Sunday to church. If you look closely, you'll see that the pearl beads are broken up to represent saying the rosary. Well, part of the rosary, anyway."

"I guess she is one, among many others I'm sure, that

I've never heard of. By the way, it looks beautiful on you."

"Thank you."

"Okay, on that note I'll take a quick shower first so you don't have to deal with caked-on blood."

"Uh, I think your forgetting that the water appears to have been shut off throughout the area. Even the rich can't get water right now."

"They can if they have a 500-gallon reserve tank out back," he responds with a smile.

"I should have known...sorry for bringing it up."

"Nothing to be sorry about. You had no way of knowing. Speaking of showers," he continues, "you obviously could use one yourself ... even with your dip in the pool earlier. Go through the opening over there and head down the hallway to the last door on your right. Help yourself to the clothes in the closet...I'm thinking you are about her size. If I'm not mistaken, there is plenty of makeup and toiletries in the bathroom. Once you're finished up, I'll meet you back here and maybe you can have a look at my back."

"Thank you...and you're definitely right about one thing...I desperately need a shower. And I know that without even having to look in a mirror. And another thing, you obviously know little about women. We never use another woman's makeup. Besides, I only use lipstick or gloss—no makeup. Oh, one other thing while I'm at it," she continues, "whose room am I reportedly stealing clothes from?"

"My sister's. She flies in every now and then…usually to hit me up for money. Come to think of it, I haven't seen her for three or four months. Must have latched onto another in a string of rich boyfriends," he remarks, with a smirk on his face. With that said, he turns and heads off for his own bedroom as Shimie finishes off her water.

5

Twenty minutes later, Brent returns to the kitchen wearing swimming trunks and nothing else. His semi-bloodied bath towel hangs down from his shoulders. His first attempt at drying his back brought silent cries of pain. So what that he was still wet—he knew he isn't going anywhere soon. He grabs a bottle of water from the refrigerator and sits down at the kitchen table and pulls a magazine toward him.

It's a full hour before Shimie appears in the kitchen wearing jeans and a tight-fitting white blouse. With Brent's back to Shimie as she enters, even from some distance away, she clearly makes out the bloodied towel hanging down from his shoulders.

"My oh my," she says, as she begins walking toward him, "donating to the local blood bank are you? Or going for a swim?"

Brent quickly swivels around in the chair and takes a quick glance at Shimie—though the look was not to be all that quick. "My oh my, yourself. You look absolutely striking. Good choice of clothes, I might add. And may I also add, you obviously clean up good," he concludes with a warm smile. He knew she was both tall and slender — much like his sister — but the tight blouse and slender slacks she wore brought arresting beauty all to the forefront.

"Nothing a long hot bath wouldn't do for any woman that had been through an earthquake. Oh, and thank you for the compliment. Your sister's clothes are a little tight in certain places, but you won't hear me complaining. I'm just thankful to have any clean clothes at all."

"Well, I'm sure when you looked through the closets you saw some pretty racy outfits. My sister always wants to look her best...never knowing where her next suitor could be lurking. She's a beautiful woman, but a little rough around the edges in terms of her lifestyle and her choices in men. And when I refer to men, that was meant to imply plural times plural."

"Ah, it sounds like your sister is attempting to enjoy the finer things in life...before she grows too old to enjoy them."

"Yep, that's my sister alright. I don't see her changing her ways until she's at least ninety."

"Okay, enough about your sister. Let's take a look at your back. I can't say that I'm thrilled seeing that much fresh blood from having just taken a shower. Unless you tried to scrub it with something rough," she adds.

"Nope. I just let the water do its thing. And I have to admit...even that hurt."

"I'm not surprised. After all of those hours in the sun, it should have permanently coagulated by now. I would expect a little bleeding from the shower, but not what I'm seeing. Where's a good place for me to have a look-see?"

"Either on one of the beds or on the massage table in the gym."

"I need to be near water, so let's go for a bed. If you have an old blanket somewhere, throw it on the bed...this might be a bloody ordeal."

"Well, no one bedroom is better than the other...they all have bathrooms. I believe my bedroom has the best lighting, however. Lots of windows."

"Okay, your bedroom it is. Where is it?"

"Follow me...it's right across from yours." Brent pushes the magazine back to the center of the table and rises from the chair, crosses through the kitchen and heads down the long hallway, Shimie but a few steps behind him. Stopping short of his bedroom, Brent opens a linen closet and pulls out what he considers to be an old blanket. To Shimie's eyes, it looks brand new. Oh well, she thinks, not hers to worry about.

After she follows him into the bedroom, she immediately comes to an abrupt stop. His bedroom was bigger than her entire apartment. The large, floor to ceiling windows take up almost two walls and are covered with long, perfectly pressed curtains and sheer drapes. She has to believe they are both electronically controlled as she didn't see any drapery cords. The bed appears to be an oversized king, or what they call a California king. Hell, ten people could sleep in that bed and not even touch one another. The oversized dresser and end tables were of a dark cherry and gave her the distinct impression they definitely would not be found at any IKEA store. As luxurious as she found the sister's room to be, and it was, this room put that one to shame. He apparently does win his cases, she concludes.

After throwing the blanket across one section of the bed, Brent pulls a floor lamp closer to the edge of the bed — lying down near, but not at the very edge of the bed. Once he settles in, Shimie sits down in the space remaining. The first thing she observes is the appearances of a number of fingernail marks dug into his back. She knew right away whose fingernails did their share of damage — though she wasn't about to bring that observation up. The other marks on his back were highly visible due to the dried blood marks following his shower. As she bends down to get a closer look, she is greeted by a glimmer of colored light from one of the wounds. And if she isn't mistaken, it appears bluish in color. She figures that it is probably glass.

"Do have any tweezers floating around?"

"In the drawer to the left of the right sink. Does this mean you're about to operate on me?"

"Well, I don't know that operate is the right word, but I

am going to attempt to remove some apparent glass pieces from your back. I have a hunch it's the reason you're still bleeding."

"Okay, fair enough, but shouldn't you put me under first before operating?" He threw out, to keep things light.

"Absolutely not—I'm into pain—as long as it's someone else's. Why do you think I became a nurse," she adds, with a lighter tone in her voice to match his. She rises from her sitting position and heads into the bathroom. After seeing his bedroom, she isn't the least bit surprised at seeing how opulent the bathroom was. Locating the tweezers and starting to soak a wash cloth in the sink, she calls out from where she was standing, "And where would I find some Band Aids, cotton balls and Neosporin—if you have any?"

"There should be some, I think, in the medicine cabinet on the right wall. If not, check my sister's bathroom."

"Found it." With tools in hand, along with a Kleenex to place the glass on, she returns and sits back down. "I don't suppose you have a magnifying glass lying around?"

"Sure do...in the center drawer of my desk over there."

Given that there was only one desk in the room—and a very large one at that—she quickly retrieves the magnifying glass and sits back down. "Okay, this may or may not hurt a little. If you need a bullet to bite down on, just let me know where you keep your ammo."

Brent couldn't see her face after hearing that, but he had to believe that she was finding this so-called "operation" rather amusing. He also surmises that she hasn't forgotten about her daughter, but was glad to see her mood lighten up a notch. "Just ignore any cries of pain and the possible tears that may fall."

"Okay, here goes nothing," she remarks as a matter of warning. Bending over with tweezers in one hand and the magnifying glass in the other, it took only a few seconds before Brent feels the first removal of glass. As she removes each piece, she holds a cotton ball in place to stop the fresh bleeding. Once assured it has stopped, she applies the Neosporin and a Band Aid. Then the same ritual continues onto the next piece of glass. The back alone takes her fifteen minutes before all the glass had been removed; or at least she thinks she's located all of it. Moving down to his legs, she removes five more pieces.

With the back and legs finished, she moves onto a more delicate matter — that of two blood stains on his swim trunks. "I'm a little embarrassed at having to tell you this, but you appear to have two blood stains on your trunks."

"I'm not surprised…it hurt to sit down. And what's there to be embarrassed about — you're a surgical nurse after all — you've seen it all before. When I raise myself up, just pull my trunks down and do your thing…but no peeking." Now this time he actually hears a chuckle from her.

Still feeling a twinge of embarrassment — in spite of the fact that she was a nurse — she does exactly that as he raises his mid-section up. The two pieces of glass, though small, were not hard to miss. A nice firm ass, she thinks to herself. He apparently uses the gym located somewhere in the house. The longer she finds herself staring at his muscular body, the warmer the room seems to be getting. If only his *Mister Philosophical* disposition matched his physique, there might be possibilities here, she muses. Knowing she was starting to get carried away with her thoughts, she finishes bandaging up the wounds and promptly pulls his trunks back up.

"Well, you apparently survived the operation in spite of my attempts to lose my first patient. And don't get up just yet...I don't want the wounds bleeding again. Let 'em dry up for a bit. All of the glass I removed was apparently from the large, stained-glass window over the entranceway. If you hadn't thrown yourself unceremoniously on top of me, that glass could have just as well embedded itself in me. And for that I thank you."

"Hey, just consider it my fifteen seconds of unceremonious chivalry."

"Your chivalry went well beyond fifteen seconds...and continues right up to this moment. I'll always be deeply indebted to you."

"If you really feel that way, you can work off your indebtedness by cooking us some dinner. You do know how to cook, don't you?"

"Unlike you, I know how to boil water. If nothing else, it will burn the mold off the food."

"Ouch again. You won't let me live that down, will

you?" Brent counters, as though being hurt by her repeated mold comments.

"Probably not. It's the only thing I have over you right now…though I'm sure I'll eventually find something else that you've neglected because you are *waaay* too busy saving clients millions of dollars ... and making million for yourself in the process."

"You're probably right about that. As I mentioned before, I'm not good around the house. Never have been—never will be. That's why I hire people."

"Along with other things, I'm guessing you were a spoiled child too?" Shimie threw out with a slightly condescending tone.

"In some respects, you're probably right. We had maids, cooks and a servant. I didn't ask for any of it—it was just there as I grew up. I eat most of my meals out, so no need for a cook, though one would come in handy right now. Do you know of anyone that can cook us up a mean meal right now?"

"You lie there for a few minutes while I go see what's still edible. Oh, and you may want to get dressed before dinner too. I don't serve dinner to half-naked men," she adds, as she rises from the bed, turns and walks out the door.

Following her instructions, he continues to lie on the bed. After what he had been through today, he could have just as well fallen fast asleep, but he knew better. Besides, the two slices of bread did little to curb his growing appetite. As far as he is concerned, Shimie was a lot more than just easy on the eyes, but she sure was a feisty one. If she hadn't chosen nursing as a profession, she would have made a great model — something his sister had done for a few years, though over the objection of his parents. And just like his sister, Shimie appears to have an air of independence about her as well.

"Whoa, my apologies for falling asleep," Brent confesses as he enters the kitchen. "I seriously tried to stay awake, but apparently the bed was too comfortable."

"I knew you were sleeping," Shimie casually replies.

"Wow, was my snoring that loud that you heard it all the way out to the kitchen?"

"No snoring. I went back to let you know that dinner would be ready in fifteen minutes. That was two hours ago. I felt you needed the sleep worse than you did a meal."

"I obviously did...it smells wonderful in here."

"Lucky for you the freezer and pantry were full. You won't be starving anytime soon...if the generator keeps running. Oh, your cell phone rang...I thought, just maybe, it was about my daughter, but it was your father wondering how you were doing. Sorry."

"Nothing to be sorry about as I have nothing to hide. I'm assuming you informed my father that all is well at the homestead?"

"I did. We talked for about twenty minutes."

"Wow again. I can't recall the last time I ever talked to him that long."

"We had a lot to talk about. He sounds like a nice man."

"I have no complaints being raised by him and my mother. His conversations anymore are usually business-related. You'll never hear him talking about the weather."

"We did talk about the weather. But enough of your father, let's eat before everything is overcooked."

"I'm all for that."

While Brent makes his way to the oversized dining room table, Shimie busies herself bringing the food to the table.

"Oh my, where in God's name did you find all of this food? And a small roast to boot."

"Check out your two freezers and your walk-in pantry once in a while. Like I said a minute ago, you won't be starving anytime soon. The roast was frozen so I defrosted it in the microwave before throwing it into the oven."

"Looking for a job as a cook any time soon?" Brent asks, jokingly.

"Nope. The thought of waiting on a man hand and foot doesn't sound very life-enriching. I went through that once already. Saving lives is what I was called to do, thank you very much."

"Okay, add another 'ouch' to your belt."

Once dinner was finished, Brent set about clearing the table while she washed the dishes by hand. With the table cleared off, Shimie hands him a drying towel. At first he wasn't sure why, until she points to the wet pots, pans and dishes lying beside the sink. Shimie isn't the least bit surprised at the stymied look on his face. As far as she was concerned, if she was to do the cooking, he sure as hell was going to help with the dishes.

With the kitchen cleaned up and everything put away, the two of them make their way to the living room. Brent makes a futile attempt at turning on the TV, but given that he was on cable, he finds nothing but snow on the screen. The radio was useless as well.

"I know you want to catch up on the latest news about the earthquake," Shimie remarks, "but right now I'm not sure I can handle anymore — sorry — it will just remind me of my daughter. Don't get me wrong — I'm not trying to forget my daughter — she's all I think about because I worry about her. I don't know where she is. I don't know if she is being well taken care of right now. I don't know if she is hurt. I don't know if she is in a hospital right now crying out for her mommy." After a short pause, she continues. "I don't know anything right now. And that is what hurts the most…the not knowing." With those lasts words, the tears begin to slowly trickle down her cheeks.

Brent, once again, is drawn into a situation that makes him feel absolutely powerless. He wants to go where she's sitting on the loveseat and take her in his arms and hold her, but feels that it may not be appropriate — that is, until she raises her hands to her face and commences sobbing uncontrollably. Putting aside everything he was just thinking as to why he shouldn't go to her, he pushes off the couch and does just the opposite. Sitting down next to her, he places his arm around her shoulder and pulls her into him. And then she really let loose with the bawling. He reaches over to the end table and pulls a wad of Kleenex out of the decorative holder. Without being asked, he slips two or three into her hands pressed against her face. Shimie wastes no time in blowing her nose.

Five minutes pass by before she shows any sign of getting control of her emotions. And even then, she remains motionless with her head pressing tightly against his neck and chest—or was it the force of his hand pressing against the back of her head that kept her against him? Five more minutes elapse before she slowly removes her head from the nook of his neck.

Looking up into the deepest blue eyes she has ever seen, she utters a one-word response, "Sorry."

Looking directly back at her, while maintaining his arm around her, he replies in a quiet tone, "Nothing to be sorry about. You have all the reasons in the world to be emotional. I don't have to be a parent to understand what you're going through. If my sister or parents were missing, unaccounted for, I would feel the same apprehensions as you. Just because I'm a guy, a member of the male species, doesn't mean that I don't have feelings for those close to me. I'm here for you whenever you need a shoulder to cry on. And just to put your mind at ease, if that's even possible right now, I offer, once again, my full support in helping you find your daughter—no matter what it takes, or for how long. I simply don't want you feeling alone in your ordeal; especially knowing that you have no family to turn too."

After a long moment of silence, and realizing that he had finished with what he had to say, Shimie nestles her head back into the crook of his neck and wraps her free hand around his back. Comfortably ensconced in his arms, she hopes he doesn't see her actions as a romantic gesture. She simply feels gratitude and an enormous release of mental pressures because of his willingness to help her. While she still didn't know the fate of her daughter, her mind was somewhat at rest for the first time today. There was hope. There was help. There was Brent.

"Well, I don't know about you, young lady, but I've got a few quick phone calls to make, check out the rest of the house for damage and then head off to bed...it's been a long day. Oh, and by the way, thank you for dinner. I had forgotten what a home-cooked meal tastes like since I went away to college or when visiting my parents. You cooked a pretty mean meal."

"You're welcome. And, like you, I'll head off to bed too. Staying up and worrying won't bring my daughter back to me, I guess."

"No it won't. And be sure to take your phone with you...just in case. I left your charger on the kitchen island...be sure to plug it in next to the nightstand. If your phone only works from cell phone towers, you may be out of luck. See if you're getting any bars. I have a Sat phone, which operates from a direct satellite link so, worst case, we have at least one functioning phone."

"Thanks. I'll do that." Pulling herself away from the comfort and security of Brent's body, she pushes herself up from the couch and heads for the kitchen.

After making two calls and checking the rest of the house for possible damage, Brent goes off in search of his own much needed bed.

6

BRENT FELL ASLEEP the moment his head hit the pillow. And he stays fast asleep until awakened by a blood-curdling scream. So deep was his sleep, he has no idea who screamed or where it was coming from—and then he fully wakes up. Flying out of the bed, he runs out of his room and directly into Shimie's room. Thanks to the night lights in the room, he is able to catch a glimpse of her sitting up in bed sobbing—hands covering her face.

Without giving it a second thought, he immediately jumps onto the bed, grabs her and pulls her into his body. She quickly throws both arms around him. Her body was trembling—even more so than on the couch earlier. He had no idea what prompted the screams, but a quick glance around the room reveals nothing remotely threatening. Her sobbing and shaking continue unabated, but he feels helpless to do anything outside of holding her close. His first thought was that she had experienced a bad dream; and given the past day, he wouldn't be the least bit surprised if that was what brought on the nightmare and subsequent screams.

Continuing to stroke her back, he became aware that she was wearing one of his sister's ultra-silky night-gowns — the type men love on a woman — short and silky. As was the case on the couch, she slowly begins to get herself under control; but not to the point of releasing her hold on Brent. He has become, unintentionally, her security blanket.

"It's okay. You're going to be okay. I'm here. Relax. Let it go. Take deep breaths. And that's okay, just hold on tight." And then he pauses before starting up again. "You're in a strange room. You've been through a lot. I promise you...nothing will happen to you. It's all okay." All of which he speaks with a soothing voice. With the final words, Brent could feel her ease up her hold on him, but still she holds on.

"I felt another ... another earthquake. It woke me up. I'm sorry." She manages to get the three short sentences out in slow motion. She is finding it difficult to talk. She just wants to feel secure in her surroundings. And in Brent's arms, she feels secure.

"Number one, it isn't necessary to say you're sorry every time you turn around. Should you deliberately hurt me in some way, then a sorry would be appropriate. Under the current circumstances...no sorry is necessary. I know what you're going through. And no, you didn't feel an earthquake. You felt a tremor, an aftershock. And there may be more to come, but a follow-on earthquake is high-ly unlikely. So relax...this house is relatively earthquake proof. You saw how well it stood up to the quake yester-day morning. Right?"

Brent could feel her going into more of a relaxed state, but still she hangs on. "It's over, so why don't you just lie back down and try to go back to sleep. We both need plenty of sleep following yesterday's activities...and who knows what's in store for us tomorrow."

"No, no, don't leave me," she cries out in desperation. "Please!"

"Okay, I won't leave you. Get back under the covers and lie down." Shimie, without having to be told twice, slips back under the covers and rest her head on the two pillows. Brent slides under the covers as well and falls back onto the two adjoining pillows. Reaching over, he grabs her top pillow and gently pulls it and her head onto his chest, before wrapping his left hand around her back.

—

Following a quick shower, Brent wanders off to the liv-ing room to read a magazine. No sense taking the golf cart down to the gate, he figures, as it was highly unlikely that the Wall Street Journal would be there anyway. After tir-ing of his magazine, he reaches for his phone and auto-di-als his mother, but it goes directly to voicemail. Not one much for leaving voicemails, he quickly hangs up.

"Good morning."

Looking up, he sees Shimie entering the room wearing a pure white bathrobe. "You look well rested. But then again, you should after ten hours of sleep," he says with a grin.

"I slept that long only because you were there to calm me down. And I thank you for that."

"No thanks needed...I was just doing my job as a slum landlord with moldy food for the non-paying guests."

Shimie immediately throws a smile his way. "Speaking of moldy food, are you hungry?"

"Am I ever! I was thinking of going into your bedroom hours ago and throwing you out of bed to get my breakfast going. Then I remembered we don't have any fresh eggs. Hell, we don't even have moldy eggs. Even those I would have eaten right about now."

"I saw lots of bacon in the freezer, though it will take some time to defrost and cook. I also saw pancake mix in the pantry. Would that be okay?"

"Bacon and pancakes sound great. If you need help, holler."

"Rest assured, I will never be asking you to help cook. Dishes...yes. Cooking...no." She immediately swings herself around and leaves.

Noticing the smell of fresh coffee, Brent rises from the couch and heads for the kitchen. "Mind if I have some of that fine smelling coffee with my breakfast?"

"That's what I made it for. Every now and then I'll have

a cup of coffee, but I don't drink it on a regular basis. And your timing is perfect; we're 15 seconds away from eating."

"Would you mind if I ask you a few questions while we're eating?" Brent asks calmly so as not to alarm her. "About you, your neighbor, your daughter, your ex, your apartment. I didn't feel that you were in any state of mind yesterday, so before going to bed last night I placed a call to the Scottsdale Police Department...to let them know what happened. As you can imagine, I was on hold for quite some time. Oh, you even found syrup in the pantry. Breakfast looks good, by the way."

"Easy on the syrup, that's the only container I could find," Shimie states, as she sits down with her own plate.

"Okay, will do on the syrup. Anyway, I talked with Detective Richards, whom I know personally, and he assures me that he'll place your daughter's name on their missing list. He wasn't sure when, but they would eventually retrieve your neighbor's body. Right now they obviously have other pressing matters...namely rescues and rampant looting. Apparently it's getting pretty ugly out there. He asked a few questions for which I didn't have the answers."

"What can I add that you don't already know?"

"Plenty. For starters, he wanted to know the name of your neighbor and which apartment she lived in."

"Gladys Broberg. Apartment 108."

"Thanks. We both know that you were at the 8 a.m.

mass. And I'm assuming you walked as you pointed out your car on its side. Have a second car by any chance?"

"No, I walked. My only form of real exercise...outside of what I get in the hospital."

"What time did you leave the apartment?"

"I left at exactly 7:35; it gets me to mass with five minutes to spare."

"And your daughter...was she up?"

"She was fussing a bit in her crib, so I asked Gladys to fire up the burner. Her bottle was already on the stove and ready to go. Why is it I feel like I'm on the witness stand?" She remarks, defensively.

"Shimie...you're not. Don't even think like that. Richards asked me a number of questions last night. He's a detective after all ... they ask a lot of questions. This isn't about a homicide or a kidnapping. It's about a missing person. The more information he has, the easier it will be for him to locate your daughter. He needs, for whatever reason, more than just your daughter's name and age."

"Okay. Sorry," she replies, in a much calmer tone.

"Your ex. Does he have visitation rights? And does he have a name?"

"He has visitation rights, but seldom exercises them. I think it was around three months ago when I took him back to court. I feared for my daughter's safety and well being, given that I kind of knew that he was probably still dealing in drugs. The judge ruled that he can't take her out of my apartment until he tests free of drugs...which he never has been tested. He knows he would flunk the test. Needless to say, he was livid with me for dragging him back into court. Oh, and his name is Paul Lewis Fredericks."

"Not a friendly divorce, I take it?"

"It was bitter to the end. He wanted full custody and child-support from me."

"Where does he work?"

"He doesn't, to my knowledge. He got fired soon after we were married. Drugs I think. I filed for divorce six months later, before I even knew I was pregnant," she states without emotion. "He has a degree in chemistry, but never found a job to match his degree. Though I got the feeling he didn't really care. There wasn't a lot of effort on his part to find a job that matched his schooling. We weren't even married for a year before I came to my senses and realized I had made a big mistake. You keep wishing, hoping, praying that things will turn around with time, but they seldom do ... or so my marriage counselor advised me."

"Sorry to hear all that. Sounds kind of messy from the get go. And Gladys, did you not say that she lived in the same complex?" Brent asks as he pushes his empty plate aside.

"Two doors down. Her apartment was one of those totally flattened. She was 70...lived alone. She adopted both me and my daughter as her own. She was always knitting stuff for my daughter. She never had children of her own."

"Okay, that helps. I'll get the information off to Richards this morning. As a favor to me, he'll put your daughter near the top of his priority list."

"Thanks, but I have no right to keep asking for your help."

"Well, if it will ease your guilt feelings any, try to look at it this way—what else am I going to do with all this unplanned free time? Besides, where else can I get a free cook?" He adds with a wink.

"Just trying to earn my keep around here. Hopefully it will only be for a few days," she replies, though unsmilingly.

"Okay then, no need to wash the breakfast plates, nary a crumb on them."

"Nice try," she fires back, "but you are not going to get out of helping with the dishes. Besides, it's about time you learned what kitchens are all about. Meals don't just magically appear out of thin air."

"Oh well, you can't blame a guy for trying," Brent replies as he pushes himself away from the table. "Oh wait; a personal question, if you don't mind my asking? Why is it I have never seen you at mass before? As beautiful as you are, surely I would have noticed you there."

"Number one, thank you for the compliment. Number two, I've only been to early mass a few times before…and I never stay for donuts afterward, but this morning, for some reason, I felt a need for a donut and coffee. I know what you're thinking … oink-oink. My mass of preference has always been the 9:30, but Gladys was invited to a brunch with some of her fellow bridge players, so I went early. It's hard to focus on mass when you have a nine-month-old to care for at mass."

"Well, that definitely solved my personal curiosity. Thanks."

7

"DETECTIVE RICHARDS, PLEASE."

"Oh. When do you expect him back?"

"No, that won't be necessary...I'll catch him on his cell. Thanks."

A short while later, Brent heads into the living room and finds Shimie curled up on the loveseat reading a book. "An interesting read?" He asks.

"It would be if I remembered what I read even two minutes ago."

"That's because your mind isn't relaxed...you're obviously not able to focus just yet. It's starting to warm up a bit, so you may just entertain the idea of going for a swim. The pool heater is shut off, but I'm thinking it should still be comfortable enough for a swim. If nothing else, you can just spend some time outdoors on the pool deck and pick up some of that vitamin D stuff. Just a suggestion. Oh, and I know for a fact that my sister has left behind any number of bathing suits.

Hanging up, in a drawer, somewhere. You'll have to look around."

"I may just take you up on that offer. I love water and sunshine. Are you up for some lunch?"

"Thanks, but no. I only eat two meals a day. An occasional lunch if I happen to be with a client. Oh, I almost forgot. I spoke with Richards earlier and gave him the details you provided. He wondered if you have a fairly recent picture of your daughter. He also asked what her legal last name was—Jamison or Fredericks?"

"It's Fredericks. I'd like to change it to Jamison, but that's another story. I have a lot of photos, but they are on my phone with no service."

"That's okay…we can tie your phone into my computer and upload them. I'll send one or two off to Richards. He wants to forward them off to the hospitals—at least those still functioning—as well as the Red Cross that maintains a comprehensive listing of missing people."

"Thanks. Do you mind grabbing my cell off of the side dresser?"

"Not at all. I have to go that way anyway. I'm assuming you have them stored under your photos icon?"

"That's where they are. Just scroll through until you see a folder with Brianna's name. The rest of the pictures I never got around to putting into folders. Maybe I'll do that while I'm here…for however long."

"Got it. Off I go." He turns around and leaves her to read a book she wasn't reading. Walking into her room, he unplugs her phone from the wall socket and makes his way to his bedroom desk. He notices right away that it is fully charged, but no cell service. After plugging the phone into his computer, he was prompted to download the appropriate software that would recognize her phone on his computer. Once that was completed, he was asked if he wanted to upload 112 new photos to his computer. After creating a separate folder and clicking yes, he impatiently waits while the transfer takes place.

A half-minute later, he clicks on the new folder and scrolls to the very bottom and, sure enough, there was Brianna's folder. Opening the folder, the first picture he sees is of a smiling little girl looking up from her crib. And what a beautiful baby, he thinks — just like her mother. He copies two of the full-faced pictures and fires them off to Richards for distribution as he saw fit. Scrolling back up near the top he stops at a picture of a young man holding the baby when she appears to be about two months old. A nice looking guy, he admits, while wondering at the same time how he had found himself involved in dealing drugs. A beautiful wife and daughter and he threw it all away because of drugs. Scrolling back up to the top, he concludes that the photo of the nice looking man was Shimie's husband, as the very first photo showed the two of them, side by side, with matching wedding bands — probably paid for by her. But none of this was really his business, so he quickly closes the folder and shuts the computer down.

As he swivels to rise out of his chair, he notices what

has to be Shimie walking past his window. Even through the sheer drapery, he could tell what a beautiful, shapely woman she was. His thoughts went instantly back to some stupid husband who threw it all away for drugs. Or was there, he wondered, something wrong with her that brought about the drug usage?

He initially was heading off for the living room, but found himself mesmerized by her image standing by the pool. She was wearing a two-piece, light blue bikini that barely covered anything. In fact, Band Aids would have covered more, he thinks. He was somewhat taken aback that she would even wear something so skimpy — before realizing the bikini came from his sister's closet. His sister's motto, *less is best*, the better to work up the appetite of a man with money — and no one knew better than she that sex sells.

Deep down, he knew that he shouldn't be staring at her, but he couldn't help himself. It had been a while since he last bedded a woman — so his hormones were beginning to kick into high gear the longer he spent looking at her. But, having a daughter whose whereabouts were unknown instantly put Shimie into the untouchable class. As much as he desires to devour her this very moment, he wasn't about to put at risk the trust she had put in him over the course of the past two days — another day, maybe.

As he continues watching, Shimie places a large towel onto the pool deck and proceeds to lie herself down on her backside. Isn't she aware, Brent wonders, that this end of the pool is right outside his bedroom window? Was she purposely trying to capture me by use of her bodily assets? That thought, if true, wouldn't bother him a bit as he moves ever closer to the window and stares at her full breasts. The bikini top hid nothing but the nipples—and even they showed through the ultra-thin material. Maybe now, he thought, was the perfect time to put on his own suit and join her. After giving it some serious thought, however, he concludes that the temptation of her almost naked body is too much to handle—so he turns and walks away.

—

"You were right," Shimie states, as she enters the living room dressed in a fresh outfit. "The vitamin D and a long swim did help."

"Exercise is not only good for the body, but the mind as well. It release feel-good endorphins, or so I've read some-where. But being a nurse, you already know that."

"You read right. Oh, I absolutely love your koi pond. I've never seen one that big with so many fish in it. As for the pool, do you use it much, or is it just for show? You know, to impress the Lolitas of the world."

"Lolitas? Who or what in the hell are the Lolitas of the world?"

"Sorry. Just a phrase I coined when I met an actual Lolita in the hospital. She came in for an emergency appendectomy. Blonde, beautiful, buxom and a real live bimbo. The four B's. Every man's dream. The male doctors, interns and orderlies doted over her like she was the last fertile woman on earth. Meanwhile, an 80-year-old woman, who had seen better days, lay in the bed next to hers and was almost totally ignored. She had one of her kidneys removed. She told me some wonderful stories about her hard life, but she never gave up on finding beauty in everything. Meanwhile, Lolita was complaining that she couldn't leave the hospital until she had both a manicure and pedicure. So that's what I mean when referring to the Lolitas of the world."

"Interesting. I'll be sure never to date anyone that goes by the name of Lolita. Now back to your original question. You'll be shocked to hear that I actually use the pool four or five times a week. I had it built extra long for the purpose of doing laps."

"So why didn't you swim today?" She inquires.

"I thought of it, but then decided to give you your privacy."

"That was very thoughtful of you, but not necessary; though I did feel a little naked out there in your sister's bikini."

"I can understand why if you wore one of hers ... which you obviously had to. She might just as well go out there naked; and probably does when I'm not around. She's told me any number of times that the naked body is nothing to be ashamed of. Of course, with her body, she's probably right. But there's a time and place for everything."

"For some reason I don't envision you as a prude," she

states, all with a slight smile. "Far from it, but like I said — a time and place for everything. Speaking of time, what are the options for dinner tonight?"

"Tonight is chicken...I took it out of the freezer this morning. Is breaded and baked chicken okay with you?"

"Sounds great. I'll get up now and go prepare it," he remarks, with a sly grin.

"Fat chance that will ever happen. I'm too young to die from food poisoning."

"Wow, you keep throwing the 'ouches' my way. I may end up developing an inferiority complex before this is over with," he counters, all with a hurt look on his face.

"Not to change the subject, but did you get the pictures you wanted?"

"Yep, got 'em and sent 'em off to Richards. Thanks."

"No, I should be thanking you."

"Hey, just trying to earn my keep around here, so no thanks needed. I'm not used to sitting around."

"I can well imagine. With your type A personality, time is money." With that comment thrown his way, she turns around and heads directly for the kitchen before he has a chance to defend himself.

—

Pushing the dinner plate away, Brent is in the process of rising when his phone begins making a series of classical notes.

"Hi mom. Returning my call from this morning, huh?"

"In court? Yeah, some of the judges can get pretty angry when a cell phone goes off."

"No, everything is fine here. We have plenty to eat thanks to the freezer and pantry."

"We? Don't you ever talk to dad? He can explain everything. In fact, the two of them talked yesterday."

"No, she's not another blonde bimbo. To be honest with you, she's kind of ugly and grossly overweight, so no way I would even consider touching her. Sorry to disappoint you again." Glancing her way and seeing the look on her face, he's glad she didn't have a steak knife close by.

"You're right, mom, the LA office will just have to step up and carry the load. The big guys want action, not some sob story about a devastating earthquake. Oh, that reminds me, I asked dad to contact the guys and gals on my team to see if they are alright...do you know if he did that?"

"Oh. Well give him a nudge...it's important that I know. Hell, it's important for the firm to know."

"No, we don't need any damn helicopter ferrying in food or anything else. Besides, every available copter should be doing rescue work...not delivering pizza for dinner."

"Okay, give my love to dad and I'll talk to one of you tomorrow. Love you too." With that he places the phone back on the dining room table.

"So, I'm fat and ugly, am I?" Shimie was quick to ask the moment the phone call ended.

"Now don't start wigging out on me until you know my side of it. My mother is always trying to get this totally confirmed bachelor married off. Every time I inadvertently mention a female's name, she instantly hears wedding bells. And no, you are anything but fat and ugly—in fact, just the opposite."

"Thank you—a woman likes to hear that every now and then—even those who are beauty-challenged need to hear something positive."

"You're absolutely right...I'll keep that in mind the next time I come across a *challenged* woman. Okay, let's get on with the dishes before I sneak out of here when you have your back turned. Once the dishes are finished, I'm going to head off to my room to catch up on some work. Are you going to be okay by yourself?"

"I've survived so far. Thanks in part to you. And I'll do my best not to wake you up screaming again."

"You can wake me up whenever the need arises. As a matter of fact, I slept very well with you beside me. Better and longer than usual, I might add."

"Good, so did I. Okay, enough of this, get over there and get your drying towel ready. But first bring the dishes over to the sink...please."

8

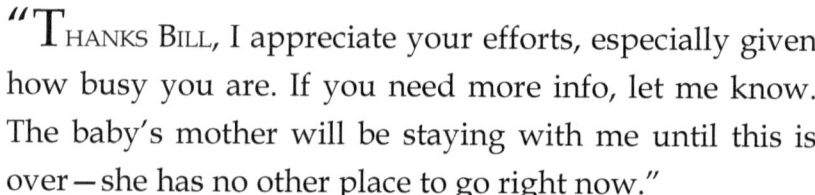

"THANKS BILL, I appreciate your efforts, especially given how busy you are. If you need more info, let me know. The baby's mother will be staying with me until this is over — she has no other place to go right now."

"No, we have plenty of food, though you could send up a cow and maybe a dozen egg-laying chickens," Brent throws out with a chuckle.

"Okay, call if you hear anything."

After hanging up, Brent makes two additional calls before picking up the book he was previously reading. With barely one sentence read, Shimie enters the living room.

"Good morning," Brent calls out, while noticing the tight, filled-out blouse she was wearing. For once he was glad his sister had good taste in clothes; her choice of men, however, was another story altogether.

"Good morning to you too. Did you sleep well?"

"Not as good as the previous night, but I still managed to sneak in five hours," Brent responds. "And you?"

"It was okay...did a lot of tossing and turning."

"That's no surprise to hear. A nap might be in order after lunch. By the way, I spoke with Richards this morning—they removed your neighbor's body and rechecked the apartment...your daughter was definitely not in there. And the note we left was still wedged in the door frame."

"I'll take that as being good news; about my daughter, that is. I just wish I knew where she was and who had her...and was she okay."

"If anyone can find her, Richards will. He's a tenacious investigator. When he takes on a case, he doesn't let loose until it's solved."

"Thanks. I know I can never repay you for what you're doing for me," Shimie replies with a deep sense of gratitude for his efforts.

"No thanks needed. I would do the same thing for any fat and ugly woman," he remarks, with a huge grin on his face.

Shimie's smile lit up the room. If nothing else, she admits, Brent has been a welcome distraction to her worries. He not only saved her life, but had taken the initiative on his own in helping to locate her daughter. For this, she was extremely grateful. How many other men would have done the same thing? Not many, she concludes. At least not the men she has been acquainted with. "I meant to ask you yesterday, but forgot. How's your back?"

"All the Band Aids have hit the shower floor. No blood on the towel, so I guess I'll survive. Though your fingernails and St. Gemma medal will scar me for life."

"Well, it serves you right for attacking me…and outside of church no less," she responds, while trying her best to stifle a smile.

"Hey, it was just my way of introducing myself to a beautiful woman. You looked a little standoffish all by yourself at church, so I had to employ desperate measures to get your attention. And it obviously worked, I might add."

"Your mother should have taught you better. If I appeared standoffish, it was only because I didn't know anyone at that particular mass."

"Hey, don't blame my mother—blame it all on my Catholic schooling—the brothers taught us to avoid girls at all cost."

"Well, whatever the reasons for your lack of proper skills with women, we'll save it for another time. I'll have a look at your back later, just to make sure none of the cuts are infected. Right now, I could use some breakfast. How about you?"

"Well, given that I've been up for three hours already, I could use some grub as well. I would have eaten a long time ago, but my personal chef was asleep on the job."

"I'll ignore that last comment. Pancakes again or cereal? Oh wait; no milk for the cereal, so pancakes and bacon it is." Shimie turns and makes her way into the kitchen while Brent resumes his reading.

—

"How was your nap?" Brent inquires, as she enters the kitchen with a look of sleepiness still in her eyes.

"I obviously needed it, though I'm still somewhat tired."

"Naps are good. They ease the mind and soothe the soul. Another thing I read."

"Sometimes I think you read too much. As for me, I'm basically not one to take naps, but that felt good. I just came in to grab some water and lay out by the pool. If you care to join me, I'll have a look at your back."

"I can do that. I'll join you in ten, or whenever." With that, Brent pulls away from the table and heads off to his room to change into his swimsuit. Once changed, he grabs a towel and goes directly out to the pool through his bedroom sliding door. He quickly snatches up two full-length lounge cushions from their respective chairs and lays them on the pool deck. He places his towel on top of one cushion and lies down on his stomach. It would be another twenty minutes before Shimie makes her way to where he was lying; though he doesn't look up.

"That sure took you a long time to change," he remarks to acknowledge her arrival.

"I took a quick shower first...I felt sweaty. Now, let's have a look at your back before I forget about it." Pulling her cushion closer to his, she kneels down and begins her examination. "Not bad...healing well. And now, if you don't mind, let's relook at the two sores on your posterior."

"Remember...no peeking," he says, followed by a laugh as he raises his torso up.

"Not to worry, my eyes are firmly closed," she throws back at him as she pulls his trunks down. "Okay, you are definitely going to live long enough to see another day." He then lifts back up while she pulls his trunks back into place. "Where might I find some sunscreen? The sores are still tender, so you don't want them getting burned."

"In the pool house on the other side of the pool. There should be some in either the men's or women's side—on an open shelf—you can't miss it."

"Okay, I'll be right back."

After returning with the lotion in hand, she remarks, "It must be nice to have both a women's and men's changing room."

"It comes in handy for pool parties. I entertain both clients and staff from time to time. The staff will oftentimes bring their children."

Without responding, Shimie kneels down with her legs straddling both sides of his torso. Squeezing the suntan lotion into her hands, she went to work, being careful on the cut areas. "Let me know if it hurts. I've had a few patients complain that I massage too hard."

"I don't think you'll hear me complaining…I like hard." As soon as that left his mouth, he wishes he had chosen his words a little better.

Shimie liked his muscular body; along with the fact that he obviously takes the time to work out to maintain his physique. Working out, she knew, requires both a dedication and, some would say, a desire to look good, not just for themselves, but for others as well. Regardless of the motivation, she finds herself getting worked up as she slides her hands methodically around his back and neck. Feeling the need to break the silence, she asks, "Do you feel that staying in shape has made a difference in your life?"

"Unquestionably. My checkups every year are perfect. I feel great in spite of the long and sometimes strenuous hours I put in. Aside from the fact that I'm on public display, shall we say, with my clients and others."

"Public display?" She responds questioningly, as she continues massaging his body. "Does that imply that you intentionally go around showing off your physique?"

"Not hardly. Body image shapes who you are. You have to remember that you women don't own the patent on the old saying, 'sex sells.' I deal with a fair amount of female clients, associates, secretaries and the like. How I look plays a big part in how they perceive and relate to me."

"Do you ever get romantically involved with the good-looking clients? You know, to create a bond with your clients?"

"Never have in the past. Oh sure, there are clients and others in the field who are knock-outs. Many of whom got their positions because of the way they look...or who they slept with. I'm not blind and I'm far from dead. I look, I admire, and I wonder what they would be like outside of the work environment. And that's as far as it goes. Sexuality is great, but not in a professional setting. There's just too much at stake to be jeopardized by a fling."

"I didn't mean to pry. It's just something I've always been curious about."

"No offense taken…I'm an open book. As long as you continue massaging me, you can ask all the questions you want."

"Thank you. Now if I can just get my patients to say that. Oh, and no more questions, your honor, you can go back to sleep," she adds teasingly.

"You keep your hands moving, I'll fall asleep for sure. Very relaxing. But if your intent is more to give me a massage instead of applying sunscreen, you may want to go back in the pool house and grab the massage oil."

"Well, given that you are an appreciative patient, I can do that. Be right back."

Shimie checks the various containers on the shelf until she finds what she's looking for. While walking back, she wonders just how many other women had used this same oil on him, or he on them. And then she quickly chides herself for being envious, or was it jealous, over women she's never met. She hardly expects him to be a virgin at his age.

Kneeling down again, Shimie decides it is best to let him rest—no more questions from her. She moves her body back down a bit to concentrate on his lower back. As she begins spreading the oil, she's pleased that he even mentioned the oil—making her hands glide far more easily along his lower back. Even though she had previously spent time on his upper back, she finds herself wanting to do so again, but this time with the oil. She knows instantly why she went back up his body—the pleasure was more for her benefit than his. She likes this way too much—and she knew it. And in some ways, she is finding it scary. She is feeling as though she were on her first high school date—wondering all evening if he was going to kiss her at her parent's doorstep.

She was both excited and nervous at the same time. With her hormones starting to get out of control, she knew better than to allow herself to get involved with a confirmed bachelor—a bachelor more married to his profession than he'll ever be to a woman. Those women—and she believed they had to be many—were simply there to meet his basic animal needs. Moving her hands caressingly down his sides, and partially to his front, she couldn't help but feel those same needs welling up in her. She knew she had to switch thoughts to something else, but wasn't sure what topics would do the trick—if any. Mind over matter, she kept repeating to herself. Mind over matter.

It wasn't helping matters any that every now and then she hears a soft moan emanating from his lips. She was finding that various parts of his body brought more pleasure than others, so she made a point of devilishly concentrating on those areas—and the soft moans would be emitted again and again. She was secretly beginning to enjoy the control she obviously had over his body. Men are so predictable, she muses. And she loves it.

Without saying anything to Brent, she rises up from her

kneeling position and relocates herself by his feet. Squeezing more oil into her hands she quickly sets about massaging his legs. Like his back and shoulders, she finds his legs to be muscular as well. Most likely, she thinks, from doing laps in the pool; or a combination of his gym and the pool. She wonders, but chooses not to ask, if he were a swimmer in high school and college. She makes a mental note to ask him—but not now—she wants him totally relaxed. She also wants to hear more moans. She wants him to know that it was she who is in control of his body—not him.

Finishing up with the feet and lower legs, she scoots herself back up a bit more to massage his thighs. This, she tells herself, is where I really have control over him. With fresh drops of oil in her hands, she gently moves them up and down his muscular thighs. Every now and then, as she massages closer to his swimming trunks, she hears another low moan. She then begins to massage farther up and into his trunks, clearly in touch with his posterior— and a firm one at that. Knowing that her thoughts and actions had already crossed the line, she envisions something else as hard too. If it wasn't, she would definitely know how to rectify that in short order. As she continues moving farther up his trunks, the intensity of his moans increases. He was clearly enjoying this—and she smiles from the knowledge of the powers invested in her as a woman. A power far too many women fail to realize and use to their advantage.

And then instantly she brings her actions and thoughts

to a halt. Realizing that she couldn't deal with the emotional ramifications of being dumped down the road, she pulls her hands back from his thighs. She knows if she allows herself to get serious about developing a romantic relationship with Brent—he would, in time, throw her to the curb. She could only imagine how many prior women he had dealt with in similar fashion. Slowly, very slowly, the urge to take him subsides within her. She finds herself quickly back in control of her physical and emotional self. She gave into her ex's needs on their first date—and look where that got her. She isn't about to make that same mistake twice. Nope—not as long as she is in control of herself.

"Okay you lazy bum...my hands can't move another inch." Shimie rises to her feet and moves over to the other mat, facing down, and supports herself on both elbows.

Brent too rises up a little and props himself up on his left elbow facing her. "That, young lady, had to have been one of the best massages I've had in a long, long time. And I'm not just saying that to make you feel good. It was a great massage...thank you."

"Can I get that in writing so I can share it with my disgruntled patients?"

"After that massage, whatever your little heart desires."

"I want my daughter back," Shimie answers, solemnly.

"Your heart gave the only possible answer it could. And you have no idea how I want the same thing for you. Outside of a few faked smiles, I've only seen you at your saddest. I'm doing everything I possibly can so I can see you smile and be happy on a regular basis. And just so you know, not only is Richards involved, but I've had hired two private investigators on a full-time basis to assist in the search."

"Oh my God! Did you really?" Shimie responds, excitedly. She immediately rises up and throws her arms around Brent—knocking him backwards onto the mat. Wrapping his arms around her, she begins to softly cry. For his part, he can do nothing but hold her tight while slowly massaging her head.

Even when she finishes with her crying spell, she makes no attempt to pull away from him. She was in no hurry to return to reality. Right now, he had made her a happy woman. Brent, without realizing it, had become her security blanket. As she lay with her head on his chest, her mind went back to the massage she had just given him. Only now she wishes she had raised the bar from one of quiet moaning to a full-blown primal scream. If, for no other reason, than to thank him for everything he was doing for her toward being reunited with her daughter. It would have been a simple gesture of giving on her part—requiring nothing more than a strategically placed hand. Given the way she teased him, she had to believe that it all ended with him feeling sexually frustrated. If the situation had been reversed, she knew she would have been frustrated as well. Her being Catholic, with a strong sense of moral guilt, ruined it for him—and ultimately for her.

She swore, then and there, to find a way to make it up to him for her failings at the pool. The church and her self-ingrained sense of guilt be damned.

"Are you ready to get up, beautiful?" What possesses him to call her beautiful, he isn't sure — nor did he feel any regrets for having done so.

"No. I'm quite content at the thought of spending the rest of the afternoon right here."

"Even though I find you fat and ugly, and utterly detestable, the sun is going to burn us both if we don't get into the house. I don't have the olive skin that you have, so ten more minutes and I will look like a lobster — except for where your body is currently covering mine."

"Are you complaining about my body covering yours?"

"Not in the least. I've always felt these mats were meant for two anyway."

"Okay, I'll get off of you...for now." She isn't sure if he caught the jest of what she had just said. He says nothing in reply as she rises up to a standing position. The two of them quickly make their way back into the house through his bedroom.

"I took out two steaks this morning to defrost. I hope you're a big meat eater."

"I'm a huge meat and potatoes man...maybe too much so," he replies. "This, I might add, is the only thing the doc yells at me for during my physicals. "Eat less meat and more fish" is all she ever says. Oh, and well-done please. The sight of blood grosses me out."

"Okay on the well-done. You have a female doctor?" Shimie asks, in a surprised manner.

"Why not? She's the best doctor in Scottsdale. And with an exclusive clientele to boot. She's available to her patients 24/7."

"Whoa, that must cost a pretty penny."

"Trust me; you don't want to know the costs."

"I'll leave it at that and head off to my room to change. You don't need to be seeing a half-naked woman running around the house the rest of the evening; especially a fat and ugly one."

"Actually, I love the attire. Don't change on my account."

"You men all think alike," she promptly remarks. Then, as she begins walking to leave his bedroom, she turns her head toward Brent and smiles. And then disappears out his door.

—

"Now that was great steak. Are you sure you won't become my chief cook and bottle washer? I pay well."

"Trust me, you can't afford me. I'm a high-class society lady. We ladies don't come cheap."

"Oh my God, that comment so reminds me of my sister and the circles she runs in."

"Whoa, I hope you don't see *her* when you're looking at me?"

"No way...you're two different people altogether. I love my little sister, but I wish she were more like you... more wholesome, down to earth."

"Well then, from the fat and ugly one, I'll take that as a compliment...unless you meant something else."

"No way, that was a full blown compliment. I see you as having big dreams, but more down to earth dreams. More realistic. My sister's dreams all begin and end with a dollar sign. Our parents, my dad in particular, spoiled the hell out of her. He spent whatever it took to keep her happy. Unfortunately for him, it's now coming back to bite him in the ass. He now sees the folly of spoiling her. Her own father spoiled her and now she expects any and all men in her life to do just the same. She has no remorse in using her body and sexual prowess to entrap a man. But, unfortunately for her, they eventually wake up and realize they are being used. And then it is onto the next man of wealth. You can tell by the very clothes you are wearing that she loves to show off her attributes. And yes, she does have them."

"You know, I haven't even met your sister and already I feel sorry for her."

"So do I, but we each have our own path to walk down. As you have seen, I like nice things, but these material items are not where my real values lie. Maybe at one time it was, until I saw the movie, *Shoes of a Fisherman*, in my law school years. The theme of the movie changed my life forever...and hopefully for the best. And now I have a long awaited question of you. Where did the name Shimie come from? It's obviously an unusual name."

"The explanation is rather simple. My father grew up in Israel, though he wasn't Jewish. He met a beautiful woman, my mother, who was visiting Israel. They fell in love and got married. Shortly after they married, they moved to Arizona where my mother had a house she inherited from her parents. As I mentioned a few days ago, my father wanted a son. So, when I was born, he named me Sheme, which is a name originated in Israel. Though it's basically a male name, my mother took out the first e, replaced it with an "i" and then added another "i" near the end to make it even more feminine. My mother, being a staunch Catholic, raised me as such. My father didn't care one way or the other. So, that's where my name came from."

"Interesting background to your name, to say the least. Male name or not, I like it. It fits you."

"In my early teenage years I used to take a lot of ribbing for my name. At the time, it hurt; I wanted to change my name to anything but Shimie. But now that I'm older, I've come to accept it without regret. Numerologically, the name represents people with gifts of understanding, charismatic and kindhearted. Oh, and stubborn. Now I have a serious question of you."

"Fire away."

"Are you asking these questions in an attempt to get out of drying dishes?"

"Damn. You saw right through me, didn't you?"

"Sure did, now get your lazy bones up to the sink. Seeing as how I cooked your steak to perfection, you should be doing the washing *and* the drying."

"Let's just leave it at drying and you won't hear any complaints from me," Brent replies, with a smile.

Completing his drying chores, Brent disappears into his bedroom to make a few calls. Shimie, meanwhile, heads off to the living room to read the book she never was able to focus on earlier. A half hour later, Brent joins her on the couch with his own book in hand. The two of them read silently for over an hour before Brent finally speaks up.

"It's 9:30 already and I'm getting tired. I have a feeling your steak is what's making me tired. It's going to be after ten as it is before I hit the sack. My first priority is to get these oils off of my back that you so lavishly spread on my body. And for that, I thank you again."

"You are most welcome. If you require another one... you know where I live. For the time being anyway. And please, don't be using one of those back scrub brushes to get the oils off. You'll just end up opening up the wounds again."

"Damn. And here I had set aside a scouring pad to clean my back. Oh well, back to plan B...whatever that is or was. I'll see you in the morning for breakfast." With that said, Brent pushes up from the couch and heads off to his room. Once he has cleared out of the room, and she figures he was safely in his bedroom, she too gets up and hurriedly heads off to her own room—leaving her door slightly ajar.

9

♦

QUICKLY SHEDDING HER clothes, she puts her robe on and cinches it loosely around her waist. With that accomplished, she stealthily walks over to her door and waits anxiously for a particular sound. She can't ever remember being this apprehensive before. A few seconds later, she hears what she had waited for — the sound of his shower being turned on. She tiptoes silently across the hallway and quietly opens his door without knocking. Walking nervously toward his bathroom door, she isn't surprised at finding it wide open. Then, just as she is about to round the corner and enter his bathroom, she comes to a complete stop. What the hell am I doing? She asks herself. This is insane. This isn't who I am. I can't let my bodily desires overrule my mind. I need to walk right back into my bedroom — and then she promptly walks right into his bathroom.

Brent, sensing movement out of the corner of his eye, instantly glances around to see what it is. He was utterly

in shock at seeing Shimie standing there in her white bathrobe—all the while staring at him through the glass-en-
closed shower stall. Though taken aback, he is also pleasantly grateful. As Shimie proceeds to walk right up to his
shower door, the blood begins to flow where it counts the
most.

"As your nurse, it is my obligation to wash the oils off
your back before you end up damaging the work I did
to heal you. Is there room in there for me to perform my
duties?" She inquires, wondering if he would reject her
unexpected advances.

"There is always room in my shower for you … and I
appreciate your willingness to look after my best interest.
You do understand the ramifications of your actions, do
you not?"

"I've never been surer of my actions at any time in my
entire life," she answers, with a serious look on her face.
Without further prompting, she loosens the cord around
her waist before letting the bathrobe fall to the floor in a
heap. Though initially embarrassed by her total nudity,
she knew she has now reached the point of no return. Unlike her hesitation on the pool deck, which she now regrets,
she is now committed to bringing him the ultimate pleasures possible—at least those within her capabilities—and
she firmly believes that she is capable of anything where a
man is concerned.

Brent couldn't help but stare at her beautiful and full
breasts—not to mention her nipples that look to have al-

ready hardened. He turns the shower head to one side and opens the shower door with the other hand. Shimie, wasting no time stepping into the warm and misty shower, closes the door behind her. Replacing the shower head back to its original position, Brent turns down the amount of water flowing out of the shower head. He has a gut feeling this is about to be a long shower.

Brent immediately brings her body into his and gives her a deep-throated kiss — one he hopes she will remember for a long time. Shimie kisses him right back with a hunger she didn't think was possible twenty-four hours ago. With his and her bodies fully engaged, she no longer gives any thoughts as to whether or not she was doing the right thing. She wanted him badly, and nothing is going to stop her from taking him — all of him. Her one goal right now is to make sure that he never forgets this one moment in time — with her leading the charge.

After a full minute of kissing, Brent releases his lips from hers and gently turns her around. Pouring generous amounts of body wash into his hands, he reaches around her and places his hands around her supple breasts. He is taken aback at how large and hard her nipples had become since entering the shower. His hands begin to move slowly and gently around her breasts, stopping only briefly to tease her engorged nipples. And with every moment of teasing, he hears soft moans escaping from her lips — much like his own moans on the pool deck earlier. Unlike her pulling back this afternoon, he has every intention of taking her completely. Even if she were to begin resisting his advances at this point, he knew deep within him he couldn't stop before being consumed by his own needs. Above all else, he knew the long deprived animal in him would drive him on until he was completely satisfied at its conclusion.

Shimie finds his touch to be almost unbearable to handle as his hands continue to massage and tease her breasts and nipples. She is fully ready to turn around and beg him to slip inside of her. She knew he is fully ready, as she could feel his hardness pressing against her backside; that by itself was bringing the passions within her to the point of climaxing. Should he have a change of heart as to what was currently happening, there was absolutely no way she would allow him to stop and walk away from her. Her loins were on fire and needed to be quenched urgently — and only he could do it by slipping inside of her.

Applying a fresh helping of body wash to his hands, Brent lowers his hands to her navel. In slow motion, he moves his hands around her mid-section, bringing forth a fresh round of whimpering from Shimie. As long as he was hearing moans, he knew she was ripe for the taking. Continuing with his unhurried, deliberate motions, he periodically slips back up to her breasts and teases her nipples before retreating back down to her mid-section. He knew, rather instinctively, that he could turn her back around at any point now and take her immediately. But he is also cognizant of the fact that the more he teases her, the greater her orgasm will be when he finally consumes her. Her total satisfaction was important to him — more so than the many women he had previously bedded.

As hands and fingers continue their teasing ways, Shimie isn't surprised at knowing that her moans of satisfaction were increasing in both numbers and intensity. She makes no attempts at hiding the pleasures he was bringing her. If for no other reason, it was her way of providing feedback that he was making all the right moves upon her body. Following a brief pinch of her nipples, she feels his hands shooting down to her loins; the very hands that wasted no time in moving ever so slowly up and down the inside of her thighs. With each movement, his thumbs would gently touch her womanhood. And with each tender touch, she finds her moans almost turning into screams. Never in her dating or married years had she felt such animalistic passions as she did at this very moment.

Brent continues his teasing ways, though he finds in so doing, it was also bringing him to a heightened level of passion and need. Fighting back the natural urge to take her to relieve his own needs and wants, he finds immense pleasure in keeping her worked up to the maximum. He knew all too well, from her heightened moaning and bodily thrusting against his hands and fingers that she could not hold back much longer before finding her release. And without warning, she does find her release. She lets out a blood-curdling scream and begins convulsing wildly — all the while pushing forcefully against his probing fingers.

The multiple orgasms she is experiencing were like no others — and still she finds herself wanting more. But more than anything, she wants, needs, craves for his manhood to enter her. That alone would bring her the ultimate satisfaction; even if the orgasms never materialized.

Knowing she was now in a weakened stage, Brent quickly brings his left hand up to just below her breasts to hold her up. Once the convulsions finally end, he again turns her around and immediately starts in again with the teasing of her nipples — but this time with his lips and tongue. Her nipples, softened following her orgasms, quickly became firm as he maneuvers his tongue teasingly over and around each nipple. And then, when she least expected it, he pulls her nipple deep into his mouth and pulls back quickly — creating a popping sound in the process — and each time he did this, her moaning instantly follows suit.

Strangely enough, in the process of satisfying her animalistic needs, he forgets all about his own needs. This, he knew, was a first for him. He could only attribute this to having been overly focused on taking care of her. Running his tongue around her breasts, he finds his way back to her quivering lips. Only this time, when he kisses her, he does so in a slow and easy motion; he knew she was spent, exhausted, out of energy. When he finally pulls his lips from hers, he looks deep into her eyes and sees for the first time from her, both thankfulness and satisfaction staring back at him with a glazed-over look.

Giving him a quick kiss in return, she steps behind him

and grabs the body wash with one hand and proceeds to gently wash the oils from his back; though she had to believe that the long shower, up to this point, had already removed whatever oils were there. But that's okay; she so wants him to experience the same pleasures he had freely given her just moments before. In the back of her mind, until he had just proven otherwise, she had seriously thought of him as one of those "wham-bam-thank-you-ma'am" kind of men; his actions upon her body ended up blowing that notion completely away.

Working down his back, her hands eventually make their way to his firm ass. Shimie intentionally runs some of her fingers slowly between the two halves of his buttocks. As a nurse, she had been taught that the nerves of a man's rectum were the same nerves as those of his member. And just to bear out what she had been taught, she glances down at his full erection while running her fingers along his rectal opening. The results of the test brought an instant smile to her face — his full erection instantly sprang to life with each caress. She was proud of herself for having stayed focused in that particular class — to not only learn that, but to actually have the opportunity to put her learning to practical use.

Following a few minutes of constant teasing, she works her way down his legs before heading back up to his buttocks. Brent was mildly surprised at her sexual playfulness. From the first time he met her, he had developed this image of a woman who was slightly on the prudish side of the sexual pendulum. His thoughts of her were now beginning to swing the other way; especially so when she shed her bathrobe and walked into his shower uninvited, unannounced. That was pretty brazen on her part, he thought, given that they hadn't even shared a first kiss or a romantic embrace. He has to admit—this was a first for him—and he finds himself liking the fact that she was the one who initiated it all.

Reaching around to his front, she places her hands on his navel and begins moving her hands around in a circular motion. Before too much time passes, she slides her hands down to the inside of his thighs—much as he had done to her. Her hands move inwards and begin fondling his testicles before moving back to his inner thighs—and then right back to his testicles again. She was going to make him pay dearly for teasing her the way he did.

Shimie observes that she was striking pay dirt with his moans increasing with each touch. As much as she loves the sounds of his moaning, she wants more signs from him that she was making the right moves—that she was bringing him, like he did her, the greatest pleasures he could ever hope for. And she knew exactly what it will take to bring him to those ultimate heights of pleasure. Sliding her hands upward from his testicles, she begins to lightly brush up and down the length of his member. With each slow move up and down, his manhood went into mini-spasms. The whimpering sounds that follow magnifies in their intensity.

Reaching over to squirt the wash into her eagerly waiting hands, she resumes her previous teasing ways—but not for long. With her left hand on his navel, she wraps her right hand around his joystick. He immediately makes a noise she was unfamiliar with from a man, though she knew it certainly wasn't the sounds of someone in distress. While sliding her hand up and down his member, she is bowled over by how well-endowed he is—her ex should be so lucky, she muses. Shimie is sensing, from his unintelligible moans, that he is about to go over the top if she keeps sliding her hand up and down. She wasn't ready for him to go that way; especially after what he did for her.

Maintaining her grip on his engorged love muscle, she moves around to his front side and immediately drops down on her knees. Moving in to get close enough, she begins licking the tip of his pride and joy—now her pride and joy to take care of. He was so rigid and trembled in her hand that she couldn't believe he could stop himself from climaxing at that very moment—and she is glad that he hadn't. From the sounds he made, she knew the moment of truth is at hand. With time running out for him, she rose up and quickly inserts his shaft inside of her.

Moving back and forth in sync with his movements and needs, the sounds of primal screams quickly pierces her ears. In a matter of seconds following his screams, she too lets loose with her own screams. The two of them immediately cling to each other for support as the climaxes play themselves out. Shimie, nestled into his chest, is pleased that her actions played out just as she had envisioned they would. He had taken her well beyond her wildest expectations—and she wanted nothing more than to reciprocate. She knew that she would do it all over again if given the opportunity—and she hopes that he would in fact give her that opportunity again and again.

She was in no hurry to pull away from him—even with the shower water starting to turn cold. Shimie finds herself exceedingly happy, satisfied and at peace with herself. As the spasms she thought would never end continue to rock him, she feels even more satisfaction. Her goal from the onset had nothing to do with being pleased herself—but everything to do with physically pleasing Brent—and she succeeded beyond her own imagination. Or at least he gave every indication that he was pleased; that is, if climaxing were to be the barometer for one's level of sexual satisfaction. She had no way of ever paying him back for what he was doing to find her daughter—if nothing else, this was a down payment on what she owes him. Though looking at the current experiences, she knew that she would have pleased him sexually anyway—even if she weren't beholden to him.

As Brent reaches over to shut the shower off, they continue holding onto one another. She feels totally secure and at peace with his arms tightly wrapped around her. Brent was extremely thankful, even though coming out of the blue, for her having made love to him in the ways she did. He wasn't entirely sure why she did what she did for him, but he was, nevertheless, exceptionally grateful that she had. He couldn't remember the last time — if ever — he felt this good after engaging in a sexual relationship with any number of his past lovers. Something made a difference this time around, but he wasn't exactly sure what made it so special.

Shimie was the first of the two to pull away from their embrace. "I don't know about you," she quietly states, while looking directly into his sexy blue eyes, "but I'm starting to get too cold for comfort."

"I hear you. Here, use this towel while I grab another one. I would have had two at the ready, but I wasn't expecting company to just barge in on me unannounced. Not only that, but to take advantage of me in a weakened state. I feel so used," he concludes, as he gives her a big smile before leaving the shower to fetch another towel.

"You're just lucky I'm in a good mood, or I would take a swing at you for that last comment. If I didn't know better, I would have to believe you dropped a Mickey into my water at dinner time. Ever since dinner I've had this strange feeling overcoming me that I couldn't control. As if someone else had control of my mind and body. And now I know both who and why. You took advantage of me. You used me. I feel so ashamed right now," she adds, all the while trying to maintain a serious look.

"You are absolutely right on all counts. I did take advantage of you. I did use you for my own wanton needs. I am sorry. And to prove how sorry I am, I will never again lay so much as a single finger on you. You can immediately return to being a vestal virgin. Okay?"

"Now just you wait a minute, Mr. Over-Sexed. I fully expect you to make amends for your sinful ways on my body. The least you can do is allow me to sleep in your bed tonight. After all, I am freezing you know. I need to be warmed up ... and fast."

"Okay, you drive a hard bargain. Besides, I wouldn't want any charges filed against me for taking advantage of a born-again virgin. That would be a big hit on my otherwise squeaky clean record."

"Smart man," Shimie responds as she stoops to pick up her bathrobe.

Shutting the bathroom light off, Brent holds out his hand to Shimie and walks her to the far side of the bed. Pulling the blanket back, she slides in. Climbing into bed himself, Brent pulls Shimie's head and her pillow up onto his chest. He wraps his left arm around her back and places his right hand comfortably on one of her breasts. In a matter of minutes, they both drift off to sleep.

10

As the early morning sun casts its light into the bedroom, Shimie slowly opens her eyes to greet the new day. Glancing to her right, she is stunned to see Brent lying beside her—not so much that he was beside her, but that he was still sleeping. She knew, or at least had come to learn, that he was always an early riser. And then she knew why— and then smiles with the knowledge that she alone was responsible for his sleeping in—she had wiped him out in the shower.

While she had almost backed out last night from her plans at seducing him, she is pleased with herself for following through. She had never been this brazen before when it came to her own sexual initiatives. It was just her nature to leave it up to her partner to make the first move. Having read countless gossip magazines in the hospital, she learned that many a man liked it when their woman makes the first move. His mentioning a need for a shower last night provided the perfect opportunity. The actual thought of seducing him began to take shape out on the pool deck. If not for that, the two of them would have been sleeping in their own bedrooms.

Lying on her side while continuing to stare at Brent, Shimie is at peace with herself—even with the knowledge that one day, when she is reunited with her daughter, she would be moving out on her own. Still, for the moment, she is at peace. She would no more undo what took place last night than sell her soul for gold. It was heavenly. She thoroughly enjoyed her sexual past, but last night's experience was more than she had ever read or dreamed of—and she knew that she would do it all over again—as long as Brent was on the receiving end. Shimie is quickly brought out of her thoughts when one of Brent's arms came to rest on her head as he stretches himself awake.

"Good morning, sleepyhead," Shimie greets him when their eyes lock onto each other.

"Oh my, I always beat the sun up. What happened? Oh, and good morning to you too." He immediately reaches behind her and pulls her part way up and onto his body. After grabbing onto one of her breasts, he continues. "I don't know what you slipped in my drink last night, but it apparently wiped me out big time."

"Uh, pardon me," she quickly replies. "I think your sleeping in had more to do with your seducing me last night than anything I might have slipped into your wine."

"Wow, I must have really been drugged last night, because I distinctly recall that you were the one doing the seducing…and I might add, you did it very well. You deserve an A+ in my book."

"Thank you. I went places last night that I've never gone before…even with my ex. I wanted it to be special for you; especially after what you did for me in the shower…and what you're doing for me and my daughter."

"While I obviously didn't initiate your coming into the shower, once you did, I wanted to do everything possible to make the experience all about you…to free up your mind."

"Thank you again. While it might sound shameful for a mother to say this, yes, I completely put my daughter out of my mind last night. I was focused on one thing—and one thing only."

"Then I'm thinking you need to continue focusing on one thing only when the need arises—and that one thing is your own pleasures. Before you can make someone else happy, you have to be happy yourself. And from this point forward, I'm going to haul you into the shower again and again to make you happy. How does that sound?"

"Absolutely delightful and delicious," she answers as she snuggles in closer.

"Before you start getting too comfortable though, I really do need to get up and make some calls, sooner rather than later. What do you think about getting dressed, though I prefer you naked, and whipping out some breakfast? I'll get dressed and make those calls right after breakfast."

"Calls about my daughter…or work calls?"

"About your daughter. I'd like to know what leads they're working on."

"Okay…we'll talk about it after breakfast, if you don't mind?" Though Brent was enjoying the cuddle time and the feel of her breast in his hand, he slides out of bed and walks directly into the bathroom—closing the door behind him. Shimie follows suit and makes her way back to her own bedroom—albeit, reluctantly. It felt so good to lie in his arms.

—

"How's the oatmeal?" Shimie asks, as she watches him spoon the last of it.

"Pretty good, actually. One can tire of pancakes every morning, so this was a treat of sorts."

"There's a lot of food in the pantry, but not of the breakfast variety." After a moment's pause, she continues. "So what's with Richards and the two investigators? At least what you know from talking to them yesterday. We never did talk about it."

"Sorry, I completely forgot yesterday, though there wasn't all that much to share. The two P.I.'s are running the trap line on every possible organization out there that maintains a listing of missing people…and those that have since been accounted for. Richards is apparently trying to track down your ex to see if he might be able to provide some leads…aside from the fact that he should be made aware of your daughter's status as missing. Just before leaving the bedroom, I received a text from Richards asking for your exes' address and phone number. He can't find a listing for either…outside of your apartment."

"I have no idea what phone number he has. The last time I tried to reach him, his number had been disconnected. Most likely for lack of payment. When he moved out of the apartment, he headed straight for his mother's place in Buckeye…in a trailer park where she's an assistant manager. I don't have the address with me, but her name is Paula Fredericks…nice lady. Unlike her son."

"Thanks…I'll relay the info. One other question while we're on the subject. When I was crawling around your kitchen, I noticed a number of pots and pans lying on the floor, as well as strewn about the stove-top island. When looking to see where they all came from, I noticed a pots and pans rack hanging from the ceiling directly over the stove. So, that explained where they came from, but something else caught my eye as unusual. I noticed that each of the big hooks was facing toward your kitchen table instead of where a person would pull a pan off toward themselves."

"You can blame my ex for that. He bought one of those already made hangers and then proceeded to hang it backward. I mentioned it to him the first time I had to use a pot. I had to lean over a hot stove to get it off the hook. My ex looked at me and said, 'live with it.' And so I did."

"Okay, that explains that. I also noticed a heavy, cast-iron skillet lying alongside your neighbor. With the hooks facing the opposite direction, I was curious how the skillet made its way over by the refrigerator. I mean, there were certainly pots on the floor, but they bounced off the stove. The skillet was way too heavy to be bouncing anywhere."

"Mystery solved. It was too heavy for me to lift up and hook, so I simply left it on the stove. When the earthquake struck, it obviously slid off the stove and onto the floor. Boy, some investigator you would make. You had better stick to what you do well…like shower activities," Shimie concludes, while giving him a wink.

"You're absolutely right. I'll hang up my private-eye hat for good and leave it to you and the professionals," Brent shot back, while also giving her a wink in return. He decides to ask no more questions of her at this point, nor share with her what was playing in the back of his mind. She is becoming more relaxed as the days progressed, so he rationalized that it would serve little purpose by sharing his own theories concerning her daughter's mysterious disappearance. When he had more concrete evidence, then he would.

"Why don't you go make those phone calls you mentioned while I do up the few dishes? Yes, I'm letting you off the hook from drying this time…but only this time."

"An offer I can't refuse," he responds, quickly pulling away from the table and escaping to his study.

After speaking at some length to his mother, and placing calls to both Richards and the lead investigator he hired, he makes his way to the living room where he knew he would find Shimie. And sure enough, there she was all curled up with a throw blanket over her shoulders. Her St. Gemma medal pressed between her fingers. He could only assume that he caught her praying the rosary.

"Why the blanket?" He asks out of curiosity.

"Well, until the sun does its job, it can get a little chilly in the mornings."

"Sorry. When hooking up the generator and the solar panels on the roof, I only had essential items and rooms wired. A/C and heat were not considered essential... though I may later regret the A/C decision when the full summer hits and I lose power again. Speaking of heat, sit up for a second while I climb in behind you to warm you up."

Without any hesitation, Shimie scoots over and makes room for Brent. Once he's in place, she leans back against him. With his arms around her, and both hands covering her breasts, she pulls the blanket back up around her and once again settles in to read. Shimie, however, was finding it difficult to concentrate on her reading—what with his hands gently massaging her breasts. A few minutes later, she reaches over and lets the book drop to floor, before leaning her head back alongside of his. The coolness she felt moments earlier is soon replaced by the feeling of security and warmth—and the longer he caresses her breasts, the warmer she begins to feel.

Brent found himself overly enamored with the fullness of her breasts, not to mention the hardness of her nipples that were clearly evident through the tight fitting blouse. With one hand remaining on her breast, he uses the other to undo the top three buttons on her blouse. Using both hands, he then locates the front two hooks holding the bra in place and slides them apart. From there it was just a simple case of flesh meeting flesh, and Brent wastes no time in doing just that. Running his hands gently across her hardened nipples, he hears some of the same moaning sounds as he had heard in the shower last night.

As he soothingly massages her firm breasts, he finds himself in no hurry, as the enjoyment was as much his as he hopes it was hers. He knew well the excitement it is bringing him by the fact that his member is now fully engorged. He had to believe that she too feels the hardness below her. After ten minutes of fondling, he lowers his hands from her breasts and quickly undoes the two remaining buttons on her blouse. Finishing with the buttons, he sets about unsnapping the button at the top of her jeans. Before he even has the chance to pull her zipper down, she reaches down and beats him to it. If nothing else, he muses, she was now an active accomplice to the seduction of her own body.

Placing both hands below her navel, he once again begins his masterful massaging techniques — techniques that he knew from last night's episode in the shower will send shivers up and down her spine. It isn't long before she begins to move her pelvis up and down against his probing fingers — a clear indication to him that she needs more of what he is doing. Brent, of course, feels that it is his duty as her now lover to take care of those needs. With her needs in mind, not to mention his own, he slides both hands farther down, well beyond encountering the first pubic hairs. With both hands in constant motion, he begins to feel the moisture appearing beneath his fingertips. He knew what it is her mind and body were yearning for.

Using both hands, he separates the two lips guarding the secretive part of her — not to mention the most sensitive. While his left hand continues to massage the left side of her opening, the middle finger of his right hand begins to disappear deep inside of her. With her head still alongside of his, he is acutely aware of how labored her breathing had become — along with the loudness and intensity of her moans. Taking all of these signs to heart, he makes a decision to put her out of her heavenly misery. Groping around inside of her, he knew when he hit her g-spot by the tightening of her entire body as it presses against him. Going into overdrive inside of her body, it isn't long before she finally lets out a series of guttural screams and explodes. He continues his animalistic-like attacks on her g-spot before she even had an opportunity to get her bearings. In short order, multiple orgasms burst forth.

Even after the orgasms long subside, Shimie finds herself still twitching with excitement as Brent tenderly plays with her nipples. She finds it inconceivable that she could experience so many out of this world orgasms barely twelve hours apart. But then again, she quickly realizes that he was a master at everything he touches. And she is extremely thankful that it is she that he was applying his craft on. She knew she had no right to be, but she was nevertheless envious of those women who were previously touched by his hands—the same hands that were currently bringing her unbelievable pleasure. Even at his best moment of giving sexual pleasure, she reminisces; her ex couldn't even begin to match Brent's level of expertise. And the more she thinks about it, the more she knew what the major difference between the two of them was—her ex was a taker while Brent was a giver. To her, and most likely to most women, that was important in knowing whether or not they were truly loved. A taker was not capable of truly giving love—at least in her mind.

Shimie eventually rolls to her side and off of Brent before looking directly into his eyes—and then tears begin to roll down her cheeks. Brent leans in closer and begins to kiss the tears away as fast as they cascade down her cheeks. But the more tears he kisses away, the more she sheds them. Knowing no reason for the tears, he feels compelled to ask.

"Why the tears? Did I do something wrong? Did I hurt you in some way?"

And the tenderness in the way he asks those questions bring only more tears—and the tears soon turn into fits of sobbing. When the sobbing begins, she straight away threw her head onto his chest and wraps her slender arms around his back—and she cries. And she cries some more.

Brent was beside himself. No woman, at least a lover, had ever cried like Shimie was doing right now. He had just finished bringing her intense pleasure—at least in his own mind it was intense pleasure. Maybe in her mind it wasn't. Just maybe she was going through the motions of being satisfied—thinking it would bring me pleasure in knowing that I had taken care of her. He is confused, but around women, that isn't too difficult to do, or so he has found out over the years. One minute they were up—the next they were down. It must have something to do with a hormonal imbalance, he conjectures. Try as he may, he fails to think of any other logical reason for such behavior. Pleasures and tears just don't go hand in hand—at least not in his world.

Even though Brent finds himself lost in an array of questioning thoughts, he continues to slowly massage her back—all in an attempt to sooth her and, hopefully, bring back some semblance of peace to whatever is currently troubling her.

Without lifting her head or moving, Shimie finally speaks up. "Brent, you did absolutely nothing wrong. In fact, you did everything right. And that's why the tears. Whenever women feel really loved—or hopefully in our situation—at least really, really liked, they get emotional. They feel so overwhelmed with gratitude. As much as women are better at expressing their emotions than men, sometimes we display those emotions via tears. For whatever time we have left together, I am and always will be grateful for your coming into my life. And when we say our final goodbyes, you can expect these same tears to fall again. Take it from me, no man will ever totally understand a woman...so I don't expect you will either right now. But that's okay, we oftentimes don't understand ourselves or other females either."

Brent is slightly overwhelmed at hearing her short dissertation on emotions and tears. It is heartening to hear that he had caused her no pain in his attempts to bring her nothing but pleasure. Taking his hand off her back, he places it on the side of her head and initiates running his fingers through and around her dark hairs. As she continues to lie there, he senses that she has finally gone into a relaxed state — and he isn't going to do anything to disturb it. He feels no remorse that his own sexual needs are not satisfied. Right now he had no needs of any kind, with the exception of continuing to relax her. Reaching down, he snags one end of the blanket and pulls it up and over her. In a matter of minutes, she is sound asleep. Brent feels some relief, though he worries for her troubles.

11

"Hɪ Dᴇʀʀɪᴄᴋ...ᴡʜᴀᴛ do you have?"

"Are you saying that she hasn't seen him since the evening before the quake? Has she heard from him?"

"Not a word, huh? Strange. Did he tell her where he was going when he left her place?"

"Left before she got up. I don't figure him to be an early riser. Did his mother appear nervous or combative, as if she were trying to protect him?"

"Good. Shimie said she was a nice lady."

"Did you ask her where he works?"

"That can only mean he's likely still in the drug business."

"Any vehicle?"

"None? How in the hell does he get around...this is a big city were talking about. Did she know of any friends he hung out with?"

"Not surprised. A loner type. Anything else of interest?"

"Okay, thanks. You would think after a major quake that

a guy would want to know about the welfare of a loved one. In this case, his own flesh and blood. I don't get it…but maybe I do. I'll relay the info to Richards. Stay in touch."

With a disappointing and somewhat perplexing call behind him, he wanders out of the study and into the living room, where he once again finds Shimie reading. As he enters the room, Shimie closes the book and watches as he approaches her.

"I just hung up with Derrick, the private investigator, he checked out your ex-husband, or I should say, his mother. He wasn't there…nor did his mother know where he was. She hasn't seen or heard from him since the evening before the quake hit."

"Why are you *checking out* my ex?" Shimie asks, with a note of indignation in her voice.

"Sorry, poor choice of words. I had asked the investigator, if he could even get there, to inform your ex of the circumstances surrounding his daughter. I know you aren't exactly fond of him, but he's still her father. Besides, if he really loves his daughter, maybe he'll do some searching on his own."

"I seriously doubt that he loves my daughter. It was a bitter divorce…he wanted custody only because it meant that I would be paying support to him…I can only assume he wanted the money for his drug habits. When the judge awarded me full custody, plus $800 a month support, he was livid. I've seen him angry before, but not like that one day in court. With his lawyer still sitting there, he got up and walked out."

"I'm just curious…and yet you married him."

"He was a different person when we were dating… only displaying his good side. He had a good job as an insurance salesman and didn't hold back on the flowers or chocolates. He was a smooth talker. I saw a future in him. I was obviously very naïve…too trusting."

"Displaying his good side…the reason for so many divorces and relationship breakups," Brent piggybacks on her statement.

"It won't happen again…if there is a next time."

"You're too caring and beautiful to remain single. You'll find the right man when you least expect it. But enough of this, I'm heading outside to swim and lie by the pool."

"Mind if I join you?" Shimie asks, not wanting to be alone.

"I thought you would never ask. And yes, I would love the company, but only if you wear that Band Aid bikini again," he adds with a big grin.

"Have you ever been called a male tramp before?"

"Probably…but not to my face. And congratulations, you're the first person to recognize me for what I am. So much for keeping it a secret from you, though I do recall a certain shower seduction," he throws back at her with a smile.

Taking his outstretched hand, she quickly places her hand in his and allows him to help her up from the couch.

—

"The roast beef tastes better the second time around," Brent remarks, just as he is about to fork another piece into his hungry mouth.

"Leftovers usually do taste better, though not sure why. There's a little more in the pan if you want it."

"Nope...this will do me. Gotta watch my youthful, manly figure," he adds, with a laugh.

"Your figure looked pretty good in the pool; especially when your trunks came off," Shimie remarks, with a big grin lighting up her face.

"Ah, if I recall, you're the one who removed them. I am only guilty of removing yours right after mine were forcibly ripped from my body." Brent attempts to maintain a serious look on his face, but fails miserably. "Oh, and thank you for the best pool-sex ever. There was no way I could do laps after that...you totally wasted me."

"Just consider it payback for the couch-sex this morning...and for kissing my tears away."

"Any time I see a tear, you better believe I'll kiss it away. You never know where that kiss might lead."

"Does your mother even know what a tramp you are?"

"My mother only knows that I attend mass weekly and that I avoid commitment like the plague. One she's happy with, the other she's not. Oh well."

"Maybe I should tell her, if you'll hand over your fancy phone there, the secret, over-sexed life you lead. That you're intentionally hiding from her, I might add."

"She'd never believe you...coming from a fat and ugly

woman." Shimie openly laughs at his remark. "But anyway," he continues, "thank you for the pool activities I hide from my mother...I didn't expect it."

"Ah, but that's why you enjoyed it...you weren't expecting it. That oftentimes makes for the best sex...when the partner isn't expecting anything. Much as I wasn't expecting to be taken on the couch, or were you in the shower. And another thing while we're on the subject of sex. For me, the pool sex was the best sex ever. Why? Because you were inside of me. Finger stimulation is great to get a woman worked up, but nothing beats having a man's tool inside of us. It's the ultimate. And you know what...it doesn't really matter if we climax or not. Women are givers. And sexuality is great...and yes, we need that too, but what we really need are the tender moments, like when we are held close to a man's body, or we lay our head down in his lap and he massages our head. It's the *goodbye* and *hello* kisses that we desperately need to assure ourselves that our men love us. I know that you single men are just interested in getting your *rocks* off. I fully understand that, but when you fall in love with that special woman, if you ever do, don't forget the other aspects of a relationship that are so important to a woman."

"Given your youthful age, how is it you know so much about what a woman wants?"

"Number one, I'm a woman. Number two, my mother was a great teacher; she shared many of the traits that made

her own marriage a success. My father loved her deeply…
even when her exterior beauty was no longer there. Third-
ly, I've spent years working around female nurses. During
the lulls in activity in the hospital, relationships, marriage,
sex and whatever, rose up. It was from those conversations that I knew something was missing from my own
marriage. I didn't say much…mostly listened. It was actually the older nurses, who were either married, or had
been married that taught me the most. They've been there,
done that. As I reflected more and more on what they had
to say, and they openly revealed more than they probably
should have, in my opinion, I began to see the things that
were missing in my own relationship with my husband."

"Wow! You are so wise in the ways of sex and relationships…way beyond your years, I might add. If I didn't
know better, I'd think I was having this conversation with
Jessica. Well, not the tenderness part. She's only interested
in the money part, which you never mentioned."

"Jessica?" She states questioningly. "I take it she must
have been your latest fling…before me, that is?"

"Jessica…as in the woman whose seductive clothing
you're wearing."

"Oh. Until now you've never called her by her name."

"An oversight on my part. Forgive me. What say we
do up the dishes and hit the living room for some reading
before bed?"

"I'm all for it, though I'm a little on the tired side, so
may go to bed early, if you don't mind."

"Fine by me. Hopefully when I come to bed I'll find you warming the sheets for me."

"Maybe…if you're lucky," she answers with a wink as she pushes herself away from the table.

12

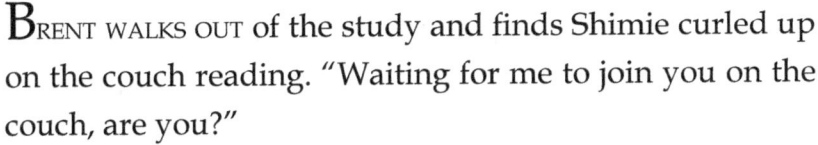

Brent walks out of the study and finds Shimie curled up on the couch reading. "Waiting for me to join you on the couch, are you?"

"I've been waiting for you alright…for breakfast, that is. Do you have any idea what time it is?"

"Sorry, but you were still counting sheep, so I snuck off to the study for work and a few phone calls. I didn't want to wake Sleeping Beauty up."

"Sleeping Beauty? Must be looking for some action later on, huh?" Shimie responds, with a smile she tries to hide, but can't.

"Action?" Brent responds with a look of shock. "That thought would never enter my mind; especially after conversing with my mother for a half hour. Oh, before I forget. The power came back on while you were still taking up bed space. How much of the city has power, I have no idea. I'm just thankful that we do. Now if we can just get water…the emergency water tank out back is getting pretty low. We may be bathing in the pool before long. And you know what that might lead to."

"I can see your trampy mind is functioning quite well without having any breakfast in you."

"Hey, don't blame me...it takes two you know. Now let's go eat."

—

"You mentioned this morning that you talked with your mother. Did she mention your office staff?"

"Yep, sure did. According to my father, all but two are accounted for—one legal researcher and a new attorney with the firm. Given the magnitude of the destruction, I'm surprised that more weren't unaccounted for...and hopefully those two will be located safely as well."

"Any new leads on my daughter?" Shimie asks in a subdued voice.

"Nothing yet. I'm waiting for a call from Richards later today. There's a possibility of getting together early tomorrow morning to go over leads, theories and that sort of stuff. One of the investigators will attempt to be there as well...if he can get there."

"Am I invited?" Shimie quietly asks.

"Per Richards, probably not. And before you get all defensive and start yelling at me, let me explain. The police department has commandeered a private helicopter for policing duties—a two-seater—pilot and passenger. Richards, without the Chief's knowledge, will attempt to divert the copter here just before the pilot's shift change. The shift change takes place at five. Richards suggest that I leave my phone here in case he has any questions of you. Sorry, but it's the best he can do under the circumstances."

"I won't yell. I won't get defensive," Shimie remarks in a calm voice. "Am I happy that I can't be there? Absolutely not. But I'm smart enough to understand helicopter limitations and resources. Of the two of us, you should be the one going. You've been dealing with Richards and the private investigators for the past four or so days...I haven't. And that's probably a good thing as I'm too emotionally involved. You have no idea how thankful I am for your taking the lead on matters related to my daughter—and for being there for me when I needed a shoulder to cry on...many times already...and probably more to come. Thank you. Thank you. Thank you." Shimie ends her words calmly.

"Gee, three thank-yous in a row. What does that win me?" Brent suggestively asks with a smile.

"You'll find out," Shimie answers, while trying to muster up a smile of her own.

"Sorry, didn't mean to make light of the situation. Like I said earlier, Richards will call this afternoon if it's a go. The pilot will be landing at the top of the driveway—cemented and flat. Being a small copter, hopefully it won't wake you up."

"No! I want to be up...I want to see you off," Shimie responds insistently.

"Okay, I'll see that you're up before I leave."

"Promise?" Shimie asks, with a sad look in her eyes.

"Promise. I may be a tramp, as you've labeled me, but one thing's for sure—I'm a man of my word. You will be up to see me off."

"Thank you."

13

♦

"SHIMIE. TIME TO get up…the copter will be here in about ten minutes."

Shimie immediately sits straight up in bed and tries to get her bearings. Brent can't help but notice her exposed breasts. Privately, he wants nothing more right now then to climb back in bed and make love to her. Catching a glimpse of her breasts is all it takes to get his blood running. Maybe when I return, he thinks to himself, she might be persuaded to hop back in the sack for a little late morning delight.

After coming to her senses enough to realize why he was waking her up, she quickly states, "Let me use the bathroom first and I'll meet you out in the living room."

"Not a problem…see you there." As he heads to the closet near the front door, Brent figures he had better grab at least a lightweight jacket to ward off the early morning chills. Two minutes later, Shimie rounds the corner and comes into the living room. She looks damn good in his sister's white bathrobe, he notices — the same bathrobe she wore and let drop to the floor at the foot of his shower. He so wants to rip it from her body and make love to her on the area rug. Or the couch. Or wherever.

"Brent. Is that the copter I hear?"

"Good ears...I guess my mind was off in some other direction."

"And what direction was that?" She quietly asks.

"The truth? I was thinking of making love to you right here and now."

"When you get back, I'll be waiting right here for you. Just like this," she states, as she opens her bathrobe revealing her totally naked body.

"Whoa. You are so beautiful in your nakedness. I'll have no choice but to take you up on that offer. And I'll be back just as soon as I can. But let's get outside — he's almost here."

Stepping outside, they easily spot the red and green flashing lights on the copter as it approaches the house. Brent, having gone out earlier, intentionally turned on every light he could think of to give the pilot a visual cue. Picking up a flashlight, he takes Shimie's hand and walks closer to the actual landing spot. As the copter gets within 500 feet of the house, Brent starts flashing the light on and off.

A half minute later, the copter begins its descent to the driveway below. Once on the ground, the pilot, keeping his head low, came over to where Brent and Shimie stood.

Making eye contact with Brent, he yells over the noise of the rotors, "Are you ready to go?"

"You bet, thanks for picking me up," Brent yells back. Turning to Shimie, he takes her in his arms and gives her a big kiss—a passionate kiss that even surprises him. "Here's the flashlight and my phone. Keep it with you." Before she has a chance to respond, he runs to the copter with his head bent down almost at waist level. After instructing Brent how to fasten the strange seat belts, the pilot wastes no time in lifting off. Brent isn't sure that Shimie could see him, but he waves anyway. With all the lights on in the driveway, he clearly sees Shimie waving to him.

As Shimie stands there watching until they were completely out of sight, she finds herself speechless. The last thing she ever expected was for Brent to take the initiative and kiss her goodbye. It was almost like an "I love you" action on his part. While the kiss was not deep, it was still very much filled with a sense of passion—as if he were saying that I'm going off to war, but I'll be back. She is deeply moved by his kiss. She is thrilled. And yes, they have made love with tremendous passion. But deep down, she knows that Brent is commitment-phobic. His commitment was to work first—not to any particular woman—and definitely not to the idea of starting a family. She tries to disprove all of these notions in her mind, but she knew better. And yet, in spite of all the obvious red flags, she still finds herself in love with him—not that she would ever tell him that. If she dares to utter those three words, he would distant himself from her in a heart-beat. She knew that. But for right now, she is content with making it a one-sided love affair. Maybe in due time, she muses.

—

"Thanks Bill for arranging the flight. I really appreciate it."

"Well, for once, you *finally* owe me."

"You know my reputation, Bill; I pay all my debts of gratitude. But what I have to say may reverse the tables. You may be owing me."

At that moment, Derrick walks into Richards' office.

"Derrick, I don't believe you've met Detective Richards before. Derrick. Bill." After shaking hands, the three of them sit down at the small conference table.

"Well, given that I asked for this meeting," Brent begins, "I'll lay my theories and facts out on the table straightfor-ward. I know both of you have plenty of other things on your minds, so let me begin. An earthquake takes place while a mother is at church. I know this to be a fact, as I was there with her...though separately. Following some treacherous struggling to get to her apartment, I go inside to hopefully find her nine-month-old daughter. I never did find the daughter, but I did find her neighbor-babysit-ter lying dead on the kitchen floor. Okay, one can easily assume that she was killed as a result of the earthquake...a blow to the left side of the head...caused by a quake-produced flying skillet; a cast-iron one at that. Everything I've said up to this point would be plausible in an investigation. But firsthand knowledge of the scene would have me believe something totally different.

"Oh, and there's the fact that a nine-month-old baby just up and disappears. A Good Samaritan comes by and hears the baby crying, perhaps? Again...plausible. Based on what I found, however, and having mulled it over for a few days, I believe the Scottsdale Police Department has a homicide on their hands...not just a missing person's case. Let me explain why I think it was a homicide. And feel free to interject if either of you have questions or think I'm blowing smoke.

"Before I could even remotely begin to enter her apartment, I had to break away huge chunks of glass that were still protruding from the base of the window frame; albeit at a 45 degree angle. There was no way I could enter the apartment without first breaking the glass away. Nor could anyone else, say a Good Samaritan. The front door was also listing at a 45 degree angle and wedged in pretty solid against the door frame itself. I assure you, no one entered through the front door after the quake hit. Bill, when the coroner removed the body, how did they gain access to the apartment?"

"As you said," Bill replies, "the window turned out to be the only access point. I was there a day before the coroner showed up. I saw it for myself. A rookie cop had to go in through the window to verify her body was there and take pictures before making a hasty retreat."

"I never thought to take pictures of the window before I entered," Brent continues, "but in hindsight, I wished I had. It would have confirmed my suspicions that we're dealing with a homicide. Anyway, I surveyed the living room...no baby, no babysitter. I then made my way down the hallway, on all fours because of the angle of the unit, to the bedroom...the only bedroom in the apartment. Her bed was obviously there as well as the baby's crib...with no baby in it. The one window, up high, was partially broken out...but in my opinion, still not accessible from the outside.

"Affirming, in my own mind, that no baby was present, I then proceeded to crawl out of the bedroom and headed just around the corner to the only bathroom. Like the front door, however, the door was closed and wedged into the frame. Just from looking at it, I knew I wasn't going to gain access without somehow breaking the door down. And, for all I knew, the door frame was the only thing holding up the rest of the apartment. I had no visions of wanting to die that way.

"I then crawled back down the hallway, made a sharp right turn and entered the kitchen. I immediately saw the sitter, Gladys Broberg, lying on the floor in front of the fridge. I crawled over to see if she were still alive. As soon as I touched her neck with my fingers, I knew she was long gone. And here again, I don't use the words 'long gone' loosely. I remembered from my law school days that it takes a number of hours for rigor mortis to begin setting in. And the warmer the temperature, the shorter the time it takes to set in. To me, she was pretty cold and stiff. Not a condition I would have expected a mere hour and a half after the quake. Yes, it was starting to get warm outside, but the temp inside of the apartment wasn't all that bad. It wasn't until a few days later that this rigor mortis condition dawned on me.

"While looking at her body, I also noticed, but didn't give it much thought at the time, a heavy iron skillet lying to the side of her. You know, the type of skillet you might fry chicken on a stovetop burner, or even in an oven, I guess. A cook I am not. I also noticed a broken baby bottle on the floor in front of the stove. Not only the bottle, but what appeared to be all the milk from the bottle. Meaning, of course, that the bottle had never been consumed by the baby. It wasn't until after I reviewed the five photos I had taken with my phone that I noticed one of the burner dials was not in a straight up position. Shimie, the baby's mother, informed me that she left the apartment at 7:35, and had asked the sitter to start warming the bottle because the baby was beginning to fuss in her crib. A bottle, by the way, that was already sitting in the pan on the stove before Gladys even arrived at Shimie's apartment. So, if the sitter followed the mother's instructions, which I have to believe she did, she most likely turned the burner on right after Shimie had left. That would be what? 7:35? 7:40 at the latest?"

"I'll admit, we never gave the broken baby bottle or

spilled milk a thought," interjects Bill. "Nor did we think to look at the burner dial in the pictures you sent us. As you said, we thought everything was related to the earthquake. That's what we get for assuming, I guess."

"Seeing so many pots and pans on both the floor and the stove area," Brent continues, "I was naturally curious where they all came from. Glancing up, I noticed one of those store bought racks on the ceiling that held pots and pans...with two pots still hanging there. Oddly enough, and verified by Shimie, the open part of the hanging hooks were facing away from where one would stand in front of the stove and oven. When I asked her about it, she said that her then husband installed it, but backward. So, if I were a betting man, I would lay money on the fact that no pot or pan could have struck the sitter on the side of the head; especially given the fact that she was found not in front of the stove, but in front of the fridge. Which, as you can tell from two of the pictures, was clearly four or five feet to the right of the stove; when facing the stove, that is. I find it inconceivable that a pan, pot or skillet could fly off the hook in one direction and then go in the opposite direction and conk her in the head with such force as to kill her. When I looked at the bottom of the skillet, which happened to be bottom side up, there was just too much hair and blood there to happen from any tap to the head. Someone wanted to make sure that she was dead. Leave no witnesses. Now, admittedly, that is all conjecture on my part.

"As you know, Bill, she was struck on the left side of her head. And this is where the person of interest comes in. If a right-handed person were to strike someone from behind with a skillet, you would expect the victim's right side to be hit…if not directly on the back of the head. Conversely, a left-handed person would hit the left side. Of course, this all assumes that Gladys was not facing the proposed assailant. I intentionally asked Shimie the predominant hand of her ex-husband. I wasn't the least bit surprised when she said he was left-handed.

"Her former husband knew Gladys well and would, in the early stages following the divorce, visit his daughter while Shimie was at church. He didn't care to be around the mother. And yes, the divorce was bitter. I strongly believe that he was parked somewhere, in some unknown vehicle, and waited for Shimie to leave for church. And when she did, he mostly likely knocked on the door and was let in. After all, he had been there before and Gladys knew him. When she had her back to him in the kitchen, he removes the skillet from the top of the stove and hits her. He then scoops up the baby, most likely from her crib, and leaves. I'm not convinced that he wanted the daughter as much as he wanted revenge on his ex-wife. The best way to get back at someone in this scenario is to deprive them of their most valuable possession…in this case, the baby.

"I hadn't thought about this before," Brent continues, "but I don't recall seeing a diaper bag as I crawled around her apartment. A person intent on taking a baby, in my opinion, would also think to grab a diaper bag as well. Where the diaper would have been, if there were one, I obviously have no idea."

"The diaper bag could be important to this case," interjects Richards. "Can you ask the mother about it?"

"I can do that...and no sense waiting and wondering about the answer. Derrick, if you'll allow me to use your phone, I'll give her a call right now."

"It's all yours," Derrick states, as he hands the phone over to Brent.

"Shimie, hi...it's me, obviously. Just a quick question. Providing you had a diaper bag, where would you have left it before heading off to church?"

"Okay, thanks."

"No, everything is going just fine. I think we'll be wrapping things up in a half hour, though I'm not sure exactly when I'll get back home...it all depends on my mode of transportation. I'll give you a call when I know for sure. See you shortly, hopefully." Hanging up, he hands the phone back to Derrick.

"Yes, she in fact had a diaper bag, which she always hangs on the corner post of the crib. When I was in her bedroom, the crib was still intact against the outer wall. I checked everywhere in the room for the baby...and never did notice a diaper bag. Not that I was intentionally looking for the bag, mind you, but I think I would have noticed one if I saw it; especially if it were hanging down from the corner of the crib."

"You know what Brent, I think you missed your calling...you would have made an excellent detective on the force," Bill comments with a smile. "And you are absolutely right about something else; I think we do have a homicide on our hands. I'll ask the Buckeye force to keep a watch on the mother's house. The question now is where is the father? It won't be easy to locate him given the current chaos in the city. Yes, even five full days later there is still a fair amount of chaos out there."

"A good place to start," broke in Derrick, "would be the known drug hangouts. Even people without jobs need money...from one source or another. Given his recent past, I would have to believe he's still dealing. Of course we have no idea if he is even still in the area. According to his mother, he was born and raised here, so I have to believe he's still here...somewhere. Not to interfere with your own investigation, Bill, but I would like my partner and I to visit some of the known drug areas...most of which are located in Phoenix."

"We here in Scottsdale, Derrick, have no jurisdiction rights in Phoenix. Any involvement in Phoenix by you should be coordinated with my Phoenix counterparts. Though you're a private eye, so I guess you can do what you want...within legal limits, of course. Though right now, I have to believe they can use all the assistance they can from folks like you. I'll also notify the proper people in Phoenix as well as the Sheriff's office."

"Okay, Bill, I'll touch base with Phoenix. Something

I've done many times before." Switching from Richards to Brent, Derrick asks, "Does the mother have a current picture of her ex?"

"I have pictures on my computer that I uploaded from her cell. I know of one or two for sure, but I'll check out the rest. Whatever I find I'll forward to the two of you. And Bill, I know you'll want to put out an APB on her ex as soon as possible. If located, however, I would highly recommend following him as opposed to apprehending him right away. I say that based solely on the welfare of the baby, which should be everyone's first priority. We need to find out where he hangs his hat at night before you law enforcement types take him into custody."

"Is he armed?" Inquires Bill.

"I have no idea, but I'll ask Shimie as soon as I get home...or do you need the info now?"

"After you get home is fine. I don't want to put out an APB without his picture anyway. We could pull one from his driver's license file, but those are usually pretty lousy, not to mention generally outdated. The days of renewing your license every other year are long gone."

"Okay, I guess you two have your work cut out for you. On behalf of Shimie and myself, I thank the two of you for your efforts. Now, Bill, any idea as to how I get home from here?"

"I had a patrol officer scope out the roads between here and your place. If you don't mind, we can get you within a few blocks of home. The copter is tied up until noon."

"I can handle the short walk, thanks." Turning back to Derrick, he asks, "Can I borrow your phone one more time?"

"Sure can," he answers, as he hands the phone across the table. Meanwhile, Richards steps out of the office while Brent places his call.

Listening to four rings, the call automatically goes to voicemail. "Hi, it's me again. We finished up and I should be home between 15 and 30 minutes. A patrol car will be dropping me off a few blocks from home. See you then."

Stepping back into his office, Richards looks at Brent, "Okay, the patrol car is outside waiting. And take these as a gift," he adds, handing Brent two cloth shopping bags filled to the brim.

"What's in the bags?"

"Well, after listening to you whine yesterday about no milk or eggs, I picked some up for you. Plus a number of other perishable staples to go with 'em. Once again, you owe me...though I really did it for Shimie," he adds with a chuckle.

"You're all heart. Thanks. You two stay in touch...and I'll send the photo and ask Shimie if she knows whether or not he owns a gun."

14

HEARING THE FRONT door open, Shimie jumps up from the couch and runs to greet Brent. When the door closes behind him, she throws herself into him and wraps her arms around him.

"Hold on a second," he says, as he sets the two grocery bags down. With his arms freed up, he pulls Shimie into him. "I see you are true to your word…you're still in your bathrobe." It isn't long after that comment when he hears what he thinks are muffled cries. He wraps his arms around her even tighter, while he strokes the back of her head.

"Okay, tell me why the tears?" He waits and waits, but no explanation appears to be forthcoming from Shimie. Pulling away from her, he reaches down, picks her up and takes her over to the couch. Setting her down, he sits beside her before pulling her down with him into a reclining position. The two of them lay there with their arms wrapped around each other. No words are spoken.

He still hears some muffled cries, but nothing like her previous crying spells. Even though it was late morning, he is feeling somewhat tired. Determining that a nap right about now sounds like a good idea, he reaches up and pulls the afghan over the two of them. The last thing he wants to face right now is having to regurgitate this morning's meeting to Shimie. Oh, he would explain it all to her, but he needs to rest up first—and she appears to be in no hurry to drill him.

An hour later, he awakens to the sound of classical music coming from his phone, which Shimie had left on the coffee table. Being in no mood to speak with his mother, he lets it go to voicemail—if she even feels like leaving a message. Shimie, with her head resting on his chest, also awakes by the phone's music. Rolling her to the side a bit, he lays one long and passionate kiss on her before settling on a whole lot of smaller ones.

"Welcome home...I missed you," Shimie says quietly, while she looks directly into his eyes.

"I missed you too...your body, that is." Instantly he goes for her neck and starts sucking on her like a half-crazed vampire. Shimie begins to squeal right away, but only because his actions were tickling her. She fights to get away from his mouth on her neck, but he is too strong and held her in place. He eventually returns to gaze into her eyes, before stating, "That's what you get for saying you missed me...it turns me into an uncontrollable animal."

Matching his stare, she remarks, "You already were an

animal before today…or have you forgotten the shower scene already? Or the pool yesterday? Or the couch before now?"

Off the top of his head, Brent fails to come up with a good comeback, so he starts kissing her again. He had photos to send off, a gun question to ask, and he had to explain the meeting to Shimie, but right now he finds himself hungry—for her body. The hunger building within him could not wait for later—it had to be satisfied now. This hunger is not solely about being sexually satisfied, though he is at loss to explain what he is feeling right now. All he knows for sure is that her passionate kisses alone could bring a dead man back to life.

With the kisses continuing unabated, Shimie struggles to get the buttons undone from his shirt. She's waited anxiously, nervously, for way too many hours for him to come home. Those hours were spent fantasizing about how she is going to rip his clothes off and take him before he knew what hit him. She wants nothing more than to hear the beauty of those screams again as they emanate from deep within his throat—not once—but many times over. As with the shower, nothing is going to stop her—and she meant nothing—not even Brent himself.

Brent was rock hard and he knew he was close to climaxing if he didn't back off a little. If he climaxes, and he knew he eventually would, he wants it to be inside her beautiful body. As he pulls away from Shimie's hungry kisses, he slides off the couch and stands up. He first kicks off his shoes and swiftly sheds the shirt she had already unbuttoned. Before going any further with his own clothes, however, he bends over and loosens the belt to her robe. Starting at her neck, he works his way down until the robe is totally parted, leaving her beautiful front side fully exposed to his lustful eyes. She is absolutely stunning in her full nakedness. As he looks down into her eyes and sees a look he has not seen before—at least on any woman he was about to seduce—he finds it mesmerizing. The look pouring forth was both trusting and wanting at the same time. There was softness in her eyes for which he has no explanation. Whatever it is, it captures him. He clearly knew that she is offering herself up to him—and there appears to be no sense of shame in her eyes from being totally naked before his eyes. All of which makes him want her that much more.

Shimie looks up at him the entire time he is viewing her nakedness with his licentious eyes. She continues watching as he loosens his belt, unzips his pants and lets them fall to the floor around his ankles. She finds herself getting hotter by the second as the strip-tease act heads to its finale. Bending over, he removes one leg and then the other before kicking the pants to the side. Grabbing his boxers by the side, he starts pulling downward until realizing that his engorged member was caught inside against the waistband. Shimie knew exactly what had happened, but held back a laugh. Pulling his boxers up and over his tool, they quickly made their way to the floor. He stands there, unmoving, while her eyes take all of his nakedness in—much as he had with her body. Her eyes eventually stop moving at the sight of his full erection—an erection that appears to be reaching straight for the sky. Just the very thought of pulling his large member into her almost causes her to climax that very second, but she wants to save herself for when he climaxes. Looking back up to his eyes, she motions for him to come to her—to take her in any way he so desires.

As he approaches, she scoots to the back of the couch to make room for him. Lying on his side, he props himself up on one elbow. He wastes no time in fondling her full breasts and already hardened nipples. Shimie finds herself turned on as she watches her own breasts and nipples being played with. Being with Brent this week has caused her to rethink the given notion that sexual intimacies should only be behind closed doors and in total darkness. Visually watching him in action was a total turn-on for her, and she had no desire to go back to her old ways of making love. This experience with Brent had opened up a whole new world for her—a world of sharing, of giving, of receiving, of trusting and forgiving. A world where nakedness was to be revered as a thing of beauty, a masterpiece of art, rather than something that should be forever hidden by clothes, or viewed only under the cover of a dimmed light.

Knowing that her eyes are still focusing on his right hand as it gently massages both her breasts and nipples, Brent knew he is at the point of having to relieve the pressures that are building up in his loins. He is finding her body to be too beautiful, too exciting to touch for anything but desire to well up in him. Her ex had to have been either absolutely stupid, or sexless, he ponders, to give up something like Shimie and all she had to offer a man like himself. What she had to offer any man far surpasses any temporary high one could get from drugs. The more he thinks about it, however, the more grateful he is for the immaturity and stupidity of the ex-husband. Shimie freely gave him the joys the ex had all but abandoned for a world of drugs.

Reaching down and feeling the hardness of his member, Shimie is amazed that he could engage in so much foreplay and not take her; if for no other reason than to seek the release that she knew has to be building up within him. Is not climaxing the ultimate goal in any sexual relationship? It is as far as she is concerned. Forget bonding. Forget the notions of love. When two people had reached the *in the moment* stage of sexuality, climaxing is the ultimate goal. Is he holding back just to please her, she wonders? Rather than wait for him to make the first move, she reaches around him and attempts to pull him on top of her. She's thankful that he gets her subtle message and quickly climbs on top of her. Reaching back down to grab his hardened member, she wastes no time in guiding it deep into her well lubricated vagina.

The very second he was fully inside of her, she experiences a mini-orgasm, his erect and large member caressing every part of her. Unfortunately, she knew she could never be satisfied with any other man who is not as well-endowed as Brent. Settling for something less was unthinkable after having experienced the best—and Brent was the best of the best.

Thankful that she had taken the initiative to bring him on top of her, and inside of her, Brent forces himself to think of anything else but how good it was all feeling. He wants to explode right now to satisfy his own needs, but he also wants her to explode with him. Shimie, however, was making it awful difficult to think of something else. She knew how to clamp down and put pressure on his erection as he moves in and out of her. The sensual movement in itself is making it difficult for him to hold back. Where she gained the knowledge of clamping he has no idea. A prior relationship? Her husband? Nursing school? Whatever the source, he is grateful that she did so for him, for tightness is where it's at; at least where he is concerned—and right now he is only concerned about himself, not the rest of the male population.

Shimie knew she is about as close to going over the top as one could get without actually going there. While she focuses on pleasing him, she privately wants the two of them to reach Nirvana together. Though not crucial, she knew it makes for an added bonus to the overall experience. Concerned that he had been inside of her for a good two minutes, she decides to step up the game. She not only increases her pelvic thrusting, but also cramps down on his member even harder, while at the same time forcing her finger up his anal opening. Fifteen seconds later, his explosion rocks both her and the couch. Shimie's own explosion follows by a few seconds. His cum flying into her was all it took. She tries her best to hold back on her primal screams, but to no avail. They have both been satisfied. Her fantasies for when her man came home are now complete. Or are they complete?

As Brent lay totally exhausted upon her, she is ecstatic at not only the foreplay, but the end result as well. It could not have been better. They both gave and they both received — she could ask for nothing more. With his full weight upon her, she shifts to one side, allowing him to slide off of her and fully onto the couch on his side. Shimie slips off the couch and remains in a kneeling position. Reaching over to grab his T-shirt, she wipes the cum off his member. When she finishes, she wipes herself as well. Tossing the T-shirt aside, she lightly runs her fingers softly around his genitals. Though flaccid now, she is still in awe of it all.

Glancing up at Brent's face, she notices the eyelids are closed. She senses that he is still awake given the minor twitches his member produces whenever she touches it. Right now she just wants to admire what had been thankfully inside of her. She no longer cares how many other women he has been inside. This day, this time, this very moment is hers to cherish. She wants nothing more than to express her feelings for Brent. If it means giving of herself sexually, so be it. He has been very giving of himself sexually as well. Her love for him right now is too strong not to make him happy. And if sex is what it takes to make and keep him happy—she's okay with that. After all, she is not exactly a virgin herself. She knows exactly how good being sexually active makes her feel. And sexually, Brent makes her feel on top of the world.

Continuing to play with him, she isn't the least bit amazed to see that the blood has begun to flow back into his member. As she reminds herself once again, the power of a woman over a man is formidable—and she is absolutely loving that power. Fortunately, what Brent needs is part of the same thing she also needs—sexual satisfaction from time to time; though most women, and she has to include herself, look for something beyond just sexuality. As great as the sexual experience can be, she is smart enough to know that it actually represents less than one percent of a couple's time together—though only one percent—it can make or break a relationship. With Brent, she can't ever foresee that being an issue in his relationships—a relationship she would love to be a part of for the long haul—but knew better.

Being three-quarters hard at this point, Shimie decides it's time to tease him some more. Leaning back in, she starts to lick the tip of his penis. At the very first lick, he starts to twitch even more than when she ran her fingers along his member. Leaning in farther, she takes his manhood into her mouth and slowly moves back and forth on it. By this time in her teasing, he was fully erect again. Thoroughly enjoying the power over him, she is in no hurry for anything to happen just yet. Brent, however, apparently has differing thoughts as he starts to thrust his pelvis toward her. Recognizing his need, she clamps down hard and begins matching his pelvic movements with her tightly closed mouth. She is promptly rewarded for her efforts when he sent his cum flying down her waiting and willing throat.

Though he is thoroughly spent, she continues to keep her mouth fully wrapped around his slowly shrinking love muscle. In her way of thinking, there is foreplay and after-play. She was never a fan of immediately rolling over and turning out the lights—though her ex was good at that. To truly show both affection and appreciation for her partner, and his efforts on her behalf, she firmly believes in staying with the moment—and Brent's member remaining in her mouth is her idea of staying with the moment.

"Come here, you little sexpot," Brent calls out to her.

Releasing him from her mouth, she rises back up and lies down beside him. He wraps his arms around her and pulls her as close to his body as he can without crushing her. Yes, he was spent, but still he needs her close to him. He so wants to pull the two separate bodies together as one—though he isn't exactly sure what makes him want her so desperately right now. Or, he thinks, is it simply an empty heart that needs filling? No, it most definitely isn't that, he assures himself. So, rather than seek an answer from within himself, he settles for keeping her body close to his.

15

"Oh my God!" Shimie shrieks in a loud voice. "I can't believe what you're saying. Paul was bitter about the divorce and custody, but to actually kill someone to get even with me? I don't believe it for a second."

"I wish it weren't true for your daughter's sake. As she gets older, she'll end up learning the truth about her father. That'll be a tough pill to swallow for her. And yes, all the evidence clearly points to your ex."

"I think you and Richards are totally wrong on this," she fires back loudly. "He may be a lot of things, but he's not a murderer. Did you ever consider that he may have been walking his daughter out in the courtyard when the quake hit? He's done that before, according to Gladys. He just walks around the courtyard talking to her."

"Anything's possible, but Richards won't know until he's located Paul. And yes, Richards originally chalked everything up to the quake, but has since had a change of heart based on new evidence presented to him."

"Sure he has new evidence...and guess who conveniently made up some cock and bull story that made him change his mind?" Shimie snaps back in an accusatory manner. "What are you trying to gain by framing my ex? A piece of ass from me? You already get that...and then some."

"Calm down, please. This isn't worth getting yourself all worked up over. We won't have answers until he's located."

"Oh sure, when the cops finally locate him, he will probably go down in a hail of bullets. I should never have told you he owns a gun. Now he's been classified as 'armed and dangerous.' Maybe you're out to get him killed for whatever reason. I've seen my share of bullet-riddled bodies come into the hospital, thank you."

It is apparent that her anger is not to be smoothed over with anything he had to say. After the bitter divorce she went through, he is astonished at her level of verbally attacking him in defense of her ex—an ex she probably wanted to kill herself a few times while he fought for custody of their daughter. None of this was making sense to him, so he decides to let it rest until she can hopefully think it through a bit more rationally. The best decision made this week was in not allowing Shimie to go with him this morning—her anger would have destroyed every aspect of the meeting.

It was challenges like these that made him thankful he isn't married—and a good reason to stay single. He thoroughly enjoys challenges, as long as they were of his own choosing. He enjoys being in control of his own destiny too, without having to take someone else into consideration. A long-term commitment of any kind would definitely put a crimp into his lifestyle. Today just confirmed his beliefs on long-term relationships—make love one minute and argue the next.

"Okay, let's close this discussion for now before it gets out of hand. With any luck, maybe I'll get this book finished before it becomes a classic," Brent offers, only to maintain some semblance of peace between them.

"Good idea…reading will help you forget everything you've done this morning." Shimie picks up her novel and heads out of the living room without saying another word.

Brent would have to settle for an unspoken truce at this point. At the same time, he is not looking forward to the inevitable resurrection of the subject—though he knew it would eventually come up again. Maybe she just needs time to think the whole thing through and will come to realize that maybe he was right in labeling her ex as a prime suspect. Of course, his primary concern right now was in locating Shimie's daughter—not placating Shimie's feelings on the course of action being taken. If, in the long run he is proven wrong, so be it.

—

"What would you like for dinner?" Shimie asks as she enters the living room.

Brent could tell from her voice that she is still upset with him. The hours alone in her bedroom obviously didn't change anything. "You know, rather than wait for tomorrow morning, I'd really like to scarf down some bacon and eggs...now that we finally have some eggs."

"How would like your eggs?"

"Over easy or scrambled...makes no difference. Thanks."

With the words barely out of his mouth, she turns and makes her way to the kitchen. Brent knew right away that dinnertime chatter is bound to be minimal. And when dinner finally came and went, that is exactly what happens. After carrying over the dishes to the sink, he immediately grabs a drying towel, but is quickly informed that she can handle it all. With her quick dismissal, he heads back to the living room and places a call to his father, before resuming his reading. Three hours later, as he makes his way to his bedroom, he sees the door to her bedroom is shut—probably locked, he guesses. He fully expects her to be sleeping in her own bed tonight.

16

$\text{\textdagger}$

FOLLOWING A RESTLESS night, Brent heads off to his study to pay bills and deal with the ever mounting paperwork—tasks he finds no joy in having to deal with on the weekends. As with most mornings, he scans the latest updates on his computer to keep abreast of the earthquake aftermath. Intently reading the news, he is startled by the sound of his phone going off.

"Hello. Oh hi Derrick...what's up?"

"Where did you spot him?" Brent asks, with a level of excitement.

"Not surprised...that's a pretty seedy part of town. A druggie's heaven."

"How could you lose him?"

"Oh. They do that just in case they're being followed. At least the smart ones. Remember, we don't want him until we know the whereabouts of his daughter. So it's imperative that he be followed to wherever he lays his head at night. If he's got the baby, that's where she'll be. While he's out dealing drugs, someone is taking care of her…most likely a female. Have you relayed the info to Richards?"

"Why don't you go ahead and do that now. Call me anytime."

"You too…talk to you later."

That was encouraging news—at the very least it meant that the ex had remained in town. The real challenge now is in spotting him again and following him to wherever he calls home. After giving it some thought, Brent decides to keep the phone call to himself. There was no sense in getting her all worked up again. She obviously has too much time on her hands right now to do anything but think of her daughter and now her ex. Her mind was temporarily freed up through their sexual escapades, but even that now appears to be out the window. He wonders if all women are capable of turning their emotions off and on like a light switch.

"Knock. Knock." Shimie speaks quietly so as not to startle him.

"Well good morning. I was beginning to wonder if you were ever going to wake up. Or, being in your bathrobe, maybe you have plans of going straight back to bed."

"I didn't sleep very well…too much tossing and turning."

"That's what happens when you choose to sleep alone. If it's any consolation, I didn't sleep well either. I've been spoiled by having a beautiful lady lying next to me."

"Don't you mean a fat and ugly lady?" Shimie remarks, with what Brent sees as the first hint of a smile.

"Beautiful and slender, fat and ugly, they all keep the bed warm," Brent counters, with both a smile and a wink.

"Sorry about yesterday afternoon. It was a terrible way to end the day after what we shared on the couch. Tomorrow will mark one week since I've seen my daughter. I guess I'm just more stressed out as the days go by without knowing anything new."

"Perfectly understandable. Stress has a way of turning normal people into behaving like they never dreamed they would. While I lay no claim to understanding people, especially women, I would like to think that I've learned to be patient with all walks of life. As an attorney, I've had to deal with every personality imaginable…and the upper echelons in the corporate world are some of the most difficult people to deal with. Unfortunately, they are my bread and butter. And you, being in the medical field, deal with diverse personalities all day long. I don't envy you."

Shimie says nothing as she walks around his desk, pushes his chair back, sits down in his lap and lays a big kiss on him. Brent is totally caught off guard, but welcomes her advances. If this was what *making up* was all about, he likes it immensely. His free hand quickly separates her bathrobe, whereupon he begins massaging her breasts. A few minutes later, he pulls away from her lips, leans her back and begins licking and sucking her hardened nipples.

Shimie was thoroughly enjoying the moves he made

upon her body. Placing both hands on the side of his head, she pulls him away from her breasts. "I love what you do to me, but this girl needs to get dressed and make some breakfast for the two of us."

"Don't change on my account; you look extremely sexy in that robe."

"Don't you worry; there'll be plenty of time this afternoon for you to take my clothes back off—if you remember how?" She adds, with a big grin.

"Somewhere on these bookshelves is an instruction booklet. Now if I can just remember where I put it," he adds, before breaking free of her hands and returning to her breasts.

"Look here, you male tramp, I'm pretty particular as to what kind of man I allow to take advantage of my body. Besides, you're making me awful damn horny. Stop it!" Shimie immediately pulls away from his hungry mouth on her breasts and stands up. "And wipe that drool off your mouth," she commands teasingly. She then turns and walks away, intentionally swiveling her hips in a suggestive manner as she walks.

"You can run but you can't hide," he calls to her back as she rounds the corner and out of sight. She is such a tease, he muses, as he sits back in his chair somewhat frustrated. Unfortunately, he knew what he is going to be thinking about until their afternoon romp—and he was going to make sure that it took place; even if he had to rip her clothes off and drag her off to bed. Who knows, maybe that's what she wants. The thought brings a smile to his face as he returns to mindlessly shuffling paperwork.

"Breakfast is ready," she yells from the kitchen.

"Okay...coming."

"Hope you're hungry?" Shimie remarks, as he enters the kitchen.

"Am I ever. It's not breakfast you know, it's brunch. All because some over-sexed woman...whose name I won't bother to mention, decided to sleep in. Oh my, look at this. French toast, eggs and ham. A feast fit for a king."

"I'm just the cook...you can thank Richards for most of what you're eating. Besides, I figured you needed lots of energy for later."

"It pays to have friends with connections," he comments, before forking in another mouthful of French toast. "As for energy later, I'll do my best to be in top form."

"Not to change the subject, but when I came into your study this morning and said I'm sorry...I meant it. But what I didn't explain is the reason, or reasons, behind my outburst yesterday. When I — "

"You don't have to explain anything," Brent interrupts. "It's behind us."

"Thank you, but I still feel an explanation is in order. I obviously had a lot of time to think over my reaction last night. When you insinuated that my ex was possibly a murderer, I believe I got immediately defensive for selfish reasons. The thought of going through life knowing that I fell in love with, and eventually married, a potential murderer was unsettling. Women, in social settings, can be awfully brutal in their need for gossip. 'Oh, what does your ex do for a living? Does he have visitation rights? Are you receiving child support? Oh, I heard from a friend of a friend that he's in prison for murder. Is that true?' Those are only a few of the questions I would have to deal with.

"To simply say that I was divorced would have been very acceptable in this day and age. But to be saddled with the stigma of a 'murderer in the family' was too much for me to handle at the time. Of course, I was also concerned for Brianna. I thought of her growing up, at least in her later years, knowing that her father was in prison for murder. That to me was far more important than anything I would be asked by busybody women. After mulling this over in my selfish mind last night, I finally realized that I can't change the hand of fate…it is what it is. And here I was yesterday biting the very hand that has been trying so hard to find my daughter; even to the point of risking your own life more than once. No matter what I say or do, I could never repay you in a million years," Shimie concludes.

"While I never asked for an explanation, I'm glad you laid it out on the table; if for no other reason than you were able to get something off your chest. Oh, and do I ever love your chest, by the way," Brent adds, to further lighten the mood.

"You, Mr. Horny, are incorrigible and should be locked away; if for no other reason than to protect women like myself who were taken advantage of in our weakest moments. Explain that to a judge."

"Your Honor, and esteemed jurors of the court, need I remind you of Exhibit A, the shower scene, where my client was physically taken advantage of by this very woman against his will?"

"Cute. Very cute," Shimie remarks.

"Thank you. I thought it was pretty good myself," Brent responds, with a wink. "And closer to the truth," he adds. "Okay, why don't we take a walk down to the gate and see if any mail has arrived; though I'd be surprised if they were even delivering mail just yet. Or, if you're feeling full, we can take the golf cart down."

"Nope, I need the exercise, let's walk. But only after we do up the dishes."

"Fair enough, but I was kind of hoping you would have forgotten about the dishes."

"No chance I'm going to allow you to skirt your one household responsibility."

"Damn, let's get on with it then."

With the dishes cleaned, dried and put away, they head out the front door for their walk to the gate. Shimie was the first to reach for Brent's hand, which he willingly accepts. He feels comfortable being around her — maybe too comfortable, he thinks. We get along quite well and our sexuality is over the top. He finds it heartening to see, and experience, that she appears comfortable in her own skin — whether it be fully clothed or totally naked — she shows no shame for what she is or was. She gives of herself beyond his wildest imagination—and he is grateful for that. He is also grateful that she was the one standing outside the church that he tackled to the ground.

"Nice grounds. You obviously have a maintenance crew, huh?"

"I have to, given my black thumb. Growing up we had a fulltime gardener, so I never learned how to maintain anything that grew."

"That's too bad in some ways. It's very therapeutic to work in a yard. At least it always was for me. I was raised middle class, you might say. We had a house with a big yard, grew our own vegetables and flowers. My mother and I spent a lot of time in the yard. While working together, we spent a lot of time talking about one thing or the other. I enjoyed that. My mother and I were very close because of it...or so I'd like to think."

"We obviously have different socio-economic backgrounds. I won't even try to hide the fact that I grew up in the so-called privileged class. As a child, I had no say in the matter...obviously. Nor did you. As you said this morning...it is what it is."

"Don't get me wrong honey...I mean Brent, every society has their privileged class." Shimie quickly regrets the slip of the tongue and starts to blush, but continues on, hoping he wasn't scared or offended by it. "They're the thinkers...the doers—the Rockefellers, Edison, Getty, Gates, Jobs and so on. Without their brains and money we would still be living in the Dark Ages. So no, I don't find fault with you at all for being born into the privileged class. That's part of why I want to be a doctor...I want a better life for myself and whatever children I was blessed with. I could lie and say it's all about the patients, about being altruistic, but it isn't. I saw my parents struggle...I wanted something better for myself. And now that I have a daughter, I want something better for her."

"Nothing wrong with that...we all have our dreams. Those dreams are what guide us along in the decisions we make for our futures. Without dreams, we simply exist day to day trying to meet our basic survival needs. My parents instilled in me the notion of being the best at whatever I do. Second place would be unacceptable in their eyes. From an early age, I didn't want to disappoint my parents, so I worked my butt off to always come in first. My sister wanted the finer things in life as well; only she didn't feel the need to work for them."

Opening the back end of the mailbox, there is no real surprise to find it empty; nor are there any copies of the Wall Street Journal lying at the gate. "Well, I'm guessing the streets still aren't passable for any deliveries. Oh well, fewer bills to pay, I guess," he adds, as they turn and begin their walk back up to the house.

17

SHIMIE WALKS OVER from the stove and places both dishes on the table. Pulling out her chair, she sits down. "The eggs represent but one day's work for a chicken. The ham, on the other hand, represents a whole lifetime for a pig."

"Cute. Where did you pick that up from?"

"Just something I saw in a restaurant on my way to the ladies room. Can you talk and eat at the same time? If so, I'd love to hear what your father had to say earlier."

"As a matter of fact, it was a very interesting conversation. He was reading bits and pieces from a Washington Post front-page article. It turns out that the earthquake we barely lived through was in fact not an earthquake at all. Well, it was an earthquake, but none like Arizona has ever experienced before...at least on a major scale.

"My father was saying, according to the U.S. Geological Survey folks, the quake was actually caused by the collapsing of an underground water aquifer. Their thinking is that it was caused by a substantial depletion in the water level; which in turn was caused by the severe drought we've had over the past five or so years in Arizona. The theory being that is this particular aquifer was more of a lake than the normal ones of rock and sand, or whatever. Without water to hold the sides together, the sides simply collapsed inward. In the process, everything above it collapsed as well. All of this apparently took place south of the metro area, but obviously produced earthquake-like movements all around it. And it was no small aquifer.

"The good news is that not all of the metro areas were impacted with what you and I experienced. The sandy sub-soil helped to dissipate the shockwaves the farther out it went. You, I, the church, etcetera, just happened to be too close to the aquifer. The areas to the north of us received their share of damage, but nothing like we did. I guess you could say we were on the wrong side of the tracks for once. When I get a chance, I'll go online and see what else they have to say."

"Wow, who would have thought. I know about aquifers from my geology classes, but can't say that I remember too much about them. Geology was not one of my favorite subjects. I do have a question of you, however, but I keep forgetting to ask. When you tackled me outside of church—and tried to take advantage of me—how did you know that an earthquake, or whatever they now want to call it, was about to happen? It wasn't until right after you attacked me that the quake actually took place."

"Damn...you caught me on that one. Yes, I had every

intention of taking advantage of you once I had you on the ground, but you were saved by the earthquake," Brent answers with a grin before turning serious. "I've had the misfortune of experiencing two earthquakes. The first being the Nisqually quake in Seattle when visiting with my parents; it was either in 2000 or 2001. Don't remember for sure. We were at the home of a wealthy college buddy of my father's. I was standing outside on the veranda with his friend's daughter. The birds — robins I think — were chirping away while their two dogs were playing and barking on the lawn below us. And then everything became absolutely quiet. The dogs quit their barking and the birds stopped chirping. It was as though I had lost my hearing, the quietness was so eerie. A few seconds later, we were hit with a 6.8 magnitude earthquake.

"The second time around, I was back in the D.C. area visiting my parents for their annual end of the summer get together with staff members and their families. The activities were taking place on the back lawn. A couple of the young children were busy chasing the four dogs around the yard — and of course the dogs were barking. And then the dogs immediately stopped barking. Once again it became eerily quiet. Not the children or adults talking, but everything else. And sure enough, we were hit with a 5.8 quake a few seconds later. I could feel the quake rolling underneath my feet. A spooky feeling to say the least.

"So, to make a long story short, when I walked out of church I heard the early morning birds chirping away and

Fr. Pat's dog barking in the rectory yard at who knows what. And then, a moment later, all became deathly quiet. The birds stopped chirping and the dog stopped barking. Just like before. It's as if someone had flipped a switch to the off position. Immediately I thought, 'Oh my God, it couldn't be.' My reactions then were almost instinctual. Lucky for us there was the retaining wall to lie against. At the time, I never even gave it a thought as to how embarrassing it would be if there was no quake. And looking back on it all, yes, it would have been quite embarrassing. A lot of people support the theory of birds ceasing to chirp and dogs stopping their barking. Of course, there are the skeptics out there too. Right now, I'm a firm believer in the theory."

"Whoa...interesting," Shimie remarks when he concludes his story. "I for one am glad you acted on your instincts...and to think that I was screaming for help and digging my nails into your back."

"And yes, you *will* be paying for that for a long time to come for the permanent scars you've left on my backside. Anyway, I knew from my earlier readings on the subject that Arizona was not sitting on any moving plates, nor had fault lines as the west coast does. In spite of that knowledge, I still had this house built to some earthquake specifications. I never gave the aquifers a second thought. As I mentioned a week ago, my architect most likely isn't laughing at me anymore. My years of living in LA, coupled with the two prior quakes I experienced, taught me not to fear quakes so much as to respect their power. This particular quake came in at 6.9, which is considered a very strong quake with a potential for major damage…and we witnessed firsthand the damage inflicted. I can just imagine the damage to the cities to the—"

"Sorry to interrupt, but is that your cell phone I hear?"

"Oh, you're right. Good hearing on your part. I obviously left it in the study…I'll be right back."

"Oh sure, anything to get out of doing dishes," Shimie jokingly remarks as Brent disappears at a fast clip around the corner and out of sight.

Picking up the phone on the desk, he notices a missed call from Richards. Brent wastes no time in returning the call, before sitting down and leaning back in his chair.

"Hi Bill. Don't you ever take a day off?"

"I can just imagine. The quake is keeping a lot of people stretched to the limit. What's up? I know this isn't a social call."

"A female driver, huh? I had a feeling a female had to be in the picture somehow. I don't see him as the type to be taking care of a baby 24/7. Was the undercover able to follow them home…or wherever they were headed?"

"I can't believe he let a flatbed with a bulldozer on it get in front of him, but at least he got the license plate number. Any leads on that yet?"

"Good. If you need Derrick or his man to help stake out the apartment, I can arrange it. Derrick continues to run the trap line on the hospitals, Red Cross and the morgue. I appreciate your update. Call me anytime."

"Say what?"

"Water by tomorrow? Good, we need it. I went out and checked this morning…only fifty gallons left in the reserve tank. I was close to pumping water from the pool into the tank. I'll catch you later…hopefully with some better news. Oh, and thanks for the food…much appreciated."

After placing the phone back on the desk, he leans farther back in his chair and mulls over what Richards had to say. Progress was being made, but he still isn't overjoyed at how long it was taking to locate Shimie's daughter. He feels a sense of powerlessness at just sitting at home waiting for phone calls to come in with the latest development. In his profession he was used to being in charge, directing traffic and getting results. He controlled situations—not the other way around. The only comfort he could find right now was in the knowledge that Richards and Derrick were the best at what they do.

After retrieving the cell off the desk, he heads off to the kitchen to bring Shimie up to date on what he learned from Richards. A quick glance into the kitchen reveals their breakfast dishes had been cleaned and put away, but no Shimie in sight. Making a quick about face, he heads off to the living room where he finds Shimie reading a book. He notices straight away that she is actually not reading the book as it sat on her lap. As soon as she raised her head and looked in his direction, he could tell that she has been crying.

"What's up with the tears and melancholy look on your

face? That's not the look you had on your face when I left the kitchen."

"I've been losing track of the days, but I just realized that today is Sunday. It has been one week since I last saw my daughter…and still nothing, no signs of hope even. Praying to St. Gemma has apparently been a waste of time."

"I was wondering this morning if you knew what day it is. And yes, there is hope. That was Richards on the phone. An undercover officer spotted your ex last night…yes, in the area of town that you and I would never be seen in. He was spotted jumping into a car driven by a young female. A tractor-trailer pulled in front of the cop, so he lost them, but he did get the license plate number. Richards had to pull some strings, but they do have a twenty-four-hour stakeout of the apartment where the plates are registered too. So see, there is hope," he adds, all in the hopes of cheering her up.

"Assuming he actually has my daughter, that is."

"Shimie, a Good Samaritan would have notified the authorities long before now. As I explained before, all of the evidence points to your ex. Both the Phoenix and Scottsdale Police Departments are actively pursuing this case… along with the two private investigators who are working this case on a fulltime basis. Because of the quake, the cops, as you can well imagine, have their hands full on a thousand and one things going on right now. Richards, bless his heart, has called in some chips with his cohorts in

Phoenix. What's the bottom line? In my opinion, they are getting close to locating your daughter. I know you want your daughter back. I know it's tough on you…the waiting and wondering. And you know what; I think you've held up well, all things considered."

"If I've held up well, then it's because of you…you've intentionally, or was it unintentionally, kept me preoccupied this past week. I really don't think I would have held up at all if you weren't around…a shoulder to cry on…a hand to lift me up."

"See, it just goes to show you that men do have some value in life. Not much, you may argue, but we do have our moments," Brent adds, with a sly grin on his face. A good choice of words, he thinks, as he notices her smile.

—

"Day ten," Shimie quietly says while they are eating a late dinner.

"Huh?" Brent responds, looking over at her with a puzzled look. "What's day ten?"

"Since I last saw my daughter," she answers, somberly.

"Oh."

"I can't take this waiting anymore. I need to go look for my daughter."

"Say what?" Brent asks in a disbelieving tone.

"We've got water now. Your mail and paper came yesterday, which can only mean that they've got the streets fixed...or some of them anyway. I don't want to sit here all day. I want to go look for my daughter."

"That's a job best left to the professionals. They're the pros when it comes to finding people."

"They haven't found her yet," Shimie responds, in a sarcastic tone.

"It's a big city...locating her has obviously been compounded by the quake. The only way to find your daughter, hopefully, is through your ex. And should you find your ex, then what?"

"I'll confront him. I'll ask him where my daughter is. If he in fact has her."

"Shimie, do you for one moment really believe that your ex would tell you where your daughter is? He took her for a reason. My guess is to get back at you for not only the divorce but for being granted custody. If my theory is correct, which I strongly believe it is, he's already killed one person and mostly likely wouldn't stop at killing another—even you—the ultimate payback."

"I doubt that. At one time he loved me."

"Yes, he probably did...at one time. That love has now turned to bitterness—as evidenced by the taking of your daughter—and killing someone in the process. And please, don't be offended when I say this, but your thinking this whole thing through is being clouded by your emotions."

"Maybe I can offer him money to get my daughter back."

"You could. And he would happily take it from you,

but don't count on his turning over your daughter. His motivation is apparently revenge—one of the most dangerous types of motivation. If he abducted your daughter for money—why no phone call? Your cell service was restored yesterday, and you yourself said the only missed calls were from Scottsdale General about working and from a girlfriend. No, he didn't do it for the money."

"So, you're not willing to help, I take it?"

Brent clearly detects the bitterness in her question. "You don't think that both Richards and Derrick aren't helping?"

"They are. Thank you, but they still haven't found my daughter."

"Your ex is obviously a smart man—he knows how to avoid detection. And the fact that the female driver no longer lives at her registered address has just compounded the problem. I'm just asking you to be patient. And yes, I know that is asking a lot of you. I'm just recommending that you leave your daughter's whereabouts to the professionals. Okay?"

"If you're not willing to help then I have no choice," Shimie responds, dejectedly.

"I'm helping...just not in the way you want right now. It's getting late, why don't we just sleep on it?"

"I'll probably be doing a lot of tossing and turning tonight, so I think I'll sleep in my own bed. Maybe do a little reading. Do you mind?"

"The dishes are on me tonight. And yes, sleep alone if

that's what you want to do, though I like having you next to me."

"Just for tonight…I promise." Shimie pulls herself away from the table and heads directly for her room, closing the door behind her.

18

—————————————— ♦ ——————————————

Reading more about the quake online, Brent loses track of the time until glancing down at the corner of his computer and noticing it was 9:30 already. He immediately thinks Shimie had experienced a restless night and was still sleeping. On any given day, they would be finished with breakfast about this time.

By ten o'clock, he is getting a little more than worried and decides to check up on her. If he finds her sleeping, he would leave her alone and get his own breakfast. Quietly opening her bedroom door, he was surprised to find the bed already made up. Going in, he silently creeps over to the opened bathroom door. Glancing in, he sees nothing but pearls from her St. Gemma strewn across the floor. Well, he concludes, she likes to read early in the morning, so just maybe she was in the living room—her favorite place to read.

Entering the living room, he sees no evidence of Shimie. At this point, he starts to worry. Quickly checking the rest of the house and the pool area, his worries now turn to panic. "Oh my God!" were the first words out of his mouth. His mind instantly goes back to last night's conversation about looking for her daughter. Running out to the garage, he notices both vehicles are still there. Once back inside, he heads directly to the front door where he notices the gate key was missing from the table—and the door is unlocked.

Going back to his study, he immediately grabs his phone and calls both Richards and Derrick to alert them about where he believes she has gone. How she could even get from one end of Scottsdale to the other end of Phoenix, he hadn't a clue. After leaving the study, he heads directly to his bedroom computer. In a matter of minutes he fires off various pictures of Shimie, from her own picture file, to both Richards and Derrick.

According to Richards, some bus lines were running, but on a limited schedule. If she didn't hop on a bus, then the only way there would be to either hitchhike or hail a cab. Going back into her bedroom, he notices her cell phone is not on the nightstand or dresser, though her purse was. Sifting quickly through her purse, he notices the absence of her wallet. Returning to his bedroom, he sits back down at his desk and quickly dials her number— after four rings, it goes directly to her voicemail.

"Shimie, I know what you're up to. Richards is not happy and feels that your actions will only jeopardize the investigation. Please call me immediately and I will come pick you up. There are way too many hours and effort involved in finding your daughter already—please don't endanger yourself, your daughter, or the investigation. Don't do anything rash. Please...call me."

By the time he finishes recording his message, he is hot. No, he isn't hot—he is downright furious with her. How could such a seemingly smart woman be so stupid as to put the entire investigation at risk? Yes, he understands her being impatient with how things were going, or, in her eyes, not going. He tried his damndest last night to convince her that any number of professionals was working tirelessly to locate her daughter, and that any involvement on her part would put those efforts at risks. Damn that woman!

Rather than sit there and fume over her stupidity—and knowing that he couldn't just sit there and await news from Shimie or the cops—he heads directly to the garage. Climbing into his Range Rover, he opens the garage door and wastes no time in getting down the hill to the gate. Turning right, he heads up to the main arterial that he and Shimie had walked along to get to his place. The streets leading to the main drag showed major evidence of fresh asphalt having been laid. Before reaching the main highway, he notices vehicles going in both directions. That is exactly what he was betting on—and most likely where Shimie grabbed a bus or taxi.

Traveling west toward his destination, he encounters fewer signs of destructions; both to the streets and the buildings themselves. Businesses appear to be operating as though nothing had happened a mere ten or eleven days ago. The only real change he notices is the seemingly fewer cars on the road, which suits him just fine right now. However, given the number of detours while the roads were being repaired, coupled with the large number of in-operative traffic signals, it would be just after one o'clock before he reaches his destination. The nervousness he was feeling earlier returns.

Outside of a number of boarded up windows, he is surprised to see this area of town as intact as it appears to be—though a small number of businesses did display large stickers on their doors indicating they were con-demned. Given the nature of this section of Phoenix, he isn't surprised at seeing a large numbers of tattoo signs, massage parlors, pawn shops and fast food restaurants. Most of the buildings looked as though they should have been taken down decades ago. Spotting a police car in front of a McDonald's, he wonders if the pictures of Shimie had reached them yet—and were they even actively looking for her. Given his sister's nice clothes that she was most likely wearing, along with her natural beauty, there was no question in his mind that she would stand out in this area of town.

Pulling over to the curb, he places quick calls to both Richards and Derrick. Rather than just drive around aim-lessly, he feels the need to get some idea of where her ex was spotted, as this section of town encompassed an unknown number of square miles. With the calls completed, he makes his way a mile farther east. The businesses here were the same as the ones he left, though somewhat seedier. Drunks were openly carrying their cheap liquor wrapped in brown paper bags, grocery carts were being pushed along the sidewalk with their worldly possessions inside, as they searched the various garbage cans lining the sidewalks. Two rookie-appearing cops were busy shaking down a young male in handcuffs—for which Brent suddenly felt a sense of empathy for the cops who were assigned to this area of town.

He knows that looking for Shimie was a crapshoot at best. Not that she isn't easily noticeable, especially to him, but he couldn't imagine that even she would know what section of this depressed area of town her ex might be working. Given her upbringing, he reasonably assumes that she had never been in this section of town before. Even though his car doors were locked, he isn't feeling totally safe here. Glancing around in all directions, and slowing down for alleyways, his stomach remains in knots. He knows he should have taken the time to eat something, but food was the last thing on his mind.

Aside from worrying about her safety, he wonders what time she had actually left the house. Was it shortly after he retired for the evening, or just before he got up? Playing with the options in his mind, he had to guess that she left shortly after he had gone to bed. If she had planned all along to sneak out of the house undetected, with enough of a head start before being noticed by him, she more than likely didn't want to risk oversleeping. Given that premise, he had to believe that she was one tired woman right now. Could she be holed up in one of those cheap motels, he wonders? With her wallet missing from her purse, he knows she had money on her or, at the very least, credit cards.

Five hours of driving around; he was feeling discouraged—not to mention a deep sense of apprehension. Spotting a fast food joint up ahead, he decides it's finally time to get something to eat. Though not starving by any means, he figures something on his stomach might just ease the pains that were growing in intensity since he left the house. Not exactly thrilled at the idea of getting out of his vehicle, he chooses to use the drive-up window. After picking up a burger, fries and coffee, he pulls into a parking space to eat—all the while keeping an eye on the people walking by.

Quickly consuming the tasteless meal, he pulls across the street to a gas station. Filling up the tank, he locks the car and walks inside to use the restroom. Taking the key from the cashier, he goes back outside and around the corner of the building. After unlocking the door and going inside, he is sorry that he chose this establishment to relieve himself. The stench and filth was almost overwhelming. He hastily proceeds to do what he had to do and makes a hasty retreat to the fresh air outside. Upon handing the key back to the lone cashier, he almost says something about the bathroom, before realizing that he probably didn't care to hear something he's probably heard a thousand times before.

Back on the road again, Brent drives east for about a mile before coming back westerly on a different street. While specifically looking for Shimie, he also keeps his eyes open for her ex as well. While he has yet to run across either of them, he knows that both Derrick and one of his employees were also driving up and down the same streets in search of Shimie. He hopes, but has no idea if any of the area cops were actively looking for Shimie as well. This was a tough neighborhood, so he can only envision the cops keeping busy on other matters. Brent is well aware of the fact that Shimie was a number one priority — but only to himself.

With darkness slowly creeping upon the city, Brent's concern was that Shimie would be harder to spot when total darkness actually set in — and that is just a matter of a half-hour away. Those patrons walking the streets during the daylight hours were slowly being replaced by the bar-hoppers, derelicts looking for a handout, and those looking to make their next drug deal. The darkness of night, coupled with this part of Phoenix, was not the place for timid souls to be out and about. Though he knows he can handle himself in a fight, he is also aware that he was no match for the many in this area that carry either knives or guns; and most of those who own guns were gotten illegally.

Driving slowly up and down each street, he learns to ignore the impatient drivers behind him. Honk all they want, but he is not to be rushed from his mission. He keeps telling himself that once he finds her – if he finds her – he will drag her into his Rover, lay her over his knees and spank the holy living hell out of her for what she was putting him through. The fast food he ate had somewhat settled his stomach, but not his mind. The monotony of driving up and down the same streets, time and time again, only made matters worse for him. The downside of having too much time to think – and to fume.

Up ahead, he spots two wobbly-walking drunks that look to be in their fifties. The same pair he had passed once before. Both had been sharing a paper-wrapped bottle of what he assumes was the cheapest bottle of wine they could afford. As they walk along the sidewalk, Brent wonders how they were even able to stand up, let alone walk. From their appearance, he assumes they drank far more than they ate. As they pass by an alley, they both stop momentarily before hurrying into the darkened alley. Brent could only surmise they had a sudden need to relieve themselves.

Continuing to drive slowly, he glances into the alleyway and readily spots the two drunkards bent over a large white object on the ground. Passing by the alley, Brent yells out, "Oh my God! My sister's jacket." He immediately slams on the brakes before throwing the Rover into reverse – burning a cloud of rubber in the process. After passing the alley by a few feet, he quickly throws the vehicle back into forward gear, goes up and onto the sidewalk and comes to a screeching halt at the entrance to the alleyway. The two drunkards make a hasty retreat deeper into the alley.

Jumping out of his vehicle, he races to where someone was lying on the pavement. It didn't take but a quick glance before he realizes it was Shimie. Going down on his knees, he quickly checks her neck for a pulse; a tremendous sense of relief washes over him at the feel of a strong pulse. Knowing that, he immediately brings out his cell phone and dials 9-1-1. When the operator came on, he fires off the situation. "Twenty-six-year-old white female is down in the alley. Strong pulse, but signs of physical trauma. I'm at Ventura Del Rio, between 16th and 17th. My Rover is on the north sidewalk partially blocking the alley."

"Yes, I'm staying with the victim. Her name is Shimie Jamison."

"My name? Brent Masterson. 6201 East Del Marco Drive, Scottsdale."

"Okay, I'll hang on until they arrive."

The headlights from his vehicle reveal numerous lacerations to her face, mainly on her left side. Feeling his way around her head, he notices a substantial lump just above her right ear. Partway through his exam, he picks up the sounds of approaching sirens. Taking off his jacket, he gently lifts Shimie's head and places it underneath.

Twenty seconds later, two police vehicles pull to a stop alongside his vehicle. He could still pick up the sounds of another siren in the distance. From the differing sounds, he had to believe it was a medic vehicle. Four cops approach Brent at the same time.

"Are you the one who called?" The oldest of the four asks, as the other three bent down, taking a closer look at Shimie.

"Yes."

"Do you know the victim?"

"Yes. Her name is Shimie Jamison. She's temporarily living with me until we can find her a place to live. The quake took out her apartment."

"How is it then that you came across her in the alley if she's living with you?"

Brent could easily see where this line of questioning was headed. "If you check your logs, you'll see where she was reported missing this morning and in possible danger. Detective Richards, with Scottsdale, made the call to one of his counterparts in Phoenix to be looking for her. I've spent the last ten or so hours driving up and down these very streets trying to locate her." While speaking to the officer, he keeps glancing down at Shimie. Not being asked to leave her side, he has no intentions of doing so until commanded.

By the time he finishes answering the last set of questions, the medics pull in from the opposite direction. A male and female medic exit the vehicle and retrieve a large medic-bag from the side of the vehicle before making their way to Shimie. Brent is taken aback by their lack of urgency in not only exiting their vehicle, but in making their way to Shimie. His definition of an emergency obviously wasn't theirs. By the time they approach Shimie, he is back up on his feet and moves out of the way.

"When doing a cursory review of her head, I noticed a large lump on the right side of her head...just above her ear." The two medics continue to check her out without acknowledging his comment—not even a "thank you."

"Do you have any idea who did this to her?" The officer in charge inquires.

"I have some idea, though it's only conjecture on my part. She came looking for her ex-husband. Detective Richards has probable cause to think her ex abducted their nine-month-old daughter out of revenge. She was in church at the time of the quake and abduction. Her ex is also being sought for the murder of the babysitter. He's known to hang out in this part of town...drugs."

"Does he have a name?"

Upon hearing the question, Brent initially wants to laugh—well of course he has a name—don't we all? "Paul Lewis Fredericks. Age 28. Known to have a gun. Address currently unknown. Richards has the full history on him. All of which were shared with the Phoenix Police Department." He figures he might just as well throw out more info now before he was asked. As Brent looks around, he notices the large crowds that had gathered on either side of the alley as well as across the street. Surely, he thinks, in this neighborhood the gawkers have to have seen it all before.

The female medic rises and approaches the officer. "We're going to transport her to the hospital...she's still unconscious. The blow to the head needs to be looked at immediately."

"Where will you be taking her?" Brent asks before she has a chance to leave.

"Valley of the Sun Hospital," she answers, retreating at once to assist her partner with the loading of Shimie onto the gurney.

"Any ID on her?" The officer asks of one of the junior officers.

"Her wallet was found zipped up in the jacket's pocket...her name is Shimie Jamison," the officer responds.

Brent chose not to say anything to the senior officer, but the fact that her wallet was still on her would give one the indication that this was not a case of robbery. Stepping to one side, he places a call to Derrick to briefly explain the situation. Now that the hunt was off for Shimie, it was back on for her ex. His next call was to Richards, but the call goes directly to voicemail. After leaving a brief message, he watches as the two medics gently lift Shimie up and onto the collapsed gurney. After strapping her down, they move her into the back of the medic van. Locking the stretcher into place, they quickly leave with sirens wailing.

Brent steps into the alley and retrieves his coat before

walking back to the officer in charge. "If you have no further questions, I'll be leaving for the hospital now."

"Nope, that should about do it. Thank you. One of our detectives may be contacting you, however. And once the young lady is able to talk, an officer will be there to get her version of what happened. The hospital will notify us when she's able to talk."

"Fair enough. Thanks for the quick response here."

19

Wanting to get to the hospital as soon as possible, he quickly heads to his vehicle — which is still running. Jumping in, he turns his GPS control switch on, speaks the name of the hospital and is quickly rewarded with verbal instructions for the fastest route. Whether or not the system takes into account the closed streets and detours due to the quake, he isn't sure. He had heard of the hospital before, but never knew exactly where it was located. Fifteen minutes later, he finds himself in the visitor parking lot.

Following a quick walk from the parking lot, he's standing before a rather nice looking Emergency Room receptionist. "Brenda, can you please tell me the whereabouts of Shimie Jamison?" He calls her by name after noticing the name tag fastened to her blouse. He figures if there was ever a time to turn on the charm, now is it.

"One moment while I look her up." A few seconds later, she looks up at Brent and asks, "And your relationship to her is?"

"Shimie's my little sister."

"And your name is?"

"Brent Masterson. I'm the one footing the bill for her treatment tonight…and however long she's here." He says this hoping that she would look at him as not just another relative. Working for a hospital, he could only assume that Shimie has her own health coverage of some kind, but that would have to wait until he had the chance to talk to her.

"Oh, in that case, would you mind filling out this patient responsibility form? I'm assuming you know her address and all the other particulars?"

"Yep, she lives with me. She moved in when her place was flattened by the quake."

"Oh my, sorry to hear that," she replies, while handing over the clipboard. "We've been busier than the dickens because of the quake," she adds, with a charming smile.

Brent hastily fills out the form and signs his name. Handing it back to the receptionist, he asks, "Can your magic fingers tell me where she is right now?"

"Well, according to the computer, she's still in emergency. I'll type your name in as next of kin, so when she's moved to another section of the hospital, say recovery, one of the doctors will come to see you in the waiting lounge… which is just around the corner and down the hallway."

"You've been a sweetheart, Brenda, thank you."

"Anytime," she responds, with a slight blush. "If you need anything else, you know where to find me," she adds.

"I'll be sure to do that," Brent replies, before rounding

the corner to a long hallway. Locating the waiting room, he enters and takes a seat amongst five other anxiously waiting people. Various doctors would come in, talk quietly to a patient's family, disappear, and then the family would, in most cases, leave. New arrivals, like himself, would come in and take their turn at the waiting game. As he glances around the room, it is easy to see that this particular hospital caters to the lower end of society.

Two hours and thirteen magazines had passed when a seasoned doctor in scrubs enters the room and walks directly toward Brent. He wastes no time in taking a seat next to him. Being the only white person in the room, Brent isn't surprised that the doctor singled him out of those waiting as Shimie's brother.

"Mr. Masterson?"

"Yes."

"I'm Doctor Walters...one of two doctors who worked on your sister. To ease any worries on your part—and I'm sure there were and are plenty—she's going to be fine. She came to us with three cracked ribs, numerous lacerations to the face and multiple bruises to the upper body—along with a heavily swollen eye. She suffered a concussion from a blow to the right side of her head. We had to go in and drain excess fluids to relieve the buildup of pressure on her brain. Though we left the drain tube in for the time being, the swelling has already gone down considerably. She's in isolation as we speak and will most likely be moved upstairs sometime in the morning. She was just beginning to regain consciousness when she first arrived, but is currently asleep due to the medications we injected prior to surgery. Given the hour of the night, I don't see her waking until sometime in the morning. At that time we'll be able to check her level of acuity. Any questions?"

"Only one. How long do you see her being in the hospital?"

"Three days...four max. Her body took a beating, but it's the head wound that needs to be watched. Looking at you, I would say that you've had a long day yourself. I would suggest you go home and get a good night's rest. You should be able to see her in the morning."

"Yes, it has been a long day, so I'll take your advice and go home...not sure about the resting part, however."

"I understand the resting part. Oh, that reminds me, does she have a personal physician?"

"Yes, Doctor Roberta Matthews."

"Ah, excellent choice," the doctor remarks. "A cut above. She was in a couple of my medical classes way back when. Okay, if there are no further questions, I'll leave you...and hopefully you'll take my advice and go straight home."

"I will," Brent remarks, shaking hands with the doctor. "And thanks for taking care of my sister," he adds.

"My pleasure. She's a beautiful young lady. Reminds me of my daughter." With that said the doctor rises and disappears through the Staff Only door.

Though not wanting to leave Shimie, he decides to accept the doctor's advice and head home. Encouraged by the doctor's overall report, his mind, nevertheless, is running in circles thinking about her, the missing daughter and her ex-husband. Arriving back home, he hardly remembers anything of the forty-five-minute drive. Following a quick shower, he climbs into bed and is fast asleep within minutes from pure exhaustion.

20

‌

Brent tries to remember the last time he slept past 6:30 in the morning. Oh wait, he recalls, there was that one time with Shimie beside him. But that was caused from physical, not mental exhaustion, as is the case this morning. Dressing quickly, he immediately sits down at the desk and fires off an email to Roberta, asking that she take Shimie on as a patient. After hitting the send button, he gathers up his wallet and keys and makes his way out to the garage.

Forty-five minutes later, he finds himself standing before a different receptionist at the information desk. With Shimie's room number in hand, he takes the elevator up to the fourth floor, stopping at the nurses' station to inquire about Shimie. "Is it okay to see Shimie Jamison?" He asks the lone nurse.

"Are you her brother?" She inquires.

"Yes."

"You might have to wait a little bit. There's a police officer in there with her right now. You can have a seat over there," she says, while pointing to a leathered loveseat lined up along the hallway wall. "If you'd like some coffee, you can find it right down the hallway on your right... in an open alcove. Help yourself."

"Thank you. Right now I could use some." After stirring two packets of sugar into his cup, he returns to the nursing station and takes a seat. With no magazines to read, his only source of entertainment is sipping his coffee and watching the hospital staff move up and down the hallway. Two cups of coffee and a half hour later, he watches as a suited, middle-aged man and a nurse came out of a room and walk past him. In his right hand was what appears to be a carrying case that would possibly contain a laptop. Brent had a feeling that he was a detective questioning Shimie about last night's ordeal.

Shortly after the two pass by him, the nurse calls out his name. "Mr. Masterson, you can go in now. Room 429."

"Thank you," Brent responds as he gets up and heads down the hallway. Sure enough, the room the man came out of was Shimie's room. Without knocking, he quietly opens the door and walks in. The first bed of the two-person room was unoccupied. The bed alongside the window has its curtain halfway draped around the bed. Peering around the corner of the curtain, he spots Shimie sitting up with her eyes closed. A large bandage covers a spot on her partially shaved head and her right eye was severely swollen. Smaller bandages cover her face in five or six places.

"Anyone home?" He whispers so as not to startle her. After a moment of no response, he repeats himself, a little louder this time, but still no response. Spotting a padded chair, he decides to sit down and wait. Brent surmises the interview with the detective has worn her out. A half hour of watching her passes when he notices a hospital worker coming in the door with what appears to be a breakfast tray in her hand. Without saying anything to Brent, she places the tray on the movable stand and leaves as quickly as she had come in.

Brent rises and once again whispers, "Anyone home?" This time around she slowly opens the only eye that was functional. She stares at him, but says nothing. Then he notices a tear rolling down her cheek. Grabbing a Kleenex from the nightstand, he gently blots the tear away.

"Morning, sleepyhead. If you're hungry, breakfast is here. Not that hospital food could be classified as edible, but you should at least try to eat something. I can only imagine when you ate last."

There was still no response from her, outside of another tear rolling down her cheek. After blotting the tear, he removes the lid from the meal plate. "Well, your lucky day… scrambled eggs and sausage with a dried piece of toast. On the side we have orange juice and a carton of milk… and what I can only assume is coffee. Just like home," he adds, giving her a wink.

"I'm sorry," Shimie says, in a voice that Brent didn't recognize as coming from her. No sooner had the words left her mouth when another tear begins to run down her cheek.

"No talking right now...concentrate on eating." Unwrapping the paper napkin tightly wrapped around the silverware, Brent picks up the fork and stabs at a piece of the scrambled eggs, bringing it up to her mouth. Opening her mouth, though not fully, he slips the egg inside. Picking up the knife, he sets about cutting the sausage into small pieces before forking one piece into her mouth. He readily sees that chewing is not an easy task for her. While her jaw was apparently not broken, he clearly sees that it had taken quite a beating. Even just the actions associated with talking, he considers, has to be difficult for her.

With half of the breakfast fed to her, he unwraps a straw and sticks it down into the milk container. Placing the straw into her mouth, he watches as she struggles to suck milk up through the straw. He knew better then to offer her any coffee. Offering up more eggs brought forth a shaking of her head. In the process of pushing the tray holder to one side, Brent hears a soft knocking on the door. Whoever it was let themself in.

"Roberta!" Brent exclaims a little too loudly as he gets up from the side of Shimie's bed and gives her a hug. "I would ask what brings you here, but I already know. Thanks a million."

"A million is what you'll owe me," she responds, with a laugh. "And is this beautiful young lady my new patient?"

"You bet. Shimie, this is Dr. Matthews, my personal

physician. You know — the one I mentioned the other day. Roberta, this is Shimie Jamison."

"Welcome to my practice, Shimie, but I'm not here to force myself on you just because Brent asked me to. If you already have a personal physician you would like to handle your recovery, just let me know."

Shimie tries to speak, but ends up shaking her head.

"Okay, Brent, I need you to clear up a puzzle. The nurses' station informed me that her brother was in the room. Did your sister undergo some major plastic surgery without my knowing about it?"

"Easily answered. How else was I to gain access to Shimie without claiming to be a relative? You know the hospital rules better than I do."

"I always knew you were quick on your feet," Roberta remarks with a smile as she moves in closer to Shimie. "And how's my new patient feeling?" She asks, while looking directly at Shimie. As with Brent earlier, Shimie gives no response outside of another tear.

"I'm no doctor?" Brent interjects," but I have to believe that her jaws are very sore, making it difficult to talk. I spoon-fed her breakfast just prior to your arrival, and it appears to be a challenge on her part to chew. A detective was in asking questions just before I came in, so I'm guessing she's all talked out."

"I'm not surprised after reading the report from the emergency room docs before I came up," Roberta remarks, while continuing to check out Shimie's wounds.

"What she needs right now is rest...and lots of it." Turning her attention back to Brent, she adds, "I would like the two of you to consider transferring her to Scottsdale General...for a couple of reasons. First of all, and it's probably selfish on my part, but I would like her closer to my home base—and yours for that matter. Secondly, while this is a good hospital, Scottsdale's diagnostic equipment is far more up to date than any of the county-supported hospitals like this one—one of the advantages of a private hospital. If you two agree, I'll make the arrangements."

"Shimie, would you like to move over to Scottsdale General?" Brent asks. Shimie responds with a weak nod in the affirmative. Turning back to Roberta, he comments, "That will be like old home week for her. That's where she works as a surgical nurse. Or I should say, used to work."

"Oh my, what a coincidence," Roberta responds. "Okay, I had a feeling the answer would be a yes, so I had already reserved a private room for her before leaving home this morning. I'll go down to the nurses' station and fill out the release form. I'll also have them call for an ambulance to transport her to Scottsdale as soon as possible. Anything else before I leave?"

"Nope, not here," Brent replies. "We'll see you in Scottsdale."

"Oh, another thing," Roberta says, while making her way to the door, "my patient needs her rest, so find something else to occupy your time with while the transfer takes place. I'll give you a call as soon as she arrives. Fair enough?"

"Fair enough," Brent replies, as she closes the door behind her.

"Okay, beautiful," Brent remarks, once again sitting down on the edge of her bed. "I had better follow the doctor's order before I catch hell. Just close your eyes and allow yourself to fall asleep and I'll see you later at Scottsdale General." With that, he leans in and gives her a gentle kiss on the lips.

Passing by the nurses' station, he notices Roberta with her back to him, apparently filling out the release form. Rather than say anything, he chooses to continue walking to the elevators. The drive home was just as long as last night's, but at least he was feeling less worried about Shimie knowing that Roberta would now be her primary physician. While Shimie's insurance, providing she had any, would cover most of the hospital fees, the private room and Roberta's fees would be borne by him alone. But he is okay with that, considering the trials she has faced over the course of the past week and a half.

The past eleven or so days have been new territory for Brent. For the first time in his life, he finds himself more concerned about the welfare of someone else than he does for himself. Even with high paying and well-heeled corporate clients, he isn't the least bit interested in them personally as he is in winning in court. Winning was the true test of a good attorney; his upbringing was by parents who were highly successful because they won the majority of their cases. The few cases he personally did lose felt as though someone had ripped his heart out — he felt total shame when he had to meet up with his clients afterward.

Right now, however, Shimie's welfare is the only thing on his mind. She is naïve in many ways — too trusting of those she comes in contact with. Apparently too trusting of a man who knew the right words to say; thereby allowing herself to marry him before she really knew him. All of which resulted in her being used, abused, the eventual abduction of her daughter — not to mention almost getting herself killed in the process. This is where she would have been better served by looking at life through a legalistic mindset, he muses. Question every action, think with your mind, not with your heart. In thirty-two years of life, he is proud of the fact that it has served him well.

His thoughts are interrupted by a ringing sound he knew came from someone at his gate. Walking rapidly to the front door, he pushes the talk button. "Yes."

"It's Bill; did I catch you at a bad time?" Richards asks.

"Come on up...door's open." After pushing the button to open the gate, Brent cracks the front door open before stepping into the living room to wait for his arrival.

Hearing the creaking of the door, Brent yells out, "In the living room."

Richards steps down into the living room and takes a seat opposite Brent.

"Well, what brings you to the slums, Bill?" Brent teasingly inquires.

"About an hour ago, I received a copy of the interview Detective Rogers had with Ms. Jamison. She apparently had trouble talking; so a large part of the interview was answered with the nodding of her head. The major thing he did get from her was confirmation that she was attacked by her ex. The only words he spoke were, "Stay away from me you fucking bitch." And then he proceeded to punch her in the face with his fists. The lacerations on her face, according to her medical report, appeared to be caused by some kind of ring on the ex's left hand. Once she was down on the ground, he kicked her in the torso twice. The last thing she remembers was seeing him pull his gun out of his waistband. She doesn't even remember how she received the blow to her head. My guess would be the butt of a gun."

"Wow. We're dealing with a real nice guy, aren't we? As in his former wife and lover. The mother of his child."

"It would appear as such. If nothing else, it confirms that he's armed…therefore considered dangerous by our standards. It may end up being a case of shoot first and ask questions later with this guy. She was lucky you found her when you did, or she may have died from internal swelling of the brain. I've already relayed the info to Derrick; advising him to be very careful…leave any thoughts of apprehension to the Phoenix cops. Have you seen Ms. Jamison today?"

"I just returned from seeing her. She wasn't able to talk given her sore jaws. My doctor, who's now her doctor, is transferring her from Valley of the Sun to Scottsdale General as we speak. I'm waiting for the doc to call me when Shimie arrives at General. I'm not sure she will be up to talking today, but if she is, is there anything you want me to ask her?"

"Nope. We know who we're looking for and why. We're just hoping that he doesn't lie low for a while after last night's altercation. We need to get him off the street as soon as possible. The Phoenix guys are well aware that the first priority is getting the daughter back, so they're still hoping he will lead them to wherever he's staying. When that happens, we'll be ready. Phoenix has doubled the number of undercover cops in the area. He'll be found... it's just a matter of when and where."

"Bill, I really appreciate everything you're doing. I really do."

"I know you do. Let's just say the next time you hold one of your parties with single women in attendance that I get a personal invite," Richards states, with a big grin on his face.

"You got it. Being single myself, I always make sure single women are invited. There'll be enough to go around for both of us, trust me. And the weather around here couldn't be better, so I'll plan for a barbeque party poolside. I have some ..."

In the middle of the conversation, his phone goes off

with Roberta's ringtone. "Hi Roberta. Did she make it to General already?"

"Room 518. I'll be there shortly. Thanks."

"Well, I see you're on a mission to rescue another damsel in distress, so I'll head back to the office for some more of that fun criminal stuff."

"Okay, thanks again for stopping by, Bill...in person sure beats phones and emails any day. Oh, let me reset the code so the gate will open when you approach it." Walking with Richards to the front door, he punches in his four-digit code and then switches the controller to automatic gate opening mode. Richards gives a final wave goodbye as he drives down the long driveway. Brent immediately locks the door and heads through the house to the garage.

21

"I'VE ORDERED AN MRI," Roberta states as Brent enters the room. "I want to have a better picture of her jaws. It's only a precautionary measure as I want to rule out any hairline fractures. An MRI can provide information that even the best radiologist may not be able to pick up on an X-ray, ultrasound or CAT scan. Emergency rooms don't always have the luxury of waiting for MRI results before dealing with the emergency at hand."

"You're the doctor. Has she been asleep since you arrived?"

"According the medics who transported her, she was awake during the ride over. The nurse responsible for her care right now said that she fell asleep shortly after being transferred to the bed. Don't be alarmed by her needing sleep…it's what she needs right now more than anything. If eating is too painful, we'll feed her intravenously."

"Okay. Thanks. I think I'll plop myself down in that comfy-looking chair over there and do some reading. I

don't like the idea of her waking up and not finding anyone here."

"Good thinking. I believe she'll look forward to seeing
that handsome face when she opens her eyes. Oh wait; her
one eye. I'll be back later once the results of the MRI are in.
They have her scheduled for three o'clock. She'll be back
in bed before four."

"I'll see you later then."

Once Roberta had left the room, Brent picks up the novel he brought with him and begins to read. An hour later,
he awakes by a tiny voice calling his name. "Oh, look who
finally woke up to keep me company. I figured I would
get a little shut eye in while you were snoring away. How
are you feeling?"

"Hurt," she replies, so softly that Brent isn't sure what
she actually said.

"Are you in pain?" He asks after getting closer to her.
She responds by moving here head up and down.

"Is it your head that hurts?" Again, the head moves up
and down.

"Well, let me summon the nurse and see what Roberta
has ordered up to control the pain." He reaches down by
the head of the bed where a contraption of some sort was
hanging down. Pushing what he thinks is the right button,
he sits back down on the side of her bed. Less than a minute later, a nurse enters the room. Before she could even
ask why the call, Brent lets her know that Shimie's head
was hurting.

"Looking at her chart here, I don't see where Dr. Matthews has ordered any pain meds." Looking directly at Shimie, she asks, "Is it your total head that hurts?" Shimie gives a negative nod. "Is it your jaws?" This time the nodding is affirmative. "Okay, let me call the doctor and see what she wants you to have. I'll be right back."

"Shimie, Richards dropped by the house a bit ago...apparently Phoenix has doubled the number of undercover cops at night. After last night's altercation with you, they're not sure if he's going to lay low or not. With any luck, providing he needs the money, he'll be hitting the streets sooner rather than later. I can just imagine ..."

The nurse reenters the room with what Brent knows was an IV bag in her hand. Brent rises from the side of the bed in order to make room for the nurse.

"Okay, Dr. Matthews has you covered. Once I attach this bag to your existing drip tube, you'll feel a lot better. As with most pain meds, you'll feel tired, but that's okay, the doctor wants you sleeping as much as possible anyway. She's also ordered soft foods for your meals. After your MRI, you'll be back to your room in plenty of time for dinner. If your brother is any kind of a gentleman, he'll help you with dinner," she finishes with a wink meant for Shimie.

Following the departure of the nurse, Brent sits back in the easy chair and takes up his reading once again. Glancing up at Shimie a short time later, he notices she had apparently drifted off to sleep while he was reading. The very mention of dinner by the nurse brought home the realization that he is hungry. Not wanting to leave Shimie alone, however, he decides to forgo eating until after she had left for her MRI.

A short while later, two orderlies enter the room and wheel her bed and IV pole away. Their activities causes Shimie to wake up, but she quickly falls back to sleep before she's even wheeled out of the room. Brent follows them out and heads down to the main level to the cafeteria. Following a remarkably good dinner, for a hospital that is, he takes a stroll outside in the beautifully landscaped entrance to the hospital. At 3:45, he heads back up to Shimie's room — coming out of the elevator at the same time as the two orderlies were wheeling Shimie down the hallway. Catching up with the orderlies, he holds the door open as Shimie passes through. She was still asleep. After the orderlies finished up and left, Brent once again takes up his novel.

"Well, not surprised to see you still watching over my patient," Roberta remarks, as she walks into the room. "Has she been sleeping long?"

"Whatever you ordered for a pain med obviously worked."

"Sleep is good for someone in her condition. Have the nurses been in much?"

"Yep. Every time I turn around they're checking on her for one thing or another. Plus all of her fellow co-workers have been streaming in and out. A guy can't get any rest in here," he adds with a grin.

"I just came up from looking at the MRI results with the radiologist, and sure enough, she has a hairline fracture of her right jaw. No surgery needed...just rest and avoiding the overuse of her jaw. So, don't look for her to be reading you *War and Peace* anytime soon."

"Then she's in luck...I've already read it. Next question. What's the short-term prognosis for Shimie?"

"Are you referring to health-wise or time-wise?"

"Both."

"The head wound should heal fine and relatively quickly. The swollen eye should be back to normal, relatively speaking, in a couple days. The various lacerations on her face will be the easiest to heal. They used dissolvable stitches, so no need to come back for that. Depending on how they heal, she may or may not want to look at plastic surgery. We'll take a look at that in two or three months. The jaw will take some time, but you'll see her talking and eating easier day by day. The pain meds will help her to move her jaws more. The parts of her that will take the longest to heal are the three cracked ribs. Don't expect her to be lifting anything heavier than a fork to her mouth over the course of the next month...maybe longer. Right now we have her ribcage wrapped tight to keep it from moving.

"Oh my God! Does this mean I'll have to take a crash course in cooking?" Brent remarks, jokingly.

"Stay away from the kitchen...I want my patient to be listed as one of my survivors. But seriously, that could be a problem. You can either hire a part-time or full-time cook for a month or two; or hire a nutritionist to pre-cook your meals. If that's not acceptable, then plan on eating all of your meals out. It will generally cost more, but one other option is to hire a nurse who also prepares meals. That, in my opinion, would be the better option—not only for yourself, but more importantly, for Shimie. If you're planning to go back to work anytime soon, Shimie will need someone around to look after her needs."

"Wow. Decisions. Decisions."

"Or you can just leave her here and walk away."

"You know that isn't going to happen."

"Must be your Catholic side speaking. The lawyer side of you is dog-eat-dog."

"Shimie, her daughter, and the ex are all aspects of my life left unfinished. I've got too much time invested right now to just walk away. She'll be on her own soon enough."

"Well, look who's awake," Roberta states, while staring at Shimie. Walking over, she sits down on the edge of the bed while Brent looks on. "That was some pretty good sleep you had. How's the pain in your jaw...better?"

"Yes," Shimie answers, though barely audible.

"Good. I'm going to order up a lot of hot compresses. The warmth on your face will increase the blood flow and reduce the pain level. You'll actually love the pampering. As a nurse here, you've done your share of pampering, so it's time you were."

A light tapping noise causes three sets of eyes to turn in

the direction of the door. They all watch as a middle-aged woman brings in a dinner tray, sets it down and quickly disappears back out the door.

Looking back down at Shimie, Roberta asks, "Hungry?" Shimie nods her head.

"Good. Sleep and food is just what you need." Turning to Brent, she states, "Make yourself useful and feed the young lady. Meanwhile, I'll disappear for the evening and see you two sometime tomorrow morning."

22

"GOOD MORNING," BRENT calls out as Roberta walks into Shimie's room.

"Good morning to you two. I see you haven't killed my patient off just yet," Roberta responds, while glancing at Shimie propped up in bed. "And how are you feeling this morning?"

"Much better...thank you," she answers, more clearly than the previous days.

"Good. You've made a lot of progress these past four days. So much progress, in fact, that I'm sending you home today. Good hospital, good care, but nothing like being home." Turning her attention to Brent, she inquires, "Did you pick up the wheelchair?"

"Sure did. It's in the back of my vehicle as we speak."

"Good. We need to keep the pressure off her ribs for a bit longer. No sense causing undue pain getting around your house. Did you meet up with the nurse yesterday?"

"Absolutely. Didn't know that nurses came so pretty...

well, outside of Shimie, that is." He notices a little smile on Shimie's face when he made that comment. "I gave her one of those store cards for groceries and I think she spent every penny of it. She'll be staying in one of the spare bedrooms."

"If I didn't know you better, I'd think you selected her solely based on her looks, not her qualifications," Roberta remarks, grinning. "Shimie, are you excited to be going home?"

"Yes, but only if Brent doesn't cook any of my meals," she responds, with a small smile.

"Ah, that is why he hired a nurse willing to cook...so he wouldn't have to. Okay you two," she continues, "I'll head out of here and get those discharge papers filled out." Glancing back toward Brent, she adds, "I'll stop by the house tomorrow and see if my patient is still alive."

"Ouch," Brent responds, "between the two of you, and probably the nurse awaiting us at the house, I don't stand a chance against three women."

"Hey, just telling it like I see it," Roberta remarks, with a wink meant for Shimie. As she pulls herself up from the edge of the bed to leave, Shimie's voice stops her.

"Dr. Matthews...thank you."

"You are most welcome, dear. And please, just call me Roberta. If Brent can, and does, you most certainly can. I don't stand on formalities."

"Okay. Thank you."

An hour and a half later, Shimie's favorite nurse and

personal friend came in to prepare her for discharge. When it came time to get her out of the hospital gown, Brent decides it is a good time to leave the two of them alone.

"Shimie, there's a full set of fresh clothes I brought from the house. They're hanging in the closet — the underclothes I placed in the middle drawer of your nightstand there. And while you're getting yourself ready, I'll head down to grab the car and meet you two outside."

"Take your time," the nurse said, "it will be a good half hour before we get down."

"Okay, fair enough. I'll stop by the cafeteria for some of their day-old coffee."

—

"Three days of being home and you and Victoria seem to have become the best of buds," Brent comments, as Shimie wheels herself closer to the couch.

"We have a lot in common...lots to talk about."

"As long as my name doesn't come into the conversation," he remarks with a wink.

"Not to worry...only half of the conversations are about you."

"Speaking of Victoria, where is she?"

"She stole your other car and went grocery shopping. She mentioned something about your eating too much," Shimie adds, with a half-smile.

"Hey, taking care of you works up an appetite in me."

"Hah! Nice try, but Victoria does everything...for both of us."

"Speaking of working, I'll be going into our temporary offices tomorrow. Our building received substantial damage, which will require a good ninety days to repair. My staff and I are anxious to get back to work. Oh, I almost forgot something, I'll be right back." Brent pushes away from the couch and makes his way to the study—returning in less than a minute.

"This is for you...even has your name on it," he says, while handing her an American Express card. "I'm going to ask Victoria to take you shopping tomorrow. It's about time you did a little clothes shopping—you know—to pick out things that are better suited to your style. And which probably fit a little better, if you get my drift," he adds.

"That's really not necessary. You've already done too much for me as it is."

"You need clothes that are you, not my sister. You lost all of the clothes you owned in the apartment. Someday soon you'll be back on your own, raising your daughter and working. You were stubborn once and didn't listen to me—please don't upset me again."

Shimie knew exactly what he was referring to when he threw out the word *stubborn*. Eight days have passed since she went against his advice not to seek out her ex— and not once has he brought the subject up. She finds that somewhat remarkable that he hasn't criticized her once for her lack of common sense. She was in the wrong and she knew it—albeit in hindsight.

"I can't believe you actually put a card in my name," she finally remarks.

"Well, don't think I didn't put some thought into it. As I saw it, I had two choices. One was to go shopping with you, or get you your own card. The second option was easier as I hate shopping...of any kind. Women will try on twenty pieces of clothing before selecting just one. I've never understood it and probably never will. Oh, and feel free to buy Victoria something nice as a way of saying thank you. I'll leave the Rover for you two...easier to get the wheelchair in and out."

"Okay, but one question. What's the limit on the card so we can max it out?" Shimie asks, with the biggest grin on her face that Brent had seen in well over a week.

"Let's just say you couldn't spend enough in a day to reach the max. Speaking of spending, I think I just heard the garage door opening. I'll make myself useful and help Victoria with the groceries. Oh, and have Victoria call Roberta to let her know that you won't be home tomorrow."

23

"ANOTHER GREAT DINNER, Victoria. I hope Shimie doesn't think of stealing you away when she gets her own place down the road. I could get used to this pampering."

Shimie, clearly hearing what Brent had just said, shudders as chills run down her spine. Maybe he can't wait to get rid of me and resume his carefree bachelor ways, she muses. She had high hopes that their lovemaking was more than just a physical conquest on his part. She gave of herself emotionally, as well as physically, because of what she saw in him — or thought she saw in him. Was he not capable of a long-term commitment? Or were all of his actions simply a case of love 'em and leave 'em?

Granted, he has never spoken the three words most women long to hear. For that matter, neither had she — but her reluctance to say anything was out of fear of losing him. She'd been around long enough to know that men who aren't ready for commitment will oftentimes pull back, or end the relationship entirely if their significant other simply *alludes* to a future together. Brent has, oftentimes jokingly, but sometimes not, made numerous references to his quest for eternal bachelorhood. It may be that he will never—

"Shimie, are you of this world?" Brent asks in a louder than usual voice to get her attention.

"Huh?"

"Victoria and I have been engaged in a long-running conversation about shopping, and I get the distinct impression you haven't heard a word either one of us has said."

"Sorry…just tired."

"Well, you've got a big shopping day tomorrow, so you may want to consider an early bedtime. Victoria, more than once I might add, keeps referring to tomorrow as a 'shop till you drop' kind of day. So get lots of sleep if you don't want to drop early. As for me, I know for a fact that I'll be going to bed early. I don't expect I'll be home for dinner tomorrow, so why don't you two plan on eating dinner out. Restaurants love American Express, so make 'em happy."

"Shimie," Victoria calls out her name to get her attention. "I don't know about you, but my taste buds can only be satisfied tomorrow with lots of escargot and caviar for appetizers, before indulging in a six-ounce Wagyu Kobe steak. Oh, and I'm thinking we should wash it all down with a bottle, or two, of Dom. Romane Conti. And to think I know exactly where Morton's Steakhouse is located…

right next to an exclusive mall. What do you think, Shimie, are you game?"

"Of course I'm game. But just how do you know all about this expensive stuff?"

"Easy. My father was in the business of writing restaurant reviews. Oftentimes I would get to go with him. I loved it. Though once I was out on my own, the fine dining came to a screeching halt and it was back to the fast-food places for my sustenance."

"Okay, ladies, have your fun while it lasts," Brent remarks as he gets up from the table. "I happen to know plenty of McDonald's not too far from here," he throws out as he walks out of the kitchen.

—

"I'm not surprised, Bill, Shimie's actions have apparently caused him to lay low for a bit. But you and I both know that he's got to feed his customers or he'll be out of business — unless he's wearing some kind of disguise and taking public transportation. Oh, my father's calling, I'll catch you later."

"Father, what do I owe the pleasure of this call to?"

"Okay, we'll take care of it right now…he's too big a client to lose. I'll give you a call later this afternoon. Thanks for the heads-up."

Trying to deal with a new office environment, welcoming back his staff and the associated chit-chat about the quake, talking with both Derrick and Richards, and then his father just now, is putting a lot of stress on him in only his first day back at work. The thought of staying home with Shimie and Victoria was sounding pretty good right about now — until he remembers they were currently out spending his money.

By the time 7:30 rolls around and the office was quiet, he is feeling thoroughly bushed. Nor was he looking forward to the longer drive home from his temporary offices — and he was hungry. Normally one to eat his meals out, he isn't sure he even has enough energy for that. Once in his car, he makes up his mind to go straight home and settle for leftovers, or whatever was quick.

Pulling into the garage at eight, the first thing he notices was the missing Rover. He finds it hard to believe that the girls were still out — until he glances in his rearview mirror and notices headlights coming up the driveway. He could only imagine how totally exhausted Shimie had to be by this late hour. Victoria, he thinks, should have known better than to keep her out this late. Standing alongside his car, he watches as the girls pull in beside him.

As soon as Victoria pulls to a stop, Brent opens up the back to get the wheelchair out for Shimie. Looking inside, he is taken aback when seeing the large number of store bags and boxes strewn everywhere. "Hold on, Shimie, I'll be right there. I just need to get the wheelchair out." Victoria, meanwhile, walks around the front of the Rover and opens up Shimie's door and helps her down. Arm in arm, they walk to the back where Brent was struggling to get the wheelchair out without destroying all the packages that had settled against it.

With Brent's back to her, Shimie casually says, "Need some help?"

Brent, caught by surprise, rises up and hits his head on the raised tailgate door. "Ouch" were the first words out of his mouth as he turns to see both Shimie and Victoria standing there laughing.

"I damn near kill myself and you two are standing there laughing at me. And Shimie, why didn't you wait for the wheelchair?"

"Simple. I didn't need it. Spending *your* money gave me an adrenaline high to push through any discomfort. Besides, we needed the wheelchair to hold our *way* too many packages." The two of them start laughing again. "Now don't just stand there rubbing your owie, get the chair out so we can start loading the loot." Once again, the laughter spews forth.

"If I live to be a hundred, I'll still never understand women and shopping," Brent remarks as he pulls the chair down. The girls waste no time in helping to load packages onto the chair and into the living room. Taking three trips of the loaded wheelchair to get everything into the house, Shimie immediately sits down on the couch while Victoria sits on the floor beside the packages.

"Well, don't just stand there, have a seat," Shimie commands, while looking up at Brent. "You need to see some of the things *your* money can buy."

"I would," Brent answers, "but I'm hungry...haven't had dinner yet."

"Don't go anywhere," Victoria says, as she gets up from the floor, "I've got a roast beef sandwich already made up in the fridge. Part of the joys of shopping is being able to show off what we bought. Don't start without me, I'll be right back."

Though tired and hungry, and in no real mood to be looking at clothes right now, he did as instructed and plops down onto the loveseat. A few minutes later, Victoria comes back into the living room with his sandwich and a glass of milk. Placing everything on the end table, she promptly resumes her place on the floor just to the side of Shimie.

"The only thing missing is a Christmas tree," Brent remarks, before taking a bite out the sandwich.

"Consider these my birthday presents," Shimie responds.

"Oh, never knew it was your birthday. When exactly is your birthday?" He inquires.

"Three months ago, but you forgot again," Shimie answers, while trying her best to maintain a straight face. Finally, however, the girls burst out in laughter.

"My bad, even though I didn't know you back then. I'll try to remember next time."

"That's what happens when all you think of is yourself," Shimie fires back.

The next half hour was spent displaying the items

they had purchased. Shimie, finishing her display of one piece of clothing, would quickly be handed up another item by Victoria. As the items were proudly displayed, Brent could only see the dollar signs associated with each item. In spite of the costs, he is warmed to see Shimie smiling and laughing throughout it all—until she starts displaying the final seven or eight items. The smiles are promptly replaced with a melancholy look as she begins sharing with Brent the clothes she had purchased for her daughter. She talks about each piece on display, but the enthusiasm in her voice is noticeably absent. Brent's heart went out to her.

"Thank you for all the clothes," Shimie says sincerely, but in a subdued voice.

"You're welcome," Brent responds. "It was worth it just to see a lot of smiles and laughter...even though the laughter was generally directed at me," he adds, with a look of having been hurt.

"And that goes for me too," Victoria chimes in. "Once I wear this outfit, I'll have to beat the men off," she adds, with a big laugh.

"You're both beautiful women, new clothes or not, the men will be beating down your doors."

"At thirty-three, the wrong ones have obviously been beating at my door," Victoria replies.

"Your time will come...and you'll be grateful you waited for the right one," comments Brent. "Oh, speaking of which, I just happen to know a certain detective with Scottsdale that would be a good match for you. Nice guy…a real gentleman. Like you, never married."

"Bring 'em on," Victoria responds with a grin. "Or are you trying to set me up with one of your loser friends?"

"Not a loser at all. He's dated plenty of beautiful women, just hasn't found the right gal to settle down with. Okay, why don't you two busy shoppers look at heading off to bed…it's getting late. Leave the packages where they are…tomorrow's soon enough to put things away. Besides, Shimie looks half-asleep already," Brent adds, while looking at Shimie's half-closed eyes. "I know tomorrow's Saturday," he continues, "but I've got some important work to catch up on at the office, so I'll see you two around noonish."

24

"Derrick's man spotted Fredericks last night," Richards begins the conversation with Brent, "but he gave him the slip again. I'll give the guy credit for being smart. At least we know he's no longer lying low, so that's a good thing in our favor."

"And the undercover cops?" Brent asks.

"They were in the area, but not close enough to where Fredericks was first spotted. They combed the area, but weren't able to locate him again by the time Derrick's man notified them. That area of the city is heavily patrolled by beat cops, so those like Fredericks know to be careful — how to avoid being tracked."

"So where do we go from here?"

"I wish I had an easy answer, Brent. Fredericks is apparently not your typical drug pusher...he's smarter than most of those we deal with. It's obviously a waiting game for all of us...and I can appreciate what Ms. Jamison is going through. It's not every day that a nine-month-old just up and vanishes into thin air. Would it do any good if I stopped by the house and talked to her?"

"That may not be a bad idea for her to hear it from someone who is actually involved in looking for her daughter. I have an ulterior motive for your stopping by, however. I just happen to have a 33-year-old guest at the house who could probably use some male companionship about now. Well, she's not a guest actually, but Shimie's 24-hour nurse I hired; considerably younger than you, but what the hell. What man doesn't like to be seen with arm-candy?" Brent adds with a chuckle.

"Are you trying to pawn off some ugly duckling on me?" Richards asks, suspiciously.

"No way. Beautiful, never married, and no children. She could easily have been a model in her younger days. I would even go so far as to say she's on par with Shimie."

"Well, in that case, I may just have to stop by the house later today. Is four o'clock a good time to visit with Ms. Jamison?"

"I think you mean Ms. Jamison and Victoria," Brent corrects him, with a good-natured laugh. "And yes, four would be fine."

Leaving Richards' office, Brent heads directly home to satisfy his need for sustenance. Between work and Richards, he never took time out for breakfast—his favorite meal of the day. Passing by the living room, where he half expects to see the girls, he quickly notes that not only were they not there, but all evidence of their shopping spree is absent as well. With pangs in his stomach growing, he goes directly into the kitchen to whip out another roast beef sandwich, along with some chips and freshly-baked chocolate chip cookies—his favorite.

After finishing off his meal—and way too many cookies—he sets out in search of the girls. It isn't until he enters his bedroom that he eventually spots them lying out by the pool in their newly purchased bikinis. The twin beauties provide for quite a view. As before with Shimie, Brent finds it hard to pull himself away from staring. The sheer curtains did little to block his view as they lay on their backs soaking up the early afternoon sun. But in the end, he finds himself walking away to a safer room.

A full hour passes before the girls come prancing into the living room full of laughter. To Brent's dismay, they had changed out of their swimsuits. "Let me guess. All that laughter can only mean that you two were discussing men again while at the pool."

"How did you know we were at the pool?" Shimie inquires. "Were you spying on us...again?"

"Guilty as charged. It's not every day a guy gets the chance to view two beautiful women sunbathing in the nude."

"We were not naked," Victoria responds loudly in defense.

"Well, you might as well have been naked...the bikinis didn't leave much for the imagination," Brent replies with a smile.

"Well eat your heart out, Mr. Gawker," Shimie responds, with her hands on her hips. "We've both decided to become born-again virgins. Men, with one-track minds, aren't worth the hassles."

"A born-again virgin, huh? A neat concept if ever I've heard one." Changing the subject, he adds, "I see you two managed to get your loot put away while I was gone."

"Yep," Victoria replies, "hanging up nicely in the closet just waiting for the right man to come along."

"Well, so much for your born-again virgin proclamation."

"Only until the right man comes along," Shimie quickly replies, "and there aren't many of those out there," she adds.

"I'll have you two—," Brent's words were interrupted by the gate buzzer. "Be right back," Brent says, as he heads to the front door. The girls hear the words, "Come on up." Brent steps outside, closing the door behind him to await Richards' arrival. As soon as Richards steps out of his car, Brent knew that he had gone home and changed clothes—and most likely shaved and showered, as well. The sports jacket he wore looked as though it was freshly dry-cleaned—or never worn before. Either way, in Brent's mind, he definitely came to impress Victoria.

"Ladies, I'd like you to meet Detective Bill Richards. Bill, this here is Shimie and the other beautiful lady is Victoria." Following the introductions, Brent motions for everyone to have a seat. At the mention of Richards' name, Shimie's jovial mood instantly turns serious.

"Brent, how is it that you ended up with two beautiful women in your home?" Richards asks.

"Beautiful, yes, but with two in the house at the same time, they've worked well together in terms of conspiring against me...too well, I might add."

"Would any of you like something to drink?" Victoria interjects.

"Water with ice works for me," Richards responds, with the others declining anything.

"Ice water it is," Victoria repeats as she heads off to the kitchen.

"Bill, this is an unexpected visit," Brent remarks, even though he knew differently.

"I figured it was about time I met Ms. Jamison...to finally put a face to a name. You've shared a lot of information about her, but you never told me how beautiful she is...how beautiful both ladies are," he adds, only because Victoria was walking in with his water. "Thank you," he responds, as Victoria hands him the water.

Looking directly at Richards, Shimie asks, "Anything new on my daughter's case?"

Richards easily senses the pain in her voice. He knew, before even arriving, that the conversation would quickly focus on the investigation. "Your ex laid low for a while, but he's apparently back on the streets. He was spotted last night by the private investigator Brent hired, but disappeared into the shadows before the Phoenix cops had the opportunity to descend on the area. Every beat cop that works that section of the city has his photo. Even when they spot him, the officers have been instructed not to apprehend him. We need him to lead us to your daughter…and she's both their and my top priority."

"Do you know for sure that he's not living, or visiting, with his mother?" Shimie quietly inquires.

"Not once has he shown up there. The authorities there have installed a motion-camera on a power pole. She has visitors, but no son. Nor has she received any phone calls from him…those are monitored as well. Unfortunately, your ex is a pretty smart man…not the typical drug dealer we're used to dealing with. Between the various jurisdictions, there's a lot of manpower devoted to his eventual apprehension. While this particular case is important to you, there are over 25,000 felony warrants outstanding in this county alone. Let me assure you, and repeat once again, that your daughter's safe return is my number one priority. I wish I could give you some guarantee that the case will be solved soon, but I can't. Those of us involved in this particular case feel your pain."

"Thank you for the update," Shimie remarks, with a notable hint of disappointment in her voice.

Victoria, wanting to change the subject for Shimie's sake, asks, "Would you like to join us for a salmon dinner?" She finds Richards attractive and was therefore hoping he would say yes.

"Thanks for the offer, but I really have my heart set on one of those big twelve-ounce steaks, a decadent baked potato and whatever veggies they throw my way. I've been thinking about this all day long."

"Oh my," Victoria states in reply, "that sounds a lot more interesting than the salmon I was going to prepare."

"Well, at the risk of appearing forward, which isn't my style, I assure you, would you like to join me for a big juicy steak? Or whatever you eat to maintain that beautiful figure. Over dinner and wine you could fill me in on what kind of a guy Brent *really* is."

"I would love that, though Shimie is the real expert on Brent," Victoria comments while glancing over at Shimie. "Oh wait; I've got to cook dinner for the two of them," she adds, turning her attention back to Richards.

"Oh no you don't," Shimie shoots back, "I've still got Brent's credit card. I think I'll have a Chinese dinner delivered...a little of everything on the menu. Though I'm not sure about being left alone with him," she adds, with a wink meant for only Brent — but that everyone picks up on.

"I'm not sure the credit card is any good now...I think you two maxed it out clothes shopping yesterday. Bill, whatever you do, don't take Victoria within five miles of a mall."

"That's the price you pay for having the two of us live here...and taking care of you," Shimie says, all with a straight face while at the same time trying to hold back a grin.

"Thanks for the tip on the mall, Brent," comments Richards, "I'll try to remember that."

"Shimie, would you like to come with me and pick out something for me to wear tonight? Plus I want to change your bandages before I leave."

"I thought you'd never ask," Shimie readily answers, as Victoria helps her up from the couch.

When the ladies were out of earshot, Brent turns to Richards, "I'll bet you five dollars we don't see them back here in under an hour."

"Sorry, but no bet. That's a sure win for you."

It was an hour and fifteen minutes before the two of them make an appearance in the living room. Richards immediately stands up, takes an intentional up and down glance at Victoria, before finally saying something. "My, oh my, you look absolutely radiant in that attire." Quickly turning to Brent, he adds, "Don't be surprised if I don't bring her back...ever." Shimie and Brent both set to laughing at his comment, while Victoria finds herself blushing from the side-ways compliment.

"Okay, were off," Richards says, as he holds out his arm to Victoria. "Oh, and are the heads ever going to be turning tonight," he threw out for good measure as the two of them head for the door.

"They make a nice looking couple," Shimie remarks, after the door closes.

"Yes they do. Speaking of couples, would you like to *couple* up tonight after dinner? I promise to be gentle."

"I'll have to check my horoscope first," she answers with a wink.

25

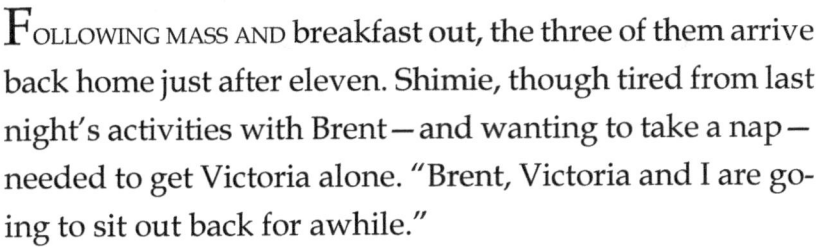

FOLLOWING MASS AND breakfast out, the three of them arrive back home just after eleven. Shimie, though tired from last night's activities with Brent — and wanting to take a nap — needed to get Victoria alone. "Brent, Victoria and I are going to sit out back for awhile."

"Well, let me guess...you're taking Victoria out behind the shed so you can hear all of the nitty-gritty from her date last night. Aren't you?"

"I am really appalled that you would think such a thing of me," Shimie quickly responds to Brent's assertion with a look of utter contempt. "But you're absolutely correct." Arm-in-arm, the two of them promptly leave the room laughing hysterically. Brent shakes his head and leaves for his study.

Emerging from his study two hours later, he is surprised to see Victoria sitting alone in the living room reading. "What happened to the gossip-gatherer?"

"She's taking a nap...some half-crazed man kept her awake during the night," she answers with a smile.

"Gee, do you women discuss *everything*?"

"Mostly, but we tend to leave out the minute details. We have to leave something to the imagination."

"In that case, I think I'll go take my own nap—given that some half-crazed woman kept me awake half the night against my will," he remarks, all the while maintaining a serious look.

Victoria simply smiles as he turns and walks out of the room. She knew full well what happened behind closed doors last night. The same thing she was hoping to happen with her and Bill Richards real soon; especially after that deep kiss he laid on her last night.

—

"Dinner's on the table," Victoria yells from the kitchen. Brent rises and helps Shimie up from the couch.

"Smells delicious," Brent comments as he walks in with Shimie on his arm.

"I hope it tastes as good as it smells," Victoria replies.

"I'm sure it will," Brent remarks. "Anyone else's cooking always taste better than our own. Not sure why that is, though. So, tell me about your hot date last night with Bill. The only thing I know for sure is that you didn't exactly break any speed records in getting home."

"Not much to say really. We had a great dinner and then he took me to a dance club where we danced the night away. And can he ever dance...so easy to follow."

"So, any future dates in the offing?" Brent inquires.

"Friday night for an early dinner and then a movie. I'll prepare a dinner and apply some more lotion to Shimie's face. The cuts are really beginning to heal nicely," she added.

"Speaking of Shimie," Brent states, as he looks her way, "you're being awfully quiet this evening. Anything wrong?"

"Tired mostly...not sure that I'm feeling all that well right now."

"If you don't really feel like eating...then don't," remarks Victoria. "Is it your head by any chance?"

"No. It's my stomach, but not real bad. Just a tiny bit upset."

"I saw some saltine crackers in the pantry," Victoria remarks as she pulls herself away from the table and makes her way over to the pantry. "I threw away of lot of pantry stuff because of the expired pull dates," she said as she set the cracker box onto the table. "Hopefully these don't taste stale. If they do, I'll pick up a new box first thing in the morning."

"Are you suggesting, Victoria, that I would have any expired foods in the house? If so, I'm hurt."

"Yep, tons of it. Unfortunately, the crackers didn't have a readable pull date on them. I guess I should have thrown them out anyway and bought fresh ones."

"No, they actually taste fairly fresh," remarks Shimie. "A miracle for sure," she adds, just to get Brent's goat.

"Regardless of pull dates," Brent quickly replies, to change the subject, "I highly recommend you heading off to bed right after dinner. Like Roberta has said more than once, sleep is good for what ails you. Besides, you've only been home less than a week from the hospital."

"I hate to agree with Brent," Victoria interjected, "but he's right for a change…bed rest or sleep is what you need right now. When you're ready, I'll go with you and change out some bandages."

"Finish your dinner first," responds Shimie.

Later that evening, with Shimie put to bed and Victoria doing whatever in her own bedroom, Brent spends his time catching on the latest news around town on his computer. A half hour of sifting through the news, his cell goes off. Checking the caller ID, he notices it's Derrick.

"Hi Derrick, what's up?"

"You're serious, aren't you?" He states, in an excited voice.

"Have you called Richards?"

"Good. Where are you right now?"

"Stay put, I'll meet you there."

Heading back to his bedroom, he grabs his wallet and keys and walks hurriedly to the garage. Five minutes later, he finds himself on the main road heading west. With light traffic and more of the roadways temporarily fixed, he spots Derrick's car at a fast-food restaurant. Jumping out of his vehicle, he walks over and lets himself in Derrick's passenger side.

"Thanks for the call…fill me in," Brent comments, without as much as a hello.

"One of my employees, Frank, was the one who actually spotted him. We were in separate vehicles canvassing the area when he noticed Fredericks going into a bar. Frank called me the minute he saw him. Five minutes later, he came walking out and headed down the street, going into another bar and coming back out five or so minutes later. My guess was to exchange drugs for cash in the bathroom—a favorite place for drug pushers.

"I made it to the area just as he was coming out of the second bar. I drove passed him just as he turned down the next street. Frank waited a few seconds before pulling out from the curb and rounded the same corner. Frank and I played tag following him for five more blocks before the same car we spotted a few weeks ago pulled over and he got in. By this time, Frank and I were both patched into two undercover cops. We took turns playing follow that car tag team— each one of us following and then eventually turning off.

"He and a young female eventually pulled into a parking lot of an apartment complex that has seen better days. The female, who we believe to be Sonya Martinez, the car's registered owner, opened the back door of the car, reached in and came out with a baby. They made a long walk down the courtyard before unlocking the door to the end unit, 115. Needless to say, a full-blown stakeout is underway. I watched as one of the undercover agents quickly placed a tracking device beneath their car."

"What do we know about Sonya?" Brent inquires.

"Age nineteen. From a large family. Born here, though her parents were originally from Mexico. No known criminal record. Apparently a victim of falling in with the wrong crowd. At this point, not considered dangerous. Worked as a waitress for a year, but no longer employed as far as we know."

"So what now?"

"Right now it's a game of wait and see. At this point, we at least know where he hangs his hat—unlike that of three weeks ago. As you know, they won't attempt to apprehend him if there's any possibility of endangerment to the child."

"Well, back to the waiting game. What did Richards have to say?"

"He was obviously excited at the news. But, as he reminded me, this is outside of his jurisdiction, so nothing he can do outside of maintaining a flow of communications with his counterparts on the Phoenix force."

"Does the apartment complex have a name?"

"The Rising Sun Apartments…on the corner of Valencia and Third."

"Thanks. I guess there's nothing I can do here, so I'll head back home. I'll call Richards in the morning and ask him not to share this info with Shimie. She's not feeling well right now, aside from the fact that we don't need to get her all worked up at this point. I'd like to wait until we have her daughter safely in our hands. Oh, and we don't need her taking off again to find her daughter," Brent adds.

"Sounds reasonable enough," Derrick answers in response. "Either Frank or I will keep you advised of any changes in the situation, though I suspect Richards will have more up-to-date info."

"Okay, thanks," Brent replies, as he exits the vehicle. Once back in his Rover, the drive home went by quickly as his mind went into overdrive. He is excited at the thought of Shimie getting closer to being reunited with her daughter and resuming a normal life without stress. As for himself, he is looking forward to once again devoting his days to his interrupted work schedule. The quake, along with Shimie and her missing daughter, robbed him of the solitude he cherishes above all else.

26

"I'LL WARM UP your dinner," Victoria states, as Brent walks into the living room.

"Thank you, I could use some grub right about now. Long day."

"We had no idea when you would be home," Shimie comments, "so we went ahead and ate."

"Too much work to do, so don't ever wait for me to show up. I'm also hiring a few more to replace those that didn't make it through the quake."

"Keep that pace up and you're going to burn yourself out before you see forty…if you see forty," Shimie adds.

"My parents are barely into their sixties and still going strong. Longevity runs in the family. Besides, I need some goals to keep me off the streets at night," he remarks with a chuckle.

"Dinner ready in five," Victoria yells out from the kitchen.

"Okay," Brent yells back. Coming closer to Shimie, and

then bending down on one knee, he looks at her face as if trying to find something. "Your face is healing really well. I take it Roberta stopped by?"

"She did...thoroughly checked out each cut on my face and the one above my ear. She wrote out a prescription for a special cream to replace the one that Victoria was using. Victoria went out and picked up the cream. The hair on the side of my head, as you can see, is already starting to grow out. She also wrote out a prescription for something to help with the nausea. She thinks it might be caused by the blow to the head. I was also a little dizzy when I got up from the table after eating breakfast. That's when Roberta asked Victoria to do a blood draw, plus I had to offer up one of those awful urine samples. She'll call me when the results come in...maybe in a few days."

"Did she make mention of any plastic surgery?"

"She won't know until the scabs completely fall off. She said to give it another month at a minimum ... most likely two months she said."

"Dinner's on the table and getting cold," Victoria remarks, as she pokes her head into the living room.

"Okay, we're coming," Brent responds, as he rises from his kneeling position and helps Shimie up.

After dinner is finished, Brent heads off to his study and places a call to Richards. Outside of grocery shopping, Fredericks and his apparent girlfriend had yet to leave the apartment. He thought of calling one of his parents, but quickly realizes the time zone difference. Given the long day behind him, he says goodnight to the two women chatting in the living room and heads to his bedroom for a quick shower and bed.

—

The following day was to be even longer than the previous one. Being shorthanded required more personal involvement on a multitude of pending cases. Each case was unique and challenging in itself, though Brent really wants to get back to managing cases, not having to work them up from scratch as he is forced to do now. Managing, however, would have to wait until a minimum of two more attorneys are hired. He's learned early on from his parents to hire only the best of the best; simply because they had a law degree was not good enough in Brent's or their eyes. To Brent's way of thinking, they had to prove to him, from prior years in the field, that losing was not an option. Winning was everything, not only to his parents, but to himself as well. Their corporate clientele came to them from word of mouth, not through any fancy and expensive advertising. In fact, even their letterhead was emblazoned with the words *Winning is Everything* at the top—in bold letters, no less. The firm was proud of their past—for the past *was* their future.

Though he finds himself mentally tired, Brent pushes himself to work right up until ten o'clock—a fourteen-hour day for him. Not being tied down to a woman gives him the freedom to work as late as he feels necessary — a freedom he couldn't see giving up for any woman or cause. In spite of his mother's desire to see him eventually married off — and with children — he knew deep down that marriage was not in his destiny. God meant for him to be forever free, to play the field without obligations of any sort. Whenever a woman appears to be getting too close, he has wasted no time in jettisoning the relationship. The very mention of the word *love* and *commitment* sends shivers up his spine. No, love to him was a sign of one's weakness of mind — and weak he is not.

"Move to the right lane," Brent yells silently at a driver doing thirty in a forty zone. He is both tired and hungry, so has little patience for others at the moment. His frustrations, however, are quickly diverted by an incoming call. Pushing the speaker button on his dashboard, he instantly sees that it is Richards.

"You should be in bed right about now, Bill, what are you doing up?"

"It's going down tonight," Richards states, with an air of excitement in his voice. "Get your ass over here now if you want in on some of the action."

"Where are you?" Brent excitedly asks.

"I'm parked straight across the street from where you found Ms. Jamison. Fredericks and his girlfriend just left the apartment…with the baby. I'm in a late model, black sedan with heavily-tinted windows."

"Okay, I'm already in my car; I'll be there in about

20–25 minutes. See you then." Pulling a fast U-turn in the middle of a four-lane road, Brent wastes no time in shaving time off a normal half-hour drive—even going through red lights when he thought there were no cops close by. Twenty minutes later he pulls to a stop behind Richards' car. In a nonchalant manner, he exits his vehicle and climbs in beside Richards.

"I have to advise you upfront, Brent, to stay in the car at all times. If my boss finds out that I called you, I'd be up on charges for violating department rules and out of a job."

"I understand," Brent responds, "and I appreciate your calling me."

"According to my patched-in radio, she's already dropped him off. She's currently driving around, which tells us that Fredericks has any number of drops to make before he's out of here. There's a whole bunch of undercover agents descending on the area as I speak...aside from the ones that were already assigned to the case. I'm not privy to how they plan to corner the car and apprehend Fredericks at the same time, but I have faith that they know what they're doing."

"What are the odds she will pick him up at the same corner as a few nights ago?" Brent inquires.

"Slim to none...he's too smart to stay in a pattern of any sort, though I'm guessing it will only be a matter of a block or two from the actual drop-off location."

"Are we permitted to drive around right now?"

"I can tell you're antsy...you'd never make a good detective. A lot of waiting takes place before the action begins. Besides, I'm out of my jurisdiction. We have good people in Scottsdale, but so does Phoenix. Trust me, they won't screw this up. Only if there is any chance of harm coming to the baby will they back off."

"You're right...I am antsy. I have a lot riding on the baby being returned to Shimie. It's been a long haul for all of us involved in this case. I just want to see it end."

"And once the baby and mother are reunited, what happens to the two of them?"

"I'm guessing they'll move out and begin life anew... like thousands of other displaced residents in the metro region. But I assure you, not until Shimie is totally healed."

"You two seemed to have hit it off very well," Richards remarks while glancing at Brent. "No plans of including her in your life, huh?"

"Nope. I'm too busy growing the business. A woman, especially one with a child, would only distract from my goals."

"Victoria tells me that Shimie would be a perfect match for you."

"Since when did Victoria become a matchmaker? I don't see any engagement ring on her finger," Brent adds.

"Not today, but maybe down the road. Like you, I have professional goals as well. The one major aspect I like about Victoria is that she hasn't brought any *drama* into the relationship. I get enough of that at work. I don't need to come home to more drama. I for one see the same attributes in Shimie. You would be a — ."

"428 leaving home," squawks a voice over Richards' radio.

"That's code, I believe, to indicate Fredericks leaving one of the bars...428 would indicate Fredericks. Code is used in case someone is listening into the frequency." The two of them sit silently as they await the next call — a call which didn't take long in coming.

"428 entering home point 2," came the unknown male voice again. Six minutes later the radio blurted out the same code as before. "428 leaving home point 2," followed quickly by another, "428 walking weasel."

"Weasel stands for west, I'm thinking," Richards remarks, without looking for a response from Brent. Richards took all of this suspense easily — such was not the case, however, for Brent. He finds himself tensing up with each passing crackle of the radio. He knew enough to stay in the car, though he finds himself wanting to be in the thick of it all. His one desire is to witness the removal of Shimie's daughter from the car.

"428 nothing on stack," came the latest in a quickening series of coded messages.

"429 circus plus 3," quickly follows.

"What's that?" Brent asks.

"That would be her vehicle circling in for the pickup. The plus three would indicate the number of blocks away from Fredericks."

"428 walking weasel," was immediately followed by "429 circus minus 1." Fifteen seconds would pass before another code was issued. "428 nine down."

"This is it," Richards says with a touch of excitement in his voice. He then turns the ignition on and begins slowly inching forward to the end of the street before making a slow right turn. Before the turn is complete, the two of them hear a series of gunshots piercing the stillness of the night. The gunshots are quickly followed by the sounds of screeching tires.

"I had a feeling he wouldn't go quietly," Richards remarks, as he continues slowly creeping down the street. Straight ahead they both watch as two marked police vehicles, with lights flashing, race to block off the street. Moments later, two more shots ring out. By this time, Brent's nervousness almost brings him to the point of throwing up.

One block away from the first police vehicle, they both notice two officers crouched over the rear and front of their vehicle with shotguns at the ready. Richards decides that now was the time to pull to the curb and wait it out. Two minutes of tense waiting occur before the radio came back to life.

"428 nine secured."

"It's all over," Richards comments, as he glances over at Brent. No sooner were the words out of his mouth than they watch as the two officers ahead stand up. Richards then reaches down alongside his seat and retrieves what

Brent knew to be a portable flashing light. Rolling down his window, Richards flips a switch on the light and places it on the top of his vehicle. Inching forward, he pulls to a stop just short of the police vehicle.

As he opens his door, he glances over at Brent, "Stay here." Brent watches as Richards approaches the two officers and pulls the left side of his sports jacket away from his body. Brent assumes that he was showing the officer his badge. After a few words are exchanged, Richards returns to his car, puts it into drive and begins slowly turning the corner. Brent can't help but notice the large number of vehicles straight ahead — all with flashing lights.

Two hundred feet later, Richards pulls over to the curb. "I don't know who's in charge tonight, so let me do the talking." With Richards opening his door and stepping out, Brent quickly follows his lead. As they slowly walk along, they notice a stretcher emerging from the alley. In short order, the stretcher is loaded into the back of the medic unit. It only took a quick glance on Brent's part to know that it wasn't Fredericks.

"Bill," a suited man calls out to Richards. "Why is it I'm not surprised to see you here?" He remarks as they shake hands.

"You know me Jerry, never one to miss watching Phoenix's finest in action. Jerry, this is Brent Masterson, the one looking after Ms. Jamison."

"Pleased to meet you, Jerry. I apologize for asking straight away, but how's the baby?"

"I don't mind your asking at all," Jerry responds. "In fact, I would be disappointed if you hadn't asked. You'll be happy to know that the baby is just fine; currently sitting in the back seat of a cruiser with one of the female officers."

"And Fredericks?" Asks Richards.

"Dead. Took a bullet to the heart...still in the alley awaiting the coroner's meat wagon. Went up a fire escape ladder, shot one of my men in the shoulder. His partner took aim and fired. Fredericks fell about a story, but he was most likely dead before he hit the ground. We blocked the getaway vehicle, front and back, and took her into custody without a struggle. Fredericks sensed something was about to come down, so he darted into the alley before reaching her car."

"So what happens to the baby at this point?" Brent inquires.

"Once we notify the mother, she's free to pick the baby up. We just called her listed number, but no one answered. Oh, and we would ask that a physical be conducted on the baby within twenty-four hours...just for the record."

"What's the possibility of Mr. Masterson here taking the baby home to her mother?" Richards asks.

"Whoa, a violation of procedures," Jerry immediately answers.

"Jerry, you and I violate procedures many times in the course of our investigations. If you can't, or won't release the baby to Mr. Masterson, would you release her to me?"

"I can possibly do that. Though I may have to run a background check on you first," he adds, with a full-size smile. "I'll note in my report that the baby was handed over to you for delivery to the mother."

"Thanks, Jerry, it looks as though I owe you one now."

"Yep, you sure do. I obviously have some work ahead of me, so I'll take you two to where the baby is. I'll have one of the officers pull the car seat out of the suspect's vehicle before they tow it away," Jerry adds, while walking to the patrol car.

Opening the back door of the patrol car, Jerry crouches down to address the officer holding the baby. "How's the little one doing?"

"Sound asleep…perfect baby," she responds.

"Mellissa, this is Bill Richards and Brent Masterson. Bill is my counterpart with Scottsdale. He's going to be taking the baby to her mother…who's not feeling well at the moment," he intentionally lies.

"Sorry to see her go," Mellissa comments. "I have two sons, but was looking for a girl to round out the family. I guess I'll have to do it the old fashion way," she adds with a smile. Scooting out of the back seat, she hands the baby over to Richards, who quickly passes the baby to Brent. Meanwhile, Jerry walks away, leaving the two of them to care for the child.

"Oh my God, what a beautiful baby," Brent remarks to himself while looking at her face peeking out from the blanket. It's obvious she takes after her mother, right down to the olive skin coloring. Not knowing how to really handle babies, he copies what he observed Mellissa doing and places the sleeping baby up onto his chest and shoulder. And like Mellissa, he reaches up with his free hand and gently rubs her back.

"Let's get out of here," Richards says to Brent, who appears to be in another world.

"Oh, good idea," Brent responds, when he realizes what Richards had just said.

"Thank you," Richards states to the officer delivering both the car seat and diaper bag. "Brent, we'll ride back in my car to yours. There's a chill in the air, need to keep her warm." Richards feels as though he were talking to the wind when addressing Brent—his attentions were clearly focused on just the baby at the moment. Brent steps ever so slowly to the car as if the baby would fall apart if he were to walk at a normal pace.

Arriving at Brent's vehicle, Richards pulls the car seat from the back and sets it inside of Brent's back seat. After strapping the carrier into place, Richards takes the baby from Brent's arms and places her into the car seat. Once the seat belts were tightened, he gently closes the door.

"Gee," Brent remarks, "you did that like a pro. Are you sure you don't have any children of your own?"

"Being the oldest in a large family, you learn quickly how to care for the younger ones."

"Uh, why didn't you put her upfront where I can keep an eye on her?"

"Always in the back seat and always facing backward… for maximum safety reasons. You obviously have a lot to learn when you have children of your own."

"Not me. I'll leave children to my sister. Though God help any children she might have."

"Whatever. I'll follow you home just to make sure there are no problems getting there. Once at the gate, you're on your own. I'll write on my report that I handed over the child directly to the mother. Oh, and don't forget to get the baby's physical taken care of."

"Will do. And Bill…thanks for everything. And I mean that sincerely."

"I know you do. I would say that you owe me big time, but if Victoria and I pan out, I'll still be owing you. Now enough of the chatter…get moving."

27

Bᴿᴇɴᴛ ꜰɪɴᴅꜱ ʜɪᴍꜱᴇʟꜰ not only driving slower than usual, but intentionally avoiding every pothole he could see from the street lighting. His one wish right now was to deliver a sleeping baby to her mother. Given that it was now just after midnight, he knew that both Shimie and Victoria would be sound asleep. And, true to his word, Richards drove away the moment they both arrived at his gate.

Once inside the garage, he unhooks the strap holding the baby in and gently lifts her to his shoulder. Going inside the house, he quickly sheds his shoes so as not to make any noises across the tiled floor. Reaching Shimie's bedroom, he gingerly opens the door and tiptoes to the opposite side of where she was lying — the two nightlights guiding his way. Pulling the covers back, he gently places the baby on the bed with her head resting on one pillow before pulling the covers back up to her neck.

Walking back over to Shimie's side of the bed, he quietly calls out her name. Not awakening, he raises his voice a little—but still no reaction. She was either in a deep sleep, or Victoria had given her a sleeping pill. Sitting down on the side of her bed, he calls her name again while gently rubbing her exposed arm.

"Huh?" She finally utters, as if in a daze. A moment later, she finally opens her eyes and stares back at Brent staring down at her.

"I'm too tired tonight for you, dear," she says, thinking that Brent wanted to crawl in beside her.

"I'm not here for any of that great action you produce. I just got home and I want to know who you are sleeping with."

"I'm not sleeping with anyone…and you know it."

"Oh yes you are. You two-timed me while I was out working."

"What the hell are you talking about?" By now she had become fully awake. "Have you been drinking?" She asks, in an accusatory tone.

"Then just who in the hell is that lying next you?" Brent responds, while pointing to the still asleep baby.

Shimie, fully curious by now, turns her head to the left and instantly spots her daughter. "Oh my God! Oh my God!" She screams out, awaking her child in the process. Shimie immediately slopes down to her daughter's side and wraps her in her arms. Somewhere around the twentieth "Oh my God," coupled with uncontrollable bawling, Victoria comes running into the room—only to come to a sudden stop after flipping on the lights and spotting Shimie clutching her daughter.

"Oh my God, I don't believe what I'm seeing. Pinch me please ... wake me up," Victoria remarks, while standing next to Brent in her nightgown.

"It's for real," Brent states to her, though he isn't sure that she heard him through all of Shimie's loud crying and rocking in the bed with her daughter. "Why don't we leave the two of them alone for a while," Brent states into Victoria's ear.

"Good idea," she replies, before going over to a small lamp and turning it on. When the two of them reach the door, she flips the main lights back off.

"I know you're going to ask how, why, where and when, but let's leave it for later. Right now I'm more concerned about what the baby needs, you know, diapers, changing table, bottles, food and whatever else babies need."

"And a crib," Victoria adds.

"Nope, already have one in the back corner of the garage. I picked one up last week, but didn't say anything to Shimie. Of course, it does need putting together. Though, if I were a betting man, I would place my money on her daughter sleeping beside her for some time to come."

"Well, given that everyone is wide awake," states Victoria, "why don't you and I go shopping for those things right now?"

"I can handle that, even though I detest shopping, but this is different. Wait, what's open at this ungodly hour?"

"A Walmart Super Store is open 24/7. I know of one

about four miles up the freeway. I also know that that section of the freeway has been repaired."

"Okay, let's go. Would you mind going in and letting Shimie know that we'll be gone for a bit?"

"Sure, if she can hear me through the crying, that is," Victoria answers, while she heads back down the hallway to the bedroom.

—

"Thanks for joining me, Victoria, that was kind of fun actually."

"I agree...if I didn't slap your hands as many times as I did, you would've bought every baby item in the store."

"What can I say; it all looked to be pretty neat stuff to me."

"While I'm making room in the pantry for the baby's food, why don't you go in and see what the two of them are up to. Oh, and think about dragging the bed out of the garage. Maybe Shimie and I can put it together during the day."

"You're in luck then, I bought one of those cribs that basically snaps together. Hammers, screwdrivers and wrenches have never been my best friends while I was growing up. If something needed fixing, my dad simply called in a handyman. I'm gone, see you in a few," he adds, as he heads off to check up on Shimie and the baby.

Slowly opening her door, Brent readily sees that the

two of them were sound asleep, with the baby lying across part of Shimie's chest, and both arms wrapped around her daughter. Closing the door behind him, he walks silently down the hallway and into the kitchen where Victoria was working in the pantry. With her busily engaged, he decides to go out to the garage and drag the crib box into the living room where he had already placed the changing table box. Given the circumstances of the previous evening, he decides to spend the day at home—the office would just have to get along without him.

Right on schedule, Roberta shows up at 11 a.m. to check out the baby and fax the requested report off to both Richards and Jerry Sellars. Brent is somewhat astonished that the exam had taken over an hour—unless she spent part of the time examining Shimie as well. Shimie had taken the news of her ex-husbands death better than Brent had expected—apparently there was no love lost on her part; especially given the beating she took from him in the alley—not to mention the abduction of her daughter and the killing of her neighbor.

With her daughter back in her life, Shimie became a new woman overnight. Gone were the rapid mood changes and the tears that seemed to appear when the wrong words were spoken. Tears were now replaced with smiles, melancholy moods were exchanged for laughter, and inner misery and apprehension were replaced with joy. A renewed woman appeared to have been reborn from the ashes of despair. And yes, Brent finds himself liking the new Shimie.

Seeing that Shimie pretty much appears to be getting along in the house on her own, Brent informs Victoria that Sunday would be her last day of employment, but that she was free to come and visit Shimie and the baby at anytime. Victoria was sad to be leaving, but knew that it was the nature of the line of work she chose for herself. She is happy for both Shimie and little Brianna Lynn, but saddened that she would no longer play a part in their daily lives. She knew, without question, that she and Shimie would remain lifelong friends.

28

"I'M SO GLAD you and Victoria picked out a high chair that reclines," Shimie remarks, while finishing up with her breakfast. "It always brings about a smile watching Brianna fall asleep after each meal in her chair."

"Like mother, like daughter...eat and fall asleep," Brent jokingly responds.

"Now was that very nice?"

"Well, it's true, at least for you."

"For a lot of people, Mr. Know it All, after you eat the blood rushes to the stomach to begin the digestive process. One can get a sugar high and then it crashes without warning. A little nap after a meal is actually quite healthy."

"Speaking of a sugar high, that cake over there sure looks yummy. Did Victoria make it?"

"We both did, though she's a far better cook and baker than I am. It was fun to spend the day with her. I'm so glad that things are working out with her and Bill. And, in case you didn't know it, he'll be bringing Victoria here for Brianna's party this afternoon."

"I forgot all about the party. What time?"

"One o'clock. Even though parties of this sort don't interest you, do your best to fake a smile."

"I have a feeling that Richards is only coming because of Victoria. The men of the world prefer cocktail or barbeque parties, not birthday parties."

"That's because you have one-track minds. Fake a smile for an hour, then you can disappear if you like."

"It's Brianna's first," remarks Brent, "that's a major milestone; plus the fact that you went through twenty-five days of hell to get to this moment. So, based on that, I'll look happy for her sake and yours. Now that we've settled on my looks for the party, I'll head off to the study, make a couple of work-related calls and then call my parents. I haven't spoken with them since last weekend."

"Do you ever talk about the fat and ugly one with your parents anymore?" Shimie asks.

"Your name comes up every now and then, mostly from my mother. She still wants the same old thing—grandchildren. And I tell her the same old thing—then adopt some." Brent then pulls away from the table and leaves for his study.

Shimie busies herself putting the leftovers away and doing up the dishes while Briana is fast asleep in her high chair. With the kitchen cleaned up, she picks up Brianna and heads off to the bedroom to give her a bath before laying her in the crib for a nap.

Walking back to Brent's study, she immediately stops when she hears the mention of her name.

"No, mother, not until next weekend. The painters won't finish up till Wednesday and then the furniture has to be moved back in from the garage. It's not as close to Scottsdale General as her apartment was, but still close enough."

Well, I'm assuming she'll go back to work there…the hospitals still have an acute shortage of good nurses because of the quake. The good part about going back to work at that hospital is that they provide onsite daycare."

"I think you're wrong on that count, mother. I'm sure she'll love the idea of having her life back—as I will mine."

At this point in the conversation, Shimie turns and walks away, feeling devastated. Only the anguish of temporarily losing her daughter brought her more pain. After three months of giving herself to Brent, she was to be let go like a hired hand—her contract was about to expire. She loved him with her whole heart and soul—a love deeper than she ever felt with her ex. She never revealed her love for him for fear of scaring him away, though God knows she longed to tell him that he was her everything.

Never once did she deny him the pleasures of her body when he slipped into her bed at night. She would make passionate love to him because she loved him—but now she felt used. She apparently was nothing more than a ready-made whore for him these past three months—and now her contract had expired—time to make way for the many conquests to follow. Yes, it was time to make room for someone else to use and then discard like moldy cheese.

His words keep coming back to her like a storm that has no end: I'm sure she'll love the idea of having her life back. Little did he know that he was her life, her dreams, her future. He, unlike any man she had known before, went generously out of his way to reunite her with her daughter. For that reason alone, she loved him deeply—and probably always will—but her contract is about to expire.

As she sat in the easy chair in her bedroom, she cries while Brianna sleeps.

—

"Well, were you pleased with my happy face at the party?" Brent inquires, while Shimie was busy spoon-feeding dinner to Brianna.

"You did well," Shimie answers, without any emotion.

"As a matter of fact, I think I had a happier face on than you did. Is something wrong? Even Victoria asked me why you were so quiet."

"No. Probably just tired."

"When Brianna was returned to you, we couldn't slow you down. Then about the time Victoria left, you appeared to lack energy. Maybe you should see Roberta…have her run some blood test, or whatever."

"Roberta gave me a clean bill of health a few weeks ago. I think I just need to get more exercise, go for more walks with Brianna in the stroller." Following a long pause, she continues, "Or maybe it's time I find a place of my own. At some point I need to start the next phase of my life with my daughter."

Brent is stunned at what she had just said. At the same time, he is pleased that Shimie is the one volunteering to leave. He could be ruthless in court, but with Shimie, he was finding it difficult coming up with the right words to inform her that it was time to move out—to give him back his freedom. Her surprise statement, however, put him on the spot for coming up with the right words.

"You've apparently given it some thought over the past few weeks. And, without sounding cold about it, I couldn't agree more with your decision. You're young and beautiful, with a daughter to care for, so yes, you have every reason to be concerned about your future…and Brianna's. Of course, I'll miss those home-cooked meals, the over the top loving and the companionship. But the things I'll miss are simply selfish on my part. This is all about what is important for you and Brianna."

"Thank you for thinking of us first," Shimie lies.

"The stars couldn't have aligned any better as I have a ground-floor condo almost ready for occupancy. It required extensive repairs from the quake, but ready to go by Wednesday or Thursday. The business, meaning me, purchased it for out of town clients, but it seldom got used."

"Thank you. I'll take you up on your offer until we can find a place of our own...that I can afford," she adds.

"Don't worry yourself about any rent. You need to get your financial footing back in order. And hopefully you and Brianna will stop by so I can see how she's growing." Brent is pleased with himself that this conversation is going so well. His worries about this very subject the past month were obviously unfounded.

"Of course we will. Besides, I think Brianna is smitten with you. In terms of my financial footing, I'll give the hospital a call tomorrow and see about getting my job back. I'm thinking Brianna will receive her first Social Security check in a month or two, now that her father is no more. I'll try to sock it all away for her college. I also received a fair amount back from my insurance company on my totaled car. At first, I wasn't sure they were going to cover it because of the quake. So, I should be in pretty good shape until I get back to work."

"You don't need to worry about a car for a while. There's a Mercedes in the garage. Nothing fancy, mind you, but it will get you from point A to point B in style."

"Thank you. It looks like all I need to do is pack—not that I have all that much here. And what I have was all paid for by you."

"Consider it all a belated birthday and future Christmas

gift. Besides, I don't think I would look good in your bikini," he adds, with a grin.

His grin, however, is not returned by Shimie. She had vowed to treat this conversation without emotion. She isn't quite sure why she is letting him off the hook, other than she is in no mood for any arguments over why he is letting her go. Why fight the inevitable? She was smart enough to know that one-sided love affairs never work out. Though somewhat discouraged by the turn of events, she wished him well in whatever relationships he found himself engaged in; short-lived as they most likely would be. She had read about commitment-phobia before, but had no idea it could be as strong as it appears to be in Brent's case.

He was good with Brianna. Carrying her on his shoulders whenever they shopped for groceries or playing with her on the living room floor. His every actions regarding Brianna gave the impression that he really cared for her. And Brianna, for her part, loved the attention he was giving to her. In terms of giving 110 per cent to the relationship, Shimie knew that she met the test—or at least she thought she did. She saw herself as a giver, but apparently her forms of giving just weren't enough to win him over. She was at a loss to make sense of it all.

29

—————————— ♨ ——————————

THREE MONTHS OF living on her own had gone far more smoothly than Shimie had originally envisioned. Returning quickly to work had enabled her to set aside some money in savings; partially as a result of the benefits of free childcare provided by the hospital, along with the use of Brent's condo and car. For this, she is thankful. Brianna enjoys the association's pool and the small park-like play area for children, even though few children actually live here. The snowbirds on either side of her unit wouldn't be returning until late fall, so Shimie makes no attempt to quiet Brianna when playing in the backyard. And now that Brianna is walking, Shimie has her hands full trying to keep up with her; even Victoria, on her many visits, has made mention of the fact that Brianna was a handful since learning to walk.

Yes, she is happy with the way things have turned out for her and Brianna since transitioning from Brent's house to the condo — except for one thing — she feels alone. Work and Brianna keep her days busy plenty enough, but the evenings, when Brianna is down for the night, are clearly the loneliest. Reading, or watching various shows on the large-screened TV, has done little to quell her sense of loneliness.

Her thoughts of late invariably lead her back to Brent. In spite of being more or less evicted, she still finds herself in love with him. When first moving to the condo, she did everything in her power to put him out of her mind—including the ignoring of his two or three phone calls. All things considered, it was easy to forget him during the first month. Getting settled and starting work left little time for ruminating about all those "what could have beens." Once her routine had been established, however, she found herself with too much time on her hands—too much time to think—too much time to wonder if love would ever find her again. Could another man fulfill her as much as Brent had done over the course of their three months together? She had her doubts—and she isn't about to settle for second-best—even if it means being forever alone.

She couldn't deny her feelings for Brent, but always in the back of her mind, she wonders what he is thinking. Did he miss her? Did he even think about her, or is he far too busy engaging in his previous free and easy bachelor life? She is too proud to ask Victoria if Derrick has even mentioned Brent—and what his social life is. She knew firsthand that he is generous—both financially and of his time. She will always be grateful for the many, many things he did for her. If it weren't for him, her daughter most likely would have grown up without her biological mother.

—

With Shimie and Brianna out of the house—and out of his life—Brent devotes every waking hour to his professional responsibilities—a responsibility interrupted by their presence. His clients, and their money, demand nothing but unsurpassed excellence out of him and his staff. His own sense of pride, coupled with his parent's expectations of him, dictate the long hours he finds himself putting in. He knew that those he is litigating against are giving it their all as well; especially since they know that they are up against one of the more successful legal teams in the country.

With the workload as such, his personal needs, desires and wants take a backseat to his professional goals—until he gets back home. Something is inherently missing—and he knows what it is. Where is the woman who greets him with smiles and open arms? Where are the dinners that used to be waiting for his arrival? Where is the little one who smiles and giggles while holding out her arms when he comes into the room? Where is the woman, who late at night and unselfishly, brought him all that over the top loving?

He knew, or at least he thought he knew, that Shimie loved him. And just possibly, he loved her as well, though the thought of commitment, of saying I love you, is foreign to him. In his entire life, he has never even come close to telling a woman that he loved her. The word love is simply not in his vocabulary. Until Shimie came into his life, he isn't even sure what "being in love" was all about.

Above all, he has to admit to himself that she was a giver with a heart of gold. He sees himself as a giver too, but it usually comes with a dollar sign attached. Looking back at the quake, he wonders if it were anyone else but a beautiful woman standing there, would he have thrown them to the ground and covered their body with his own? He has to admit that the chances of that happening were highly unlikely. If it were anyone else but her, would he have given up the time, the monies expended, and taken the risks he did to help find her daughter? Again, most likely not. He immediately chastises himself for his prejudicial, non-Christian attitude.

Yes, she is stubborn, but always where it centers on her daughter. She never once argued with him, except where the finding of her daughter was concerned. He is convinced, if it came down it, that Shimie would have freely given up her life to save her daughter. To Brent, that is the ultimate sign of her capability to love deeply — or anyone's capability for that matter — a trait most likely missing in him, he had to admit.

Though he encouraged an open door to her visiting, she apparently has chosen not to. Even the phone messages he previously left have gone unanswered. Is she mad at him, he wonders? If she is, he knew that he is partly to blame for making no outward effort in persuading her to stay. That single omission has been playing on his mind ever since she left. Try as he may to justify his inaction, he couldn't then or now. If only he could go back in time, he would do a lot of things differently.

The weekends, like today, are particularly hard — the quietness in the house is unnerving. With the exception of church and some minor food shopping, he finds himself forever lost in his thoughts. Afternoon naps, something unheard of pre-Shimie, are now sought out with regularity on the weekends — more as an escape mechanism from his thinking of her. Upon awakening, however, she fills his mind again — there is no escaping her. Taking pen in hand, he begins to write.

30

⚶

Pᴜʟʟɪɴɢ ᴜᴘ ᴛᴏ the garage after work, Shimie is pleasantly surprised to see Roberta standing by her front door. After parking the car and taking Brianna out of her car seat, she hurriedly makes her way out of the garage to meet Roberta.

"Oh my," Roberta exclaims, "Brianna is growing like a weed."

"Yep, that's my girl...and racing around like a speed demon too. It's hot out here, please, let's go inside." After unlocking the door, the three of them step into the coolness of the living room. "I must admit, I never expected to see you standing at my doorstep."

"Well, given that I hadn't heard from you in a few months, I decided to stop by the house last weekend to see how you were getting along. That's when Brent informed me that you had moved here. I hope you don't mind his giving me your address."

"Of course not," Shimie answers, as she lifts Brianna up

to the couch. "You're welcome to stop by anytime, but just so you know, I can't afford your services."

"You needn't worry about any costs, Shimie, I don't charge by the visit. My clients, Brent in this case, pay a retainer for a full year, so you're covered for a good seven or so months. Do you have another doctor now?"

"No. I've been meaning to get around to it, but haven't. You would think being a nurse that I would know better."

"So tell me, how are you feeling…any more nausea?" Roberta inquires.

"No, that was short-lived. I actually feel pretty good right now. And Brianna, bless her little heart, keeps me moving. By the end of the day I'm exhausted, but that's okay, as I sleep better."

"Any regrets about moving out on your own?"

"To be honest with you, yes and no. If I didn't move on my own, it was just a matter of time before I'd be asked to leave, so I saved him the trouble. I like Brent. I like him a lot, but he's not one for permanency. Plus having a child of my own runs counter to his lifestyle."

"Well, although I'm a firm believer in doctor-patient privacy, I can say, however, that he didn't appear to be his normal self when I saw him…his usual happy go lucky demeanor wasn't there. Maybe it's just stress from his workload. In hindsight, I should have inquired, but I didn't. Bad doctor."

"You're right; it's probably work-related—what with his being in temporary offices, and the loss of some of his staff due to the quake. He's a perfectionist, so when things go awry, it shows."

"Perfectionist? That's an understatement when referring to Brent. But then again, that's what got him to where he is today...a very successful attorney. Anyway, I've got a client to see at six, only a few blocks away, so I need to get going. Unless you choose to go with another doctor, I fully expect to be hearing from you. Not only for your ongoing medical needs, but Brianna's as well. Do you hear me?"

"Yes...I hear you, and thank you for making me well."

"You're welcome. Now go get some dinner in that child before she eats her toy."

With Roberta's surprise visit behind her, Shimie heads off to the kitchen with Brianna in tow to prepare dinner. When the dishes were eventually set into the dishwasher, Shimie asks, "Brianna, would you like to walk to the mailbox with mommy?" Brianna, never one to be left behind, lifts up her hand to meet Shimie's. Even though it was 7:30 p.m. by this time, the heat of the evening hit her hard as she opens the front door. The one block walk to and from the community mailbox is suffocating.

Setting the mail on the coffee table, she scoops up Brianna and heads off to the bathroom to give her her nightly bath. By 8:30 p.m., Shimie has barely gotten into *The Tale of Peter Rabbit* when Brianna's eyes close for the night. With her daughter fast asleep, Shimie makes her way back to the living room, plops down on the couch and begins sifting through the mail. Cancer Society. Toss. One-half off pizza circular. Toss. An HOA barbeque notice. Set aside. And then her heart stops. A business-sized envelope with Brent's return address on it.

Why would he be sending me something? She wonders. Wouldn't it be easier to just pick up the phone and call her? And then she realizes that she has never returned his previous attempts when he's called. Carefully opening the envelope, the first thing she notices is that it is hand-written — something that is totally uncharacteristic of Brent — given that he seemed to spend half his life on his computer. With her heart beating way faster than it should, she leans back on the couch and begins to read.

My Dearest Shimie,

I know what you're thinking: Why is Brent sending me mail? And just so you know, this is the first time in my entire life that I have ever written a letter to a woman — well, if you don't count those Valentine cards in grade school, that is. This letter should be taken as legal notice of your pending eviction of the premises you currently call home. Now don't get all bent out of shape with what I just said — at least until you have read the rest of this letter.

I entertained the idea of just dropping by, but had second thoughts when considering your rights to privacy — and possibly wanting to ignore me. For all I know you could have another man in your life, given how beautiful you are. I thought of calling you, but my earlier calls were never returned. Of course, I haven't a clue as to why the calls weren't returned. For some unknown reason you had to be either mad at me or, at the least, upset with me. Having had three months to think it over, I realize now that I should have strongly objected to your wish to move out. Or did you feel forced out? Which is probably closer to the truth, I'm sorry to say. At that moment, I failed not only you, but myself as well. And for that, I deeply apologize.

So, after two paragraphs, you have to be still wondering why I'm writing to you. I can best sum it up by paraphrasing a line from My Fair Lady: "I've grown accustomed to her face. Her smiles, her frowns, her ups, her downs are second nature to me now." Yes, Shimie, over the course of three months together, I've grown accustomed to everything about you — your smiles, your laughter, your idiosyncrasies, your off-tune singing, and all the parts of you that you have freely shared with me — both emotionally and physically. When did I begin to fall for you? When you first slipped your hand in mine on that fateful Sunday some six months ago.

And right now, I am missing you — missing you terribly. I miss the soft breathing that accompanies me when I awake. I miss watching your eyes light up when I come home from work. I miss your off-key voice when singing your favorite song while cooking our meals in the kitchen. I miss watching your many interactions with Brianna — oh how the child loves her mommy — and how her mommy loves her child. I could only hope one day to be so loved. And maybe I am, but never realized it at the time.

It was only after watching you two that I finally began to understand what love was all about. The word "love" has always been foreign to me. Come to think of it, I don't even recall my parents speaking of love before; either between themselves or with my sister and me. I never gave my parent's relationship any thought — until now. I'm sure, in their own way, they love each other. If they do, it is a love that has never been openly displayed on the outside. Maybe that's what happens with us attorney types; there is no room for emotions in our legal dealings. Our emphasis is always on the written word, the fine print, not on how someone is feeling on the inside. I'm very much guilty of thinking just like that. Until there was you.

Because of you, I now believe I know what real love is, or what I think real love is. It's the needing of someone special — someone who completes a person and makes them whole without shredding their individuality. It's the absence of loneliness. It's love when we began putting someone's needs and happiness above our own. It's love when one begins to think of futures and memories as a couple, as a family, rather than as an

*individual. Love is accepting one another without res-
ervation, and knowing that their lifetime partner will
always have their back. Love is accepting someone for
who they are – not what we would like them to be in the
present or future. I have no desire to change any part
of you. I love you just the way you are – idiosyncrasies
and all.*

*Never in my life – until the past three months –
have I ever devoted so much time to thoughts of love –
until there was you. And it took my missing you for it
all to come together – to learn the real meaning of love.
Not just to be loved, but to love someone else with every
fiber of my being.*

*Shimie, I need you. I love you. Yes, I miss you. I
want you back into my life – a life I should have fought
for three months ago, but didn't. And because of you, I
now know what they mean when they say, "you don't
know what you've missed until you've lost it." Can
you see it in your heart of hearts to return what I've
lost? You have my promise that I will cherish your love
forever, as my wife. And I promise you more tenderness
than you can handle – as you so eloquently explained
the concept of tenderness to me following our tryst in
the pool one afternoon. I know this letter isn't exactly
the most romantic way to say that I love you and want
you in my life forever, but it's the best I can do under
the present circumstances.*

Oh, before I forget it (how could I?), I would love

very much if you would allow me the honor and privilege of adopting Brianna. She's a beautiful child – who takes after her mother – who could definitely use a father to spoil her. Oh, and by the way, any chance of your wanting to expand the family? I really believe that Brianna should not have to grow up as an only child. Of course, you should be forewarned that we may have to engage in a lot of lovemaking in order to create an additional child (or children).

Or, if you prefer, we could forego children for a while so that you can attend medical school. It never hurts to have a doctor in the house. Think of all the free physicals I could get (but no peeking – remember?).

Anyway, my love, think about all that I have said above – even the parts that don't make any sense – and let me know your decision. But please hurry…I'm dying on the inside.

Missing You,

~ Brent

"It's about damn time you learned something about love," Shimie states to an empty room. Is he serious about all of this, she wonders, or is he just in need of physical companionship? Well, that can't be totally true, as he could get just about any woman he wanted, whenever he felt the need to get a little action. She had taken care of his needs for almost three months and, admittedly, he had taken care of her needs as well—at least the physical needs.

The thought of being able to go medical school is enticing, but she knows the timing isn't quite right. She has other, more important priorities to deal with at the moment. Or is he simply trying to buy me by offering to see me through medical school—free sex in exchange for free schooling? No, she really didn't like the idea of using her body for other than what God had intended it. Her religious beliefs were too strong to allow herself to be used in that way.

But, she admits, there is always the chance that his letter is sincere—written from the heart. For a man, he did a decent job of expressing many of the feelings and traits that one would normally attribute to the meaning of love. She considers herself smart enough to know that people fall in love for any variety of reasons—there is not, nor will there ever be, a formula or textbook to follow for any two unique individuals. Each and every love affair is of its own making.

No, she decides, she is not about to get back to him anytime soon—if ever. She and Brianna are comfortable now with their daily routines. She would move out of his condo if it weren't for the need to set some more money aside to live on; at least for when she and Brianna are totally on their own. There is always the possibility of moving to another city—maybe another state even. She has no relational or emotional ties here to hold her back. A fresh start—that's what she needs, and she would see to it that it happens—and the sooner the better.

31

———————————♪———————————

"Yes, mother, I went to church this morning. Though it's farther away, it's actually a pretty good parish. Crowded though, as many other families from the old parish are apparently attending mass there as well."

"Not to worry, I'm spearheading the drive to rebuild. Scottsdale families have a lot of expendable income, so I don't see the fundraising taking that long. The parishioners are anxious to get back to their home parish. A new church. A new beginning."

"The fat and ugly one? I have no idea what she's up too or how she's doing. She and her daughter, as you know, left approximately three months ago...haven't heard a word since. I did send her a brief note this week, asking if there was anything else I could do for her, but haven't heard back. I gave her some extra cash before leaving, so I'm sure she's doing just fine without further assistance from me."

"Oh mother, the pearly gates aren't going to open up

for me just because I did one good deed in my thirty-two years of life. Okay, you'd better get back to your guests. Tell father I send my love."

If he didn't talk to his mother once a week she'd think he was dead or dying. She ought to know that her only son couldn't die yet—too much work to do. Was that the doorbell? He wonders, as he cocks his head to one side; though he has to admit it would be hard to hear over the music playing in the background. After ten seconds passes, he realizes that he was only hearing things. Besides, only close friends with knowledge of the gate code would be ringing the doorbell—and they always call ahead.

A half-minute later, he thinks he hears the doorbell again. Not taking any chances this time, he hurries out of his study and heads to the front door.

"Oh my God!" Were the first words out of his mouth. After that, he was totally speechless. A long silence ensues between them.

"I understand you have a room to rent...females only." Shimie states without emotion.

Brent has never been at a loss for words in his entire life—until now. Before he could find the right words, however, Brianna pulls her hand away from Shimie's and walks quickly over to Brent's leg—wrapping her tiny arms around his leg and giving it a big hug. Brent wastes no time in bending down, picking her up and holding her close to his chest—all the while staring into Shimie's eyes.

With the front door wide open, Shimie hears *I Can't Help Falling in Love with You* playing in the living room — by Elvis no less — the version she loves to sing the most. When the song ended, it automatically began playing again. Shimie curiously wonders as to how many times Brent had listened to that one song this morning.

"Oh my God!" Brent exclaims for the second time while looking at Shimie. Followed quickly by, "You're pregnant!" After a long pause, and still not believing what he was looking at, he asks, "Would it be too much to ask who the father is?"

Shimie, without answering him, simply continues to look him square in the eyes. A single tear manages to fall from her left eye.

"Does your silence mean that I'm the father?" He inquires, still in shock at the possibility that he was, in fact, the father. "Why didn't you tell me?"

After some hesitation, she finally speaks in a quiet tone. "Because you didn't know the meaning of true love and weren't ready to be either a father or a husband when I lived here." And then she pauses for a few seconds before saying, "After reading your letter…now you are."

Reaching into his pocket, he pulls out her restrung St. Gemma medal. Setting Brianna down, he steps behind her, slips the medal necklace around her neck and secures it into place. With that being done, he bends down and scoops Brianna back up before reaching out his hand to Shimie. She in turn reaches over and slips her hand into his as another tear rolls down her cheek. All reminiscent of that fateful Sunday not so long ago. But this time, neither one was about to let go of the other's hand or heart.

About the Author

MICHAEL JENNINGS WAS raised and educated in Seattle, Washington. He was the fourth born of a large Catholic family of eleven children. He remained in Seattle until joining the Navy shortly after graduating from high school. After completing his naval service, he went to work for the Boeing Company while attending college.

In late 1971, he relocated to Denver, Colorado, where he pursued his college degrees on a full-time basis — graduating from Loretto Heights College (now Regis University) in 1973 with two B.A. degrees (Behavioral Science & Sociology) before moving on to the University of Colorado where he obtained his M.A. degree in Sociology (1974). In 1978, he returned to Seattle and The Boeing Company before taking early retirement in 2003. Aside from writing his debut novel, *Flight Surgeon* and *Understanding Woman (A Guide to Male Survival)* with two fellow authors, he has written a full-length musical play, *Blind Love*, which awaits musical composition of the lyrics. He has also written, in conjunction with his son Ryan, a play for his eighth-grade class, *The Man Who Lost His Way*. In addition to plays, lyrics and short stories, he has crafted over two hundred and fifty poems, along with an animated story for young readers, *Fluffy*.

He has two adult children, Brendan and Ryan, and has joined up with them in the summer of 2013 in Great Falls, Virginia in a large house located on six forested acres. A father couldn't ask for two better sons. Michael formerly spent eighteen months in Scottsdale, Arizona (where he still winters). He currently spends his days and evenings working on his next novel. He is a voracious reader of novels and attends mass weekly at his local parish.